<u>DEDICATION</u>

"For my mother.....just cause that's the way it should be.
I love you."

ACKNOWLEDGMENTS

First, before I go any further, I have to thank God. Thank you for my blessings and thank you for the hard times I've had in my life. Because I've come to learn that those times were some of my best blessings. Those times made me the strong person I am now. I figure if you are a person living through or that has lived through a struggle you have hands on experience with reality. My mother, thank you. Thank you for everything. Thank you for having my back and my front at all times. When people compliment me I always think it should be you they compliment. Because you're the one that did a good job. My children. Donlynn, Quintin, and Lyric. It's you guys that made me realize I had to grow up. Mommy loves you! To my Lil' Sis, Cee Cee. You're a young woman now, make sure you watch your steps. Thank you for holding down mommy. I love you.

Cee you have come into my life and changed it. I love you for that. Thank you for always having my back. We've been through so much together in our short time together, but we still here. I love you baby!

Kashan, thank you for believing in me when I didn't myself. Thanks for always being there. Kalisha and Khjim we've been through a lot and we're still going. Thanks for holding me down the way big sisters should! Aunt Nita, Aunt Diane, my cousins Zahn, Zarae, Sabrina, Uncle Gerald, Aunt Thedra, Aunt Colette....My family. I got to thank you all, cause without family there's nothing. You got some that's not fortunate enough to have family, so I thank God and I thank you for being there.

My grandmother, Annie Walters... I don't know where to start. You're the back bone and have been for a very long time. I love you!

Auntie Sherly, Uncle Keith, Asia, Ashley, Kia, and Lil Keith. I like to thank you guys for holdin' me down wit' Lyric and always being a phone call away...I love ya'.

Prime Time Management, much love. Thank you.

All my friends in Brooklyn, I'm scared to start naming. I don't want to forget anyone! You guys know who you are. To Sticky, Monty, Jus, Zu,......the whole crew, BS ya' heard!! Thank you guys!

Nancy and Sha... it goes without saying.....Thank you, I love ya'! Big Jackie, Rena, Melinda, Becky. Ya' stay goin' strong! My girl Teri Woods, I love you! You my dog wit' ya' crazy ass!!! My homie da Brat, M.C. Lyte, Queen Latifah, my friend Monifa, my homegirl Candice.

Everybody at Felon magazine...Good lookin'!

There's a few people I need to thank that never played that industry bullshit with me. They always saw me as the person I am and didn't go by the entertainment guidelines a lot of fake people do in the business....... Jamie Foster Brown, thank you for being a friend. Thank you for always finding a way to keep me out there when my record label didn't have a clue. Wendy and Kevin, thanks for looking out and not being full of shit like so many in you guys positions are, good lookin'!! Vinny, at WBLS, I got to thank you cause you did something for me nobody else in New York would. You are a real person and in this business that's hard sometimes. But you are one of the few people that seems to stay well grounded. Thank you and your staff for everything! Lynn Scott, at Motown, you're my girl. Thank you for just being you. Even though your people are grimy, you alright with me. D.O., Leland (even though you could be kind of flaky sometimes you my boy Lelo). Kay Kay, Elise, you've always been real with me. I love ya'. Beverly Ali, Shaka Don, Onika, Beatrice, She She, Tracey, La La, Missy Loo, Ina, Dez, Big Nell Dog, Wanda. All my friends thank you for being just that.

Sharon Page, Pam Crockett, Rogina Scott. Thank you guys for jumping on to this project. Pam thank you for being so real and down to earth. That makes it even easier to work with you. You have truly held me and this project down and I love you for that. Sharon you my girl!!! You know we got each other's back. It's time for people to know you are one of the hardest working black women out here!! Rogina, you are so sweet and hard working. Don't let nobody's negativity stop you!

Dave Mays and Ray Benzino. Thank you guys for being there when I call, I got love for ya' for life! You're my peeps! Teddy, I love you no matter what. Don't forget it. I get on your nerves sometimes and you make me mad sometimes, but we got a bond that can't be broken. Tone Copone, Markell, Nicole, Donna, and the whole Lil' Man crew.

To Nas I would like to just say thanks for recognizing our struggle and not being afraid to talk about it. We have alot of power with our tongues and words, and I think you are realizing it. Brother I see ya' vision and I'm down with it!! God Bless you.

Mark Pitts & Wayne Barrow, ya' know ya' my dogs for life!! Damn, we been through some shit together! If nobody else knows how real I am, I know ya' two do. Can't wait til' the day we connect again. I Love you guys. Kelly, thanx for jumpin' aboard and doin' ya' thing...Good lookin' out.

To my homie Shine, hold ya' head baby. You now know how a lot of cats is fake and phony in this biz. I got ya' back regardless. You and ya' family are in my prayers every day. Just remember, God sees everything, so He knows ya' heart is cleansed. And he's all that matters! I love you, Shine.

To everybody that's been down wit' me. My fans, without you it would have been extremely hard for me to be QueenPen. All my peoples locked down, I got love for you and got your back!! All the ghetto's (What society considers the ghetto. Ghetto is mental.) around the world, remember without us this world could not go round.

And to all my peps in the struggle remember, we work better together than apart. With struggle and hard work comes blessed rewards! We all are blessed, just 'cause we woke up this morning!!

Sorry if I forgot anyone. If that's the case sign your name at the line, that way you won't be forgotten

Peace, Love, and God Bless.............Hope you enjoy!

QueenPen

*_____ (Sign here)

SITUATIONS

SITUATIONS

A Book of Short Stories

Lynise "QueenPen" Walters

A QP
Publication

Published by
QP Publishing

Printed in the United States of America

2nd Printing April 2002

ISBN: 0-9714246-0-8
LCCN: 2002090230

Cover design: Cee
Edited by: Charmaine Roberts-Parker & Amanda Perkins

USA $15
Canada $18

<u>CONTENTS</u>

Crossing The Line

"A black guy, Jen?" Terry asked her friend with astonishment. She couldn't believe what her best friend was saying. She didn't know if she should laugh or take her seriously. She didn't know if this was one of her friend's idea of a joke.

"Yes, a black guy." Terry responded nonchalantly.

Jen had souped herself up for this moment. She knew she had to tell someone sooner or later. And the fact that she felt she was in love with this guy helped. She was at the point where it didn't matter what her friend or anyone else thought. Terry plopped on the futon style bed with her mouth dropped wide open. "So, you mean to tell me you've been fucking some black guy for six months and I didn't know about it? I mean what would make you want to sleep with some black guy? And where did you meet him...? What do your parents think? Do they even know?" The questions just started flowing out of Terry's mouth.

Jen didn't expect her friend to react the way she had. She took a deep breath and set her hands in her face before she replied. "Look, I didn't tell you this for you to judge me, dude...I mean come on you're supposed to be my best friend."

Terry jumped up off the futon. "Look, you are my friend I'm just saying how did you expect me to react? You just told me you're in a relationship with some black guy... I mean where did he come from? We never had a black person living on our block growing up. Maybe a handful in school. What is he some rap guy or something? Oh! I hope he's not some drug dealer. And I hope he's not taking you for your money... And what about Johnny?"

"Johnny?! You have the nerve to ask me about Johnny! You know he's a total idiot. You can't even stand Johnny anyway!"

"Yeah, but at least he's white!! What the fuck is going on in your head?" She walked over to her friend and looked her in her eyes. "Jen if you're having drug problems you can talk to me I'm here for you..." Jen cut Terry off with anger. "Look I'm not on no drugs! I smoke a little pot here and there just like you, but I'm not on no hard-core drugs! I mean get real, because I'm in love with a man who happens to be black I got..."

Terry turned blood red in the face. "In love!!!! Are you trying to tell me you think you're in love with some... some..."

Jen cut her back off, sharply. "Go ahead say it, Terry!! Some what? Say it! Nigger? Is that the word you're looking for?"

"I wasn't going to say that... you said it not me!" Terry shouted and stormed out her friend's guest bedroom and straight down the steps and out the door. Leaving Jen standing in the middle of the room. Ending their afternoon plans. Tears ran down Jen's face for an hour and a half. Was she out of her mind? She thought to herself. She couldn't be. She knew how she felt. Was it the sex? She thought. Maybe her friend was right. It wasn't like she and him had anything in common, as far as backgrounds. She never even had black people as neighbors. Not even as friends. She fell asleep with her thought.

Jen jumped up out of her sleep dazed. She looked over to the clock on her night stand. Eight-thirty! Shit! She thought. She overslept. She was supposed to meet TJ at seven. She looked over to her answering machine and the red light was still. Not even a slow flash. She went into the bathroom and washed her face off. The earlier incident with Terry played in her head. She picked up the phone and dialed TJ's pager number. She paged him three times in a row. He always called her back within minutes. But not this time. An hour had passed since she paged him and the phone hadn't rang yet. She thought of everything to justify him not calling back. TJ just looked at his beeper and shook his head. He knew he couldn't be bothered with Jen. He didn't even know how he had let it get that far in the first place. They were two different kinds of people. With different lifestyles.

By the time TJ and his friends got to the club the line was down the block around the corner. But the crew of guys went straight through to the front without a thought of standing on line. TJ was popular with the girls, always had been. Only Jen saw him as the shy bashful type. His beeper kept vibrating and each time he looked at it it read duplicate. Jen wouldn't give up. After a while he didn't bother to look.

Jen couldn't understand what was the problem. He had never done anything like this before. She didn't even know if she should go looking for him. She didn't know why she bothered to come down to the bar. She couldn't enjoy herself. She kept beeping him the whole night. Until she convinced herself, rather the shots of Tequila convinced her, to go looking for him. She slid off the bar stool and said her good-byes. She tried to gather her thoughts. She had an idea where he would be partying, but she didn't know if she should go there. So she decided to go to his house. When she got there she looked up to his window and noticed all his lights were out. She thought either he was out or he was in there with company. She rang the bell and got no answer, so she went back to her car and sat at the corner.

She was staking out his apartment.

She lit a joint and moved her seat slightly back. About a half hour later, she saw his Benz pull up in front of his place. She sat up and squinted her eyes to see. When she saw the passenger door open and TJ passing a set of keys to a young lady, heat took over her body. She unlocked her door as she watched the medium built young lady walk up the stairs to the front door. She noticed the plump sized ass on the girl. She also noticed her skin color. It was about ten shades darker than hers. That explained the size of her ass. She knew that the black girls usually had big butts. She got out the car watching the girl open the front door. She noticed the girl went straight to the right key. With all the keys on the ring, she seemed to know which was the correct one. Either he showed her before she got out or she's been there before. Jen knew where he was going. He was going to park his car in the garage underneath the building. She waited for him on the stoop. She looked up to his apartment and saw the living room light on. "Fuck it" she thought to herself. She rang the bell. To her surprise it rang back giving her entry into the building. She went upstairs and knocked on the door. But there was no answer. She stood there until TJ came up. He wanted to piss on himself when he saw her. "Yo, what the... What you doing in front of my door? How'd you get in?" He asked puzzled.

"I rang the fucking bell. Why didn't you answer my pages?"

He ignored her question. "Rang my bell? You didn't talk to Sharon did you?"

"Who the fuck is.... Oh that's her name?... No I didn't. And I asked you a fucking question!!" She started to get loud.

"Shhhhh. Yo, stop yelling." He whispered.

"Why! You don't want to let your girlfriend hear what's going on out here, TJ!!!"

He grabbed her by her arm. "No, I got neighbors! Now take your ass on out of here!" He shouted back. Out of all the days the building security wasn't there, it had to be today.

"Get your fucking hands off of me!!" she shouted with tears running down her face. She was hurt and ashamed. "Why did you even bother with me? You lead me on!" She snatched her arm back.

"Look, I don't know what you're talking about, but you better leave from in front of my door!!!!" Just as he finished his sentence his door unlocked. Sharon came out wet with a towel wrapped around her. She was in the shower so she didn't hear Jen knocking and she didn't catch the beginning of the argument.

"Excuse me, but what the fuck is going on out here?" She asked dripping wet.

Jen and Ty looked at each other. Jen crossed her arms with a smirk on her face. Sharon walked up to them. "What the fuck, y'all need a battery for y'all miracle ear? I said what the fuck is going on?"

"Tell her Ty." Jen said.

He looked at Jen like she was crazy. "Man, you better get your white ass out my face! Before I call the police!"

"Oh, you know her?" Sharon asked.

"Yeah this motherfucker knows me.... for six months he's been knowing my WHITE ASS!!!!" She shouted.

Sharon turned to Jen. "Ain't nobody talking to your ass!! I'm talking to Ty, Bitch!!!!" She shouted in Jen's face. Ty jumped in the middle of them. He knew Sharon wasn't nothing to fuck with. He felt good though, Sharon having his back. Jen reached over Ty and tried to mush Sharon, but missed. Sharon grabbed her by the neck. "Bitch, I will break your face!!"

Ty snatched them apart and Sharon's towel dropped. Her belly popped out. Jen's mouth dropped. "You're pregnant?"

"Yeah, Bitch." Sharon answered.

Jen turned to Ty. "You bastard!...."

Sharon cut her off and threw her finger in Jen's face. "Yeah and I got this!!!" Showing off the seven carat engagement ring she was sporting.

Jen stood in Ty's face in shock. "I should call ESPN on your black ass!!!" She walked straight out the building completely numb.

Sharon stormed back into the house and started getting dressed. Ty followed her. He knew shit was serious. He couldn't even think of what to say. He just watched her as she threw everything she had at his place into a travel bag. He had to think fast. She was pissed! He grabbed her arm, but she snatched away without looking at him.

"Look Sharon..." she cut him off. "Look what!! Tyron, what?!!! What you got to say? She didn't mean nothin' or you're sorry? Fuck you!!" She shouted. Then rage took over. She picked up an ashtray off the coffee table and threw it at him, just missing his head. Instead it crashed into his screen television breaking the screen. That just got her more hyped. She began breaking up everything she could get her hands on.

"A white bitch, Tyron?!!!!" She shouted while throwing stuff. "You fucked...excuse me...you BEEN fucking a white girl? While I'm here pregnant!! What you thought the ring made everything okay? You bastard, I was with you before the NFL! I was with you in the projects. I had ya' back and you do this to me!!!! Of all people. You couldn't even keep ya' dirt away from home front? Well, guess what? You can keep da' fuckin' NFL, you can keep ya' white bitch, and you can FORGET about me!!!" By this time she was crying.

"Sharon... It's not what you think." He couldn't even finish.

"I don't have to think nothing Ty! I saw. Why a white bitch? What you thought you had a trophy or something? The only white people we ever saw around our way ain't do nothin' but give us problems! And now all of a sudden you play pro-ball and you running around here fuckin' white bitches for six months!!!! Six months at that!!!! You were willing to throw away us and our baby, for some white cave bitch!!!?" She looked him dead smack in his eyes and waited for an answer.

"NO! No..I...I wasn't and I'm not willing to throw away you or our baby." He reached for her, but she just backed up holding her bag.

"Well, you did. And I'm out. I told you when you got drafted I wasn't putting up with no bullshit." She turned around and walked out the door. What could he do? He was wrong and he knew it. He got busted. He couldn't believe what just happened. Maybe he should have answered her call. Out of all the girls he had fucked, Jen had to be the one that flipped out. He wanted to go to her house and wring her neck!

The next day at practice, Ty couldn't focus on the game. He didn't know where Sharon was. He called her condo all night and morning before he left out. By the end of practice he ended up in the coach's office. He sat with his head down and his sweaty fingers crossed into each other. "Tyron, what's going on with you? And don't tell me it ain't shit coach...because I know it is".

"I'm straight coach...I'm straight."

He looked Tyron dead in his face and replied. "I'm not going to push you, but if and when you're ready to talk I'm here. My office and my home is open for you. No matter what time. You're more than an $80M investment to me." Tyron just thanked him and walked out. He knew he had to talk to someone sooner or later. He was too embarrassed. The whole drive to his place he just kept thinking about what Sharon had said to him last night, about being with him before the NFL. He remembered the times when she would take her summer job money and treat them both to a movie and dinner. He had promised himself he wouldn't get into the NFL and start doing bullshit. He ended up riding pass his exit to his place. He decided to go over, unannounced, to his homeboy Jeff's crib.

He and Jeff had been friends since second grade. When the boys were in sixth grade Jeff's mother died from a drug overdose. About a week after the funeral Jeff moved with his Grandmother, over an hour away. Jeff hated it. Said she was a mean old bitch, so he would spend every weekend at Tyron's house and go to school on Mondays from there. Before you knew it he had moved half way in with Tyron and his mother. Tyron's mother had a motherly instinct for him, so it wasn't a problem with her. It seemed like his grandmother didn't mind too much either, rather she didn't seem to care.

Tyron pulled into the gated townhouse community where Jeff lived. He swiped his card to enter the private entrance. Jeff gave him a set of keys the day he moved in. Tyron insisted he didn't, but Jeff wouldn't take no for an answer. Tyron didn't want Jeff to feel like he had to, because Tyron was the one who bought him the townhouse. About a week after his draft he went and purchased the three bedroom townhouse for his boy Jeff, a duplex for Sharon, and a mini-mansion for his mother. The house he had his eye set on for his mom was a six bedroom, three floor, brick Victorian. But she wouldn't go for it. She said it was too big and she would lose herself in the home. She was a very simple woman. She rather see her son happy. So, they found a four bedroom home with three levels, a swimming pool and sun deck in the yard. She always dreamed of having high ceilings and windows...and she finally got it. Tyron made her quit her job the very next day. On draft day he was handed an envelope with a signing bonus check. He walked off the stage, handed the envelope to his mother and kissed her on the cheek. He would have it no other way.

He heard the smooth sounds of Mary J. Blige's "My Life" through Jeff's front door as he put his key in. Mary sang soulfully as Tyron turned the volume arrow all the way downward. He walked through the townhouse calling out for Jeff. "Yo, Jeff! Yo, you here man?" There was no sign of him. He ran upstairs to the master bedroom, but there was no sign of him there either. He went back down stairs and snatched a beer out of the refrigerator. He walked over to the plush white leather couch and sat down. Just as he closed his eyes Jeff walked in with Fred. "Hey, Ty. What's up?" Jeff walked by and slapped him on the back of his head.

"Yo, what's da' deal? Hey, Fred what up?"

Fred walked over and slapped him five. "Hey, man how you?" Fred was this cat Jeff had met in college. He always seemed to be a cool guy to Tyron. But Tyron never really paid him that much attention. He was one of those good guys that came from a good household. You know the kind where both working parents reside. Tyron never did understand how Jeff could be cool with a cat that had no idea or clue about a struggle. But to each his own. He didn't have to deal with him. And it always seemed to Tyron that Fred was always pushing himself to be nice to him. The more Jeff brought him around the more he began to avoid eye contact with Tyron. "What's going on, Ty? You look kind of fucked up." Jeff asked and stated in the same breath.

"Man, me and Sharon got in to it last night. Some real fucked up shit."

"What happened? Where she at?"

"I don't know. I've been trying to reach her at her place and her mom's, but I can't find her." Tyron avoided the first question about what had happened. He didn't feel like getting into it with Jeff. Especially with Fred there. Plus, he had kept his little fling with Jen from his best friend. He actually kept it from all his friends. He knew Jeff wouldn't ever let him live it down. A white girl? Jeff always was fond of Sharon. She was there and down with Tyron from day one. Before there even was an NFL. She saw through all that and that's what Jeff liked about her. Jeff broke Tyron's thoughts. "Hey, man what's going on?.... The baby's all right, right?"

"Yeah, the baby is fine...it's just us.... . I think I really fucked up this time, kid."

"It can't be that bad....Or is it?"

Tyron got up from the couch and put the beer bottle on the counter. "I'm going to go ahead over to my place. You know to collect my thoughts and shit. Let's talk later. I don't want to hold you up." He didn't wait for a response he just walked out the door. He left Jeff puzzled. Fred came from downstairs and tapped Jeff on the shoulder.

"You all right? What's up with Tyron?" He asked. Indicating he was eavesdropping.

"Yeah I'm straight. Ty is a'ight. Come on you ready?" He brushed off his inquiries.

Fred stood behind him and took a deep breath. "Can I ask you something, Jeff?"

"What up?"

"Has Tyron ever told you why he doesn't like me?"

Jeff got up and walked into the kitchen. "Oh, come on where'd that come from?"

"Well has he? Me and you both know he doesn't and you always try to ignore the fact that he doesn't"

"Nigger 'you buggin'."

Fred folded his arms and walked into the kitchen behind him.

"Nigger? How many times have I asked you not to refer to me as a nigga? I'm not one of your around the way homeboys!"

Jeff turned and looked at him. "You really got a fucking problem, FRED! I don't know what it is but I do know you got one!"

He moved a little close up into Jeff's face. "I got a problem cause I know who I am and it's not nobody's nigga!" He replied.

"What the fuck is that supposed to mean? Huh? I don't know who I am? NIGGER', I went to the same school you did, got the same amount of years under my belt as you, and I got mine's through scholarship! Which means I probably had to bust my ass a little more than you did! I didn't have my mamma and papa to pay my way! So, here's a news flash....You ain't no better than me, Fred!"

"Yeah? Well news flash to you, NIGGER! At least I'm not ashamed of who or what I am. He curled his lips together so that his words barely could get out. "What about you. NIGGER??"

"Oh, trust I'm far from ashamed of what I am?"

Fred smirked. "Yeah? Then why can't you tell your homeboy Ty about us? Huh? What, I thought you weren't ashamed of who you are. Cause guess what? Another news flash, NIGGER.... You a faggot! Ain't no other title for what you are!!!"

Bang..Bang!

It was two hits. Jeff fist hitting Fred's face and Fred's body hitting the kitchen floor! Fred had touched a soft spot and the result of that was not in his favor. When Fred woke up from his twenty-two minute knock out rest, he found himself lying outside Jeff's door surrounded by his belongings he had in Jeff's place. His face throbbing and aching, he pulled himself up off the floor and rang the bell, but no answer. He put his ear to the door and heard nothing. Pure silence. Filled with regret and pain he rang the bell again and began speaking through the door. "Hey, Jeff come on open the door....Look...just open the.....". He stopped in the middle of his sentence when he noticed a piece of paper lying on one of the two duffel bags that sat outside the door. He reached down and picked it up. It was a note from Jeff. He unfolded it. It read... .

Fred,

Sorry for hitting you, but I'm not sorry for the things I

said. We're two different people and that always seemed to get in the way. So, here's your things. I've gone out for a little while, with hopes that you'll be gone when I get back. And please no phone calls or visits, I need to be alone to get my thoughts together. I wish you the best. Oh yeah, I wouldn't consider myself a faggot being you were the only man I've ever been with in my life...I would look at it more as an experience. You were just an experience, that I wish not to revisit again.

Peace, Jeff

He stood holding the letter in his hand. His chest ached with hurt. Not the kind of hurt he was feeling in his face, but a different hurt. He felt betrayed. How could Jeff refer to him as an "experience"? He thought to himself as he gathered his things. Two and a half years, an experience? He was so hurt and confused, he didn't even once think about his swollen face. He just walked to the parking lot and loaded his car with his bags. He drove straight out the complex without looking back.

Part Two

Jen paced her bedroom floor for hours. She kept looking over to her nightstand where the phone sat. She was full of rage and some type of sick hurt. She wanted revenge and she wouldn't stop for air until she got it. Her Plan A kept running through her mind. She was trying to give Tyron the benefit of the doubt before going through with it. But he didn't call, so there was nothing else for her to do but go through with her plan. She knew that it could destroy him. She thought for the last two weeks about her plan. She had to have her story straight. She took a deep breath and walked over to the night stand. She picked up the phone and started dialing. *Ring ring, ring.* "Hello." Terry answered on the other end of the line.

Jen started crying and whining. "Terry....Terry is that you?"

"Jen? Oh my God Jen is that you?... . Are you okay? What happened.....what's going on?" She asked in a concerned tone. The two hadn't spoken since Jen told her about Tyron.

"Terry...He raped me!"

Her cries got louder. "I don't know what to do! I've been trying to get over it on my own, but I can't...I just can't, I don't know what to do, Terry!!"

"What the fuck are you talking about, Jen?! Who are you talking about?!" By this time Terry was just as hysterical as she was. "Look, I'm on my way to your place. Calm down and don't move." Terry hung up before Jen could answer her back. Jen knew Terry would react the way she did. That's why she called her first. Jen knew that Terry was her friend regardless. She knew she would forget about their disagreement and run to her aid.

She quickly ran through her house throwing items down, mostly things in her bedroom. She took a miniature bat out of the hallway closet, took a deep breath, and banged her left wrist. She dropped to the floor. Tears filled her eyes. Still with no time to waste, she didn't stop there. She took the other hand and began squeezing her neck. She needed to make some type of marks on her neck. She had pleaded last night, with Tyron, but he wouldn't hear it. He told her he didn't want nothing to do with her and for her to stop calling him and sitting outside of practice waiting for him. He didn't even want to go over to her place but she wouldn't give up. She started threatening her life if he didn't come. So he gave in and decided to go. He spoke his piece and stormed out. He stormed out so quickly, he forgot his baseball cap on her bed. She would use that as evidence that he was really there.

While Jen was setting up her big pay back, Tyron was on the other side of town. Jen was the furthest thing from his mind.

He sat outside Sharon's place holding his cell phone to his ear. He had dialed Sharon's number about fifteen times. He knew she was there. The security guard had no problem upping info on Sharon and it didn't take Tyron long to convince security to offer the 411.

"Hey, how is the star quarterback doing this evening?" He asked Tyron when he'd pulled up, two and a half hours earlier. He had sat outside Sharon's for what he didn't know himself. Hoping to get a glimpse of her. To see if maybe she was with someone else. "How stupid is that? She's pregnant." He said to himself. He rang and rang and rang. She just wouldn't pick up. He knew she saw his number on the caller ID. He tried to think of a way to call without his number coming up. In the middle of his brainstorming, a yellow cab pulled up across the street. There she was. "Why's she in a cab? Where's her car?" He thought out loud. Before he knew it, he was out his car and heading her way.

Without looking his way Sharon put her hand up and shouted. "Tyron Jackson don't even bother! Just turn around and go 'bout ya' business, boy!"

He ignored her demand. "Look, Sharon....Just listen to me. At least let me help you with your bags. And where the hell is your car?" She stopped and stared at him. A part of her wanted to hear him out and the other part wanted to bust him over the head. "I parked it at ya' mother's house this morning and dropped the keys in her mailbox."

"Why would you do some shit like that, Sharon?" He asked. By this time they were already walking inside of her duplex apartment and he had an arm full of bags.

"Why wouldn't I, Tyron?"

"Because, it doesn't make any sense."

"You would think so. Look, I don't want nothing from you. As a matter of fact I don't want nothing to do with you." She was very calm and certain with every word that flowed from her mouth. He listened and tried to take in what she was saying, but he just couldn't digest it. He noticed luggage sitting in the corner of the living room.

"Where did that luggage come from?" He asked

"From you. You don't remember? You bought that set of Gucci luggage last year." She replied nonchalantly.

He stood up with anger. "Don't be fuckin' funny, Sharon. You know what I mean. Why do you have luggage out?"

"Oh....I'm leaving in the morning." She replied.

"Leaving?! Leaving and going where?!!!! Where do you think you're going with my baby?!!!" He shouted.

She stopped in her tracks. "Your baby?! You selfish mothafucker! You should of thought 'bout ya' baby before you fucked that white cave bitch!!! You should have thought about us!!!! Should have remembered when all we had was each other!! When we penny pinched and when I had to work 'til closing at Burger fuckin' King so we could have extra money to go to the movies, and buy all the latest gear, and shit!!!" Tears rolled down her face. "I would have done anything for you, Tyron. I don't give a fuck 'bout the NFL. I would have had five babies for you with or without a big football contract. That was before now. Now you have proven to me that you aren't worth all that love! So, don't go telling me nothin' 'bout *your* baby. Me and your baby are going to my sister's in L.A."

"Going where?! What the fuck are you talking about?!"
She continued on shuffling around between the living room and the kitchen, acting occupied. She felt it was best that she just ignored him, act as if he wasn't even there. He stood up and looked at her like she was out of her mind. He knew her just as well as she knew him. So he knew she wasn't in her bluffing stage. He knew she was dead ass serious when she said she was leaving. His baby girl, out of his life. He couldn't have that. He rushed over to her and snatched her by her arm. "Sharon, don't start no shit...you hear!"

She pulled away, with tears in her eyes. "Me don't start no shit!? You already started!" She bit the corner of her lower lip, trying to hold back the break down she felt coming on. "You started when you disrespected me, Ty." Ty. She had called him Ty. He knew right then and there that she was serious and that it was over, for now. Filled with guilt and consumed with hurt and pain, all he could do was wipe the trail of wetness that crept out the corners of his eyes. They locked eyes for a few seconds, then he turned away and walked to the door. His every step painful. He stopped at the door and held the door knob with his sweaty palms. He spoke soft and in a whispered tone. Not able to turn and face her, he talked with his back turned. "Umm...You know if you need..." He struggled with his words. "If you need anything you know I'm here. You know how to get to me."

She stood with the same trail of wetness from her eyes down her cheeks and chin. With her right hand sitting gently on her stomach and her left hanging on her side. She too spoke in a soft whispered tone. The softness they both had not spoken to each other with since the other night. "I know. Thank you, I'll...." Her too struggling with her words. "I'll hit you up if I...if *we* need anything." He slowly opened the door with tears running down his face, in a way that some may think men aren't supposed to cry and walked out. "Take care of ya' self, Ty." That was Sharon's words as Tyron closed the door behind him.

That was that. She took a deep breath, cried a little more, and continued packing. She was tempted to pick up the phone and call him several times, but she didn't. She just let him go. Her mama always told her. "If you let a man get away wit' his bullshit...He'll keep doin' the same bullshit that you kept lettin' him get away wit'!" In other words, she felt like if she forgave him and stayed with him he would have tried it again. And she wasn't about to set herself up for anymore pain. Give a motherfucker an inch and he'll take a yard. That's how she felt. She gave him enough rope to hang himself and that's just what he did.

****

As Tyron approached his block he noticed police cars and news vans. So caught up in his world and his own situations he didn't bother to think about who, what, where, or why they were there. Just as he was passing the large news van he noticed a reporter pointing at him. He brought his car to a halt. Suddenly, five police officers surrounded his car with their guns drawn. "Step out of the car!!" One officer shouted. Stunned, he just sat behind the wheel looking at the officers. One of the officers stepped over to the car with one hand clutching his weapon and with the other he snatched opened Tyron's door. "I said step out the car with your hands up!!!" He shouted.

Tyron stepped out in confusion and embarrassment. "What's this all about....what's going on?" He asked the officers.

The officer's words became a drifting echo to Tyron, as he read him his rights. The ride in the back of the cop car was insulting. Reporters, cameras flashing, questions shouting at him from every direction. It seemed like the distance from the cop car to the front of the precinct was miles. He couldn't believe what was going on. Rape, he was being charged with rape.

Ring, ring, ring. Sharon ran back into the apartment to catch the phone.

"Hello." She answered out of breath.

"Sharon, this is Jeff....umm....I need to talk to you."

"Look, Jeff, I don't know what Ty told you but I don't want to hear it! It's over and done with us!"

Jeff took a calm disposition. "Look, Sharon. It's nothing like that. Some bullshit went down with Tyron and his coach and the lawyers want to speak to you." She stood on the end of the phone with wrinkles in her forehead displaying confusion. "What....what...are you talking about, Jeff?"

"Just come down stairs. I'm in front." He hung up, not waiting for a reply.

Tyron was bailed out and rushed through the crowd of reporters within an hour of his arrest. He went straight to his coach's house to avoid the press. To his surprise, but relief. Jeff, Sharon, and his mother were sitting in the living room. Sharon, eyes red and full of tears. Unlike his mother. His mother had that firm blank look. Tyron knew that look. He knew that look meant hurt. She turned to her son, as if they were the only ones in the room. "Did you rape that girl, Tyron?" He walked over to his mother and held her in his strong arms. "No, ma. No, I have never raped anyone in my life." She pulled from him. "So why would that child say some shit like that?!" He turned and looked at Sharon, who watched them in curiosity.

"Ma....I fooled around with her and she wouldn't leave me alone. I told her I didn't want to be bothered. She just wouldn't give up." She walked over to Sharon and sat beside her. "Sharon explained to us what happened at your place when the girl popped up. Me and Coach Simmers had a talk and we came to the conclusion that it's gonna be important for your family, including Sharon, to stand by your side."

It was decided to be in Tyron's best interest if he and Sharon moved in together and be seen in public together during the trial. He went from practice straight home. The mornings and nights were filled with silence in their home. That's why it was very confusing for Ty when he heard the sounds of Luther Vandross playing in the living room when he walked in from practice. The smell of southern food filled his nostrils as he walked deeper into the six bedroom home he had purchased three weeks ago for him and Sharon. Sharon popped out of nowhere. "Hey, you hungry?" She questioned in a perky disposition.

"Hell yeah. We had one of those three hour meetings after practice today." Coach was in one of his dictating moods. She walked over to him and stood on her tippy toes, wrapped her arms around his neck. "Well, you got you some good ole' southern grub coming right up." She kissed him on the lips and walked into the kitchen. Every day and night from that evening on was smooth for the two. It was like there was no trial, no rape, no problems.

One night, while lying in bed, Sharon reached over and kissed him on the cheek. "Ty, you woke?"

"Yeah, baby. What's up?" "I love you, you know." He sat up. "Of course I know, boo."

"We got too much past and shit with us for me to let some stringy headed bitch come between us. Let alone a mistake separate us......It was a mistake, right?" He laid her head on his shoulder and stroked her head. "Yes, baby. A bad mistake. One I wish I'd never made." "Baby, everybody makes mistakes." She lifted her head from his shoulder and looked him dead in his eyes. "Just promise me you won't make it no more."

****

There she was. Sharon stopped in her tracks. She couldn't believe she was face to face with Jen, in a crowded department store. They had run dead smack into each other. Standing in the middle of the cosmetic department, staring at each other. Sharon's belly standing out further than the last time they had bumped heads. Jen noticed she still sported that seven carat square shaped diamond ring. Sharon broke the silence. "Do you realize what you've done to that man's life? Do you have any idea what he went through to get where he is now? Did you ever consider him, just once? Before you started this sick twisted game?" Jen just held her head down. She knew Sharon was right, but she couldn't let her see that. Jen had no idea that it would come to this. She never thought that her life would be turned upside down. The more she got deeper into her lies the more she realized she couldn't live with herself. She was tired. Tired of the whole ordeal.

Sharon moved closer to Jen and spoke sternly. "Huh, Jennifer Russo? Do you know anything about him, besides his dick!? Do you know anything about his struggles in the ghetto? And how he had to claw and fight his way out to chase his dream? Well I do, cause I was there. And I'm still here, I'm not going anywhere. NFL or no NFL, I'm down with him." She turned away from Jen and started to walk away, but turned back and headed her way. "I hope you'll be able to live with yourself, Jennifer. Cause when the press dies down and the trial is over you're going to have to look yourself in the mirror everyday. And all you'll see is a lying, obsessed, fucked up, bitch!"

Tears ran down Jen's face as she spoke softly. "I'm sorry.....Tell Ty I'm sorry." And she walked away. Sharon took a deep breath. She realized that that was Jen's way of saying she was lying. She rushed through the crowd after Jen. She caught up with her on the escalator.

Sharon grabbed her arm. "Hey, you sorry? For what.....lying?" Jen grabbed her arm away, turned her back to Sharon, and walked off the escalator. Sharon wouldn't give up, she followed. Sharon jumped in front of her and blocked her way. "What are you saying, Jennifer?"

She looked Sharon eye to eye. "I'll fix it. Tell him I will fix it." And she rushed off. This time she wasn't trying to be found.

When Tyron walked into Jeff's apartment, he was upstairs

fussin' out somebody on the phone.

"Look, I can't be bothered with you or your shit! I asked you not to call me no more. I need time to get my thoughts together! I don't want to be nasty and shit, but you keep pushing the issue giving me no choice! No....No! Why? Because I said so that's why! Because I don't see no sense in us meeting to talk, when there's nothing for us to talk about!" Jeff slammed down the phone and ran downstairs. Tyron was standing at the foot of the stairs.

"God damn, man! Who the hell you fussin' out like that man?" Ty asked.

"Man, nobody. This chick just won't give up." He replied, brushing Ty's curiosity off.

"Seems like it's a lot of that going on these days, huh."

"How's shit with you?"

"It's the same. This bullshit with this bitch is slowing my shit down. Can't get no endorsements. Motherfuckers scared to touch me until the trial is over. People staring at me like I'm a god damned serial killer."

"Damn man, you gonna need a little vacation after the trial."

"Shit that's if I don't blow trial." He put his head into his hands. Jeff got up off the couch and went in the kitchen.

"You want a beer or something?"

"Yeah."

"How's shit going with Sharon?"

"Believe it or not, shit's great. The best it's ever been."

Ty noticed Jeff was being distant. "Man, what the fuck is up with you?"

He snapped out of his trance. "What....What you talking bout'?"

"Ya' ass all dazed and shit. You still on the phone or something. Who was that you was talking to?"

"Nobody important."

"Man, I don't know you to be with nobody but Kim."

Kim was Jeff's ex. He was with Kim practically his whole life. But after he started messing around with Fred he started pushing her away. It was his own guilt. The phone would ring constantly. And Jeff would act like he didn't hear it. That told Ty he didn't want to be bothered.

"Yo, don't you hear your phone ringing off the hook man?"

Before Jeff knew it, Tyron had picked up his cordless. "Hello. Yo, what up? That was you calling all this time? Oh, hold on." He handed the phone to Jeff. "Here, it's Fred."

Jeff took the phone, hiding his real reaction. "Hello. What up man? What you up to?"

Fred spoke shallow on the other end of the line. "Oh, didn't know you was busy." Jeff gripped the phone tightly and held it firmly to his ear, scared Ty would hear him through the phone. "Yeah, yeah. We just over here kickin' it and shit. Let me hit you back in a minute, my nigga'." Fred hung up on him before the 'ga' could roll of his tongue. Jeff still continued his conversation. "A'ight. One." He hung up the phone.

Tyron insisted on pushing the issue. "So, what is up with Kim? I know you'll gotta be getting back together, man."

"She's doing real good. But I don't think she's really feeling me right now. I would love to try to make it work with Kim that's my girl."

"Then do it."

He paused for a few seconds. "I wish it was that easy." He knew she didn't want nothing to do with him. He had hurt her so bad she just washed her hands of him. A few months ago was the last time he had spoken to her, and it was very briefly.

Ty wrapped up his visit and headed home. He had all kinds of thoughts floating through his head. He thought a lot about Kim and Jeff. He came to the conclusion that he was gonna step in and make something at least try and make something happen with the two. He picked up his cell and dialed his mother.

Ring. Ring. Ring. "Hello."

"Hey, Ma. What you up to and why it took you so long to answer your phone?"

"Well, like you young folks say 'I'm chillin'. And I was letting my company out, so I couldn't get to the phone."

"What company you got at 12:50 in the morning?"

"Excuse me boy? And you called for what again?"

He didn't push the issue. "Oh, what's Kim number?"

"What Kim? Jeff's Kim?"

"Yeah."

"Oh, hold on. I just spoke to her yesterday. I invited her down to see me."

"Yeah, what she say?"

"You sure are all up in my mix tonight, huh?"

"All up in your....What you talking about, Ma?"

"You know, all up in my business."

"I know what it means, I meant where you get that from?"

"Look, I maybe ya' mamma, but I'm still in tune with the world you know."

"You funny. Look, that's Sharon beeping through. Call Kim and give her my cell, tell her to call me now. Ok?"

"Yes, sweetie. Love you." She hung up.

He clicked over to the next line. "Hey, what's up?"

"Hey, baby. Look your lawyer called, he said something came up and he needs to speak to you right away. It sounded like it was important. You know he's always so calm and soft spoken, well he was just the opposite." "Okay, I'll be to the house in about 15 minutes. I just left Jeff's crib."

"Alright. See you in a minute."

His cell rang just as he hung up with Sharon. "Yo."

"That's how you answer your phone?" A female voice asked on the other end of the phone.

"Who this?"

"Kim. What's up? Your mother told me you wanted me to call you." +"Oh, hey girl what's up? I didn't pick up on your voice. How you? Why you haven't been down to see us yet. Let me find out you don't love us no more."

"Whatever, Ty. I don't see nobody running to come see me either. But I told your mother I would come down next week. How's Sharon?"

"She's fine. Getting bigger and bigger everyday."

"To what do I owe this call?"

"Why can't I just be checking on you, big head?"

"Cause you don't do shit like that. It's always gotta be a specific reason with you." "Well...you're right. I was calling to see what was up with you and Jeff?"

"Shit." She replied dryly.

"Well, is there ever gonna be anything up with y'all?" "Look, Ty. Where is this leading?"

"I'm just saying...You know maybe you two should try to give it another shot or something." "Yeah, or something is more like it."

"What's that mean?"

"It means it would never happen."

"Why?"

"Because I said it won't." "That's not telling me why."

"Yes it is.....That's your god damn boy. Won't you ask him."

"Damn Kim. I was just saying...."

She cut him off. "Yeah, I know what you're saying and I'm just saying. And I'm just saying your boy fucked up big time with me."

"Ok, fine. But just for the record, yes he is my boy but you're my girl too."

She laughed. "You know I didn't mean it like that. But I'll be up there next week. We gotta hang. You need to be hooking me up with one of those NFL cats you play with."

"Yeah, a'ight whatever. I'll see you next week."

"Love you."

"Love you too, big head." He hung up.

"Shit must have gone real sour with them." Sharon climbed into the bed next to Ty. "Why you say that?" "Cause the way Kim was talking. I don't remember Jeff ever saying anything about them having no big fall out."

"Maybe she just got tired of him." "Naw, she said he fucked up big time with her. That means some shit went down."

Changing the subject. "Did you call that man back?" "Oh, shit! I sure didn't. I'll call him soon as I get up." He reached over and kissed her. "Good night."

Sharon woke up the next morning to Ty's screams. "What!! Get the fuck out of here!!! Well....what...what happened? ....All right I'll be right down." Sharon ran down stairs. "What's going on?" He picked her up and started spinning around. "That was my lawyer. Shit changed with the case. He said Jen dropped the charges and admitted it was all a lie." Sharon immediately thought about her brief encounter with Jen in the store. "Well...what...when? Where does that leave her?" "Shit I don't know and don't care. Probably leaves her ass in jail for perjury. I really don't give a fuck." He kissed her on the cheek and walked out the door.

When Jeff got home there was a vase with two dozen roses in front his door. No note and no card, but he knew where it was from. He picked them up and walked into his house. He walked straight to the phone and dialed Fred's number. No answer, so he left a message on his machine. "Yo, stop doing this shit. I'm throwing the flowers in the garbage, just like I did the last four times. Stop calling me, leaving messages. It's over!"

Fred had been sending flowers, sorry letters, and calling non stop. He even left a note on his car at the supermarket. Which made Jeff think maybe he was following him. It was getting out of hand. He thought maybe he should meet with him and let him know face to face how he felt. Especially with Kim coming into town. He didn't need no interruptions. He had made up his mind, he was going to try to get back with Kim and he didn't want Fred in his way.

Fred had been following Jeff all day. He had rented a van so he wouldn't make him out. He couldn't understand why he was going to the airport. He didn't come out his townhouse with any luggage. He pulled three cars behind Jeff. Peeping through the rushing crowds of people, trying to pick up people. Just then he realized he was at the arrival section of the airport. Jeff got out and hugged a tall olive colored girl, with slightly chinky eyes. Fred noticed that it was more of a personal hug. She was very attractive Fred thought to himself. He watched as Jeff loaded her bags into his trunk.

Suddenly Fred screamed. "Kim! That's fucking Kim! That motherfucker!" He caught himself and looked around to see if anyone noticed his out burst. But all the windows were up.

He sat in shock for a few minutes. He pulled out right behind Jeff and Kim. He couldn't hold back. He picked up his cell and dialed Jeff's cell phone. He could see Jeff picking up his phone, looking at the number and putting it back down. "Why you not answering your phone?" Kim asked

"Oh, it's the office. I don't feel like being bothered. So how was the flight?"

"It was okay, I guess. You know I was never really with that flying shit."

"So, did you make up your mind if you were going to stay with me, or with mamma?"

"I guess I'll do both. If that's okay with you?"

"Sure, it's okay. You hungry?"

"Yeah, but I rather cook something. I'm tired from the flight. Don't feel like being in any restaurants." She reclined her seat back and closed her eyes. Fred felt like that was a gesture of comfort.... And he didn't like that.

Kim walked around Jeff's townhouse smiling. "Nice. Looks like you had a little help with decorating." He replied with a big fat lie. "Naw, not at all."

Out of nowhere Kim asked, "Hey, how's Fred?"

Jeff became numbed. "Huh....?"

"Huh, what? How's Fred I asked?"

"Oh, he's fine. I haven't seen him in a minute. I've been working like crazy."

"Tell him I asked about him."

"Will do....So what we having for dinner?"

"What you have in your fridge?" "Not much, but the supermarket does deliver."

"How about some barbecue chicken breast, sweet peas, and macaroni and cheese....homemade that is. I don't do the Kraft Mac and Cheese no more, since college." Kim still had hidden feelings, but she still couldn't forget all the pain he had put her through. He was looking so good to her she was thinking maybe she should let some of her bitterness go. And she too was looking very good to him. He hadn't really looked at too many women while he was with Fred.

After dinner, Kim loaded the dinner dishes in the dishwasher while Jeff opened up a bottle of champagne. "You want to chase yours with orange juice?" He asked.

"Sure do. That ain't change."

The bell rang and Jeff's heart jumped. He didn't trust Fred at this point. He didn't know what to expect from him. Before he knew it Kim had jumped up to answer it.

"Hey, y'all what's up!" She shouted and hugged Sharon and Ty. Tyron was holding a bottle of champagne. "What up baby?" He hugged her and slapped Jeff five.

"I hope we didn't interrupt anything." Sharon said noticing the champagne.

"No, you straight." Jeff answered.

"Well, I don't care I'm here with a bottle and I'm ready to celebrate!" Ty said jokingly.

"What we celebrating?" Jeff asked pulling out two more glasses.

"I'm off the mother fuckin' hook!! Homegirl dropped the charges."

"Did she really!!" Kim shouted.

"What!? What happened, when?" Jeff asked.

"What ya' don't watch t.v.? That's all they've been talking about."

"No, we've been cooking all day." Kim replied.

"Well, the bitch couldn't front no more."

After drinking and talking about old times, Tyron and Sharon got up and headed home. Which left Kim and Jeff alone and tipsy. Not a good combination for two people with an unsettled past. Jeff walked behind her and wrapped his arms around her waist. Something that she wanted him to do all night. She turned around slowly and looked him in his eyes. "You know you broke my heart, Jeff. You were all I knew, all I ever loved." She whispered

"I know. I'm sorry, baby. I fucked up." "You know that was the first time you've told me sorry." "Really?" He asked surprisingly. Nothing more was said. From that point it just was kissing and foreplay. He had not touched or caressed a woman in such a way in a long time. Matter of fact he hadn't since the last sex episode the two had, years ago. And she hadn't been touched so good like that since him. Now, she had been touched but not like this and not by him. Soon foreplay turned into the actual thing. For a minute she couldn't believe what she was doing, but that moment faded. Love and lust replaced it quick.

After making love for over a good two hours, they fell into a good hard sleep. Kim cuddled deep in his arms. Then the ringing of the phone began. He jumped out his sleep and looked at the phone, and Kim at the same time. Kim didn't budge. She's always been a deep sleeper. After the ringing, three different times, he finally decided to answer. Even though he knew who was on the other end. "Hello." Jeff answered in a sleepy tone.

"OH, don't play sleep now motherfucker!!!" Fred shouted on the other end.

Jeff continued in his sleepy push off tone. "What? Look, I'm sleep. I'll call you tomorrow or something."

Just as Jeff was hanging the phone up, Fred shouted threats. "Motherfucker!!! I'll come over there now!! You talk to me now or I'll come. God is my witness I'll bang down your door!!! And you wouldn't want that!! So talk now or I'll embarrass you in front of fucking Kim!!!!!!!!!!!!"

Jeff sat in amazement. How did he know Kim was there, he thought to himself. "Look, now you're being disrespectful. I'm hanging up now and don't call back. I don't have shit to say to your ass!" Jeff slammed down the phone and fell back to sleep.

Bang, Bang, Bang. Jeff jumped up and looked over to the other side of the bed, Kim was still sound a sleep. He noticed it was his door. He looked over at the clock. It read, 4:25 AM. He leaped out of the bed and ran down stairs. He looked through the peep hole. "How the hell this nigga' get through the gate?" He whispered to himself.

Bang, Bang. Fred knocked on the door again. "I saw you come to the peep hole, Jeff!" "Yo, what the fuck you doing at my door Fred?" Jeff asked. Not at all losing his cool.

"I got some shit to discuss with you."

"You ain't got nothing to talk to me about at no wee hours of the god damn morning. Now get the fuck away from my door." He whispered sternly through the door.

"I'm gonna tell you this one time and, and one time only. Either you open this door and talk to me or I'm gonna make sure Kim knows about us." Jeff opened the door, with intentions on kicking his ass, but caught himself. He remembered Kim sleeping upstairs and didn't want to wake her.

Jeff stepped outside the door and into Fred's face. "Look, you little bitch, don't threaten me. You need to move on with your life. It's a wrap with us." "Just like that, Jeff. Huh?" Fred asked.

It wasn't until then Jeff realized how much of a bitch Fred was. That was some shit a female would say he thought to himself. Jeff stepped back and asked. "What..?"

"Over two years, all that we had and that's it? It's a wrap is all you got to say? What about what we shared?" Jeff just stood speechless. He felt like he was breaking up with a childhood girlfriend. Then he thought briefly, that's probably the same words Kim would have said if she had had the chance years ago.

He stepped back halfway into his townhouse. "Look, Fred.....It's just not the time or the place." He proceeded to close his door. Fred put his foot in the door. "Then when is? When do you think you'll get around...." His words stopped short by the presence of Kim. She appeared out of nowhere. "Hey, Fred. What's up? I asked Jeff about you today." She reached out and hugged him. Both, Jeff and Fred were shocked and lost for words. Fred just looked, trying not to let his real feelings of disgust show. She stood in front of him with a kool-aid smile, wearing the four-hundred dollar Gucci robe Fred had brought Jeff last year.

"Why are you'll standing outside?" She asked.

Jeff quickly replied. "Oh, Fred was just leaving, baby." Fred asked, paying Jeff no mind. "Why do you have on that robe?" Kim and Jeff looked at each other.

Fred continued, "Jeff, you would stoop that low??"

Kim turned to Jeff. "What's he talking about, Jeff?"

"Look, Kim this is between me and Jeff. I've never had anything against you."

Jeff had it! "Look, Fred you better get your monkey ass from in front of my door!!" He ripped the robe off of Kim's back and threw it in Fred's face.

Kim stood naked in front of the two, in shock, trying to hide her body with her hands. "What..... What are you doing, Jeff!!!?" Jeff pushed her back in his place and followed. "Oh, don't worry, he's a fucking faggot!!!!!! He ain't worried about your naked body!!!!!!!!!!!!!" He shouted.

"What about you, Jeff?! What are you?! Tell her the whole story!! If I'm a faggot then I guess you're a Homo!!!!!!!!!!!!" Fred shouted through the door that was slammed in his face. He continued. "Tell her about us, Jeff!!!!!!" Kim's mouth dropped to the floor and tears attacked her eyes. Fred's comments rang in Jeff's ears.

When Sharon opened the door and saw Kim standing outside in a robe with red eyes, she was shocked. "Kim, what's up? You okay.....Jeff okay?" She asked pulling her into the house. Kim just dropped to her knees and started crying,

"Ty! Get down here!!" Sharon shouted.

He ran down stairs. "What's going on....What happened, Kim? Is Jeff ok?"

Kim looked up at the two with pure hate in her eyes. "Fuck Jeff, that mother fucking faggot!!!!!"

Tyron just sat in the T.V. room listening to Kim as she told him and Sharon what had happened at Jeff's place. Sharon sat with her mouth twisted in amazement. Tyron sat with his forehead wrinkled, his heart pounding, and anger boiling. He jumped up, grabbed his jacket from the coat rack and headed out the door. The two women followed. "Where you going?" Sharon asked, even though she already knew the answer.

"You know where, I'm going over to Jeff's!"

"Are you sure that's a good idea. You're really upset right now. Just wait until the afternoon." Sharon pleaded.

"Fuck the afternoon! I gotta see that nigga' now!!" He jumped in his truck and sped off, leaving the two standing outside the front of the house.

"I'm gonna throw some sweats on and give you some to put on. Come upstairs." Sharon said.

"I'm sorry, Sharon. Maybe I shouldn't have come over here like that. I just didn't know what to do or where to go. I just grabbed his car keys and made him tell me where you guys lived."

"Girl don't even worry about it. We just need to get over to Jeff's, cause I don't know what's going to kick off with him and Ty."

When the girls got to Jeff's, Tyron was sitting across from him with sweat beating down his face.

"Oh, my god!" Sharon shouted. "Baby, give me the gun please...." She pleaded.

It was like she wasn't in the room when Tyron spoke. "You fucking faggot ass nigga! You like fucking men?! I should have known you and that sissy ass cat was a little too close!!!" He cocked back the gun and moved closer to Jeff.

"NO! Baby please give me that gun! It's not worth it, you just got out of trouble!" Sharon pleaded again.

Tyron finally acknowledged Sharon's presence. He snapped at her. "What?!!!! I don't give a fuck about no trouble!! This here has been my friend for as long as I could remember!!! I'm the only one that's walking this earth that can check his homo ass!!"

"Look... Tyron...." Jeff tried to explain.

"Look what bitch!!! You been walking around me gay as fuck!!!." He jumped over the chair and stuck the gun in his mouth. "You like sucking dick?!!! Huh? Answer me faggot!!!!" Tears ran down Jeff's face. He couldn't believe what was going on. "Please...Ty....." He mumbled.

"Oh, my God, Ty." Sharon ran over to him and Jeff. "Look, just think about this. It's not worth it!! Leave him be!!!" Sharon screamed.

Kim walked over to Jeff and punched him in the face. "You lucky I don't have a gun right now. I would shoot you until your brains covered the walls!!"

Suddenly Tyron pulled the gun from Jeff's mouth and passed it to Sharon. "She's right...Ain't no homo, sissy, faggot worth my career. I want your ass out of this townhouse by the end of the week!! I don't want to see your face again!!! You hear me?!!" All Jeff could do was agree. "Yeah....."

Tyron and the girls walked out the door.................. And didn't look back.

When It's Said & Done

Toni sat stiff in the hard wood chair. Even with all the commotion in the room, the back and forth debating, Toni still sat stiff, staring at the wall in front of her. It was like she wasn't in the crowded room. If she could have it her way, she wouldn't be there. She sat and thought, thought about the beginning. And as she forced the voices around her to fade, she went deeper into thought. After a while she wasn't in the room no more. She was in her own world. She asked herself why? Why was she even there? How? How did she get herself there? She remembered the beginning. She remembered when she first got with him.

****

It was a cold winter night. Toni had been chillin' at her girlfriend Stacy's crib. They had planned on going out that night, so Toni brought her clothes with her to avoid going all the way back home. The girls were shootin' the shit while they waited for the rest of the girls. "You know that boy asked for you, Toni." Stacy said with a smirk on her face.

"What Boy?" Toni asked.

"J.R. I saw him on the block, when I went to cop some trees."

"Whatever. He's too shady for me. All anti-social and shit. And why does he always see one of my friends and ask for me, but when he sees me he acts like he ain't got much to say?" Toni replied, pullin' on a dutch full of haze and chocolate.

"Toni, that's just how da' nigga is, girl."

"Well, I ain't got time for da' shit. Ya' heard?"

"I can dig it. He asked me 'bout ya' show Friday."

"Word? How he know?"

"You know the boys probably mentioned it or something."

"Oh. Ain't like his shady ass comin' anyway."

"You never know. If the boys go he might go."

"Like I said, what da' fuck ever."

When the girls pulled up to the club, three cars deep, it was packed outside. You could tell they wasn't letting nobody else in, but the girls knew that didn't mean them. Shelly jumped out the car and went towards the door. "Let me handle this." She said and walked over to the door. The girls watched anxiously in the car. They knew they had to be up in there. Everybody who was somebody was up in that motherfucker. They watched every gesture Shelly and the bouncer made trying to figure shit out. In no more than two minutes, Shelly came walking back over to the girls with a big grin on her face. Trina rolled the window down. "What happened?" She asked.

"What da' fuck you think happened? We goin' up in that piece. He said they wasn't lettin' nobody else in."

"So, how we goin' in? Trina asked.

"I used Toni's name." She replied.

Toni eyes popped open. "Me? He knew who I was? What you said?"

"Hell yeah he knew who you was, he better had recognized. Bitch you blowin' up! You don't see it, but everybody else does. Now, let's park these cars and roll in that shit. He said he'll have one of the security walk us back from the lot straight in."

The girls went and parked the cars. All eyes was on them when they stepped out the cars. They all had minks on. In all colors and styles. Don't get it twisted these was some bad ass chicks half of them had skills in the store. The best boosters in their borough. It was all about survival with them. Some had jobs, some didn't, but food hit their tables, clothes covered their kids backs, and bills got paid. One way or another.

The girls walked back towards the club with the bouncer. People were whispering and mumbling, about how the girls were allowed to enter the club after they were told it was shut down. A few girls noticed Toni and made comments. One girl standing with a group of her friends pointed to Toni and her crew as they walked in and said to her homegirl. "That's that new girl....umm... Big T. I like her, she dope. And she keep it real." Toni caught an ear full as they were walking in. She stopped and turned in the girl's direction and smiled. "Thank you. Ya not goin' in?"

The girl that had noticed her smiled back and said, "You're welcome. Na, they said it's closed down."

"Who you wit'?" Toni asked. The girl pointed to two of the girls in the group. Toni didn't bother to ask about the other four that she didn't point to. She just pulled them in with her and her friends and once in the club they said thank you and went their way. Toni just had a heart like that.

The girls went straight to the bar and from the bar to the VIP. It was packed wall to wall. But it seemed nobody minded, because it wasn't like it was packed with a bunch of nobody's. Everybody was in there. The music was pumpin' and the drinks was flowin. The DJ gave Toni and her crew a shout out. "We got Big T in the house!! Doin' it up with her fly ass crew!!!" Then they dropped Toni's single. Toni couldn't believe how people was breaking to her shit. They played it four times. The rest of her entourage was scattered throughout the club doin' them. Getting numbers and drinking. Toni and Stacy stayed in

VIP socializing. Stacy tapped Toni on the arm and pointed out into the crowd. "There goes ya' brother and them."

Toni eyes dodged in and out the crowd. "Where? I don't see them." Stacy pointed in the boys' direction. "Right there at the bar. And look who's with them." Toni spotted them. Not caring too much for the fact that J.R. was with them. She was more so surprised.

The girls made their way to the bar where the boys were standing. Toni snuck up behind her brother and tapped him.

"What up? I thought you wasn't comin' out." She said to Link, her brother.

"We changed our minds. Who you wit'? Want somethin' to drink? I heard ya' little shout out, you blowin' up!"

"I'm wit' da' girls. I want Red Alize, you can get Stacy that too."

He turned back to the bartender and ordered the girls' drinks. J.R. was standing a little ways down from Link. It seemed like as soon as she noticed him he noticed her. They made eye contact and smiled at one another. It wasn't until then she had noticed how cute he really was. She knew at that point she wanted to fuck with him. Could it be the six drinks she had, she thought to herself. Naw. It had nothin' to do with drinks, she wanted him.

It was four-o-clock and everybody started exiting the club. It took ten minutes for the girls to find one another. Most of them had slid off with one of their beats. Stacy and Toni rode together with two other friends, but by the end of the night only Toni and Stacy ended up left in the car. The same bouncer that walked them in the club had offered to walk them back to their car. Toni told him thank you, but her brother was there and she was fine.

Link and his friends waited for Toni to pull her car out of the lot. Toni was hoping J.R. was still around. The funny thing was J.R. wanted to see her too. He knew he probably wouldn't say nothing to her. He just wasn't the type to rap to girls. And who was the first face she saw? His. And from then on he was her mission. And discreetly she was his.

Toni's Mission

It was two days since the club and Toni still hadn't seen J.R. She was leaving in a week to go do some promo stuff and she hadn't even begun her mission. She went on the block and still she didn't see him. She figured the one person that would know his whereabouts was Stacy. She knew everybody's biz. Toni jumped out the bed and started dialing Stacy's number. Before the phone could reach the second ring Stacy answered. With her thirsty ass.

"Hello!" Stacy answered breathing hard and out of breath.

"Damn, girl what you doin'?"

"Oh, what up Toni? I was thinkin' 'bout you this morning. I just got out the shower and I heard the phone ring. What's goin' on, what you doin' today?"

"Nothin' I wanted to go to the movies or something. Why, what up with you?" She was hoping Stacy would give up the info, like she usually does.

"Who you goin' to da' movies wit'?"

"I don't know. We all can go I guess."

"Oh. I thought you meant on a date or somethin'."

"Whatever. Who I'm goin' on a date wit'? I don't got no beats. I got rid of all of them."

"What about Fred?"

"Fuck Fred. He be playin' hisself. Man, I'm tired of these men. They treat us fucked up 'cause we let them. We don't give a fuck about ourselves, if we did—they would know they can't treat us anyway. I'm tellin' you I'm not goin' for da' shit no more." "You right, girl. That's why when J.R. asked for ya' number I told him no."

Toni's heart skipped a beat. She tried to sound uninterested. "What? When he asked for my number." She asked.   "Last   night. He was on da' block.

Oh! Yeah. Girl, guess who got locked up last night!" She said, changing the subject. "Who!" Toni asked, wanting her to get back to J.R. "Timmy, girl!!"

Toni's mouth dropped.   "Get da' fuck out of here! When...where..?"

"On da' block, last night!"

"For what?"

"How you gon' ask for what? What you think? Da' big boys came for his ass."

"Feds?"

There was a brief silence on the phone.

"Stacy, who else de' got?"

"Nobody. He had a federal warrant."

All Toni could think about was her brother and how she knew Timmy was a weak nigga'. She knew he could get in there and get under pressure. Stacy broke the silence.

"Toni?"

"Yeah, I'm here. Man, that's fucked up."

"Ain't it? But anyway let me tell you 'bout ya' boy J.R. He asked me for ya' number, you know I'm not goin' to give ya' number out like that. I asked him for what? You know his shady ass, talkin 'bout just give it to him. He said he got to ask you 'bout somethin'. I told him I couldn't give ya' number out like that. Plus I knew you wasn't tryin' to see him like that. So, he gave me his number for you to call him."

If Stacy only knew how bad she was trying to see him.

"What is it?" Toni asked

"You want it?" She questioned her, with curiosity.

Toni thought about how big her friend's mouth was and changed her mind, real quick. "Forget it. I don't want that shit."

"You know ya' right." Stacy answered. Stacy would go along with anything you go along with. If Toni wanted the number she would have been down with it.

After the girls hung up, making plans to hook up later, Toni sat and wondered how she could get J.R.'s number. She knew if she asked her brother for the number it will be a million and one questions. Fuck it, she thought, she might as well ask. She picked up the phone and started dialing Link's number, practicing what she was going to say. The phone rang, but the voice on the other end wasn't familiar. "What up?" The person answered.

"What up? That's how you answer a phone? Where Link at? Who's this anyway?" Toni asked the person, with an attitude.

"What? Who's this?"

"This is his sister, Toni. Who is this?"

The person calmed down their voice. "Oh. What up? It's J.R. He went in da' store. He'll be right back."

Shit! She thought to herself. What a fucking coincidence. What was she supposed to say? "Oh. Stacy said you wanted to ask me something." She replied.

"Forget it now."

What the fuck was he talking about, she thought.

"Excuse me?" She asked.

"You heard. Forget it."

"A'ight." She answered with a whatever attitude. "Tell my brother to call me when he comes out of the store."

"One." He answered. And then the line went dead.

He just hung up. Toni was stressed. J.R. had memorized her number from the caller ID on Link's cell phone. He had planned on calling her later. Once he got rid of his baby mother, who was sitting in the back seat of the car when Toni had called.

When Toni got around the way, Link and his boys was standing outside their cars, like they was getting ready to break out. And there he was, J.R., standing next to her brother. She was glad she had put on her tight jean set. Yes! She thought to herself. She didn't hold back. She doubled parked and jumped out the car. She knew he would have no other choice but to look at her. That type of shit didn't move J.R. though. He saw chicks every day. All shapes and sizes. Toni walked over to the crowd of guys.

"Link, why you ain't call me back." She asked.

"When." He replied.

"Your friend ain't tell you I called earlier?" She asked, pointing to J.R.

"Naw." He turned to J.R. "Yo, why you ain't tell me my sister called?"

J.R. gave him a smile and took a pull off of the blunt he was holding. "I forgot son." Toni just looked at him. His smile was so cute. She wanted to melt.

Link turned backed to his sister and put his arm around her

shoulder. He playfully pulled her to the side, to talk to her in private. J.R. kept his eye on her, on the low. "Yo, you better watch ya'self ." He said to his sister with a warning look on his face.

"What you talkin' 'bout?" She asked with a confused look on her face.

"What you think I'm stupid. How long have I known you?" He asked her.

"What? All my life."

"That's my point. You can't pull no wool over my eyes. I'm tellin' you I know him better than you. He's my friend, I'm with the nigga' almost everyday. Don't come runnin' to me when shit don't go ya' way."

No more needed to be said. It didn't make sense to even deny or question his assumptions. He was right, he was her brother, and he knew her well. Wasn't no doubt Link loved the hell out of his sister, but at the same time she wasn't a little girl no more. He smiled and changed the subject.

"So, did them car people call you back?" He asked her. Still thrown off by what he had just mentioned to her, she snapped back into the conversation. "Huh...Oh yeah. That's what I was calling for earlier." She put a big fat smile on her face. She felt good being able to do for her brother, considering everything he did for her and her sister.

"Well, what de' said?" Link asked.

"They said everything is straight. We just got to take them the money."

He smiled. "You want to come with us?" He asked her. "Where ya' goin'?" She asked?

"Look you want to go or not? Don't worry 'bout where we goin'."

"A'ight." She replied with a smile.

"Park ya' car and get in wit' me and J.R." She parked and jumped in the back of his car. She had no idea where she was going, but she knew that she was straight once she was with her brother and them. After riding around for half hour getting weed and drinks they finally started towards the highway. Listening in on Link's conversation, she realized that they were going to Great Adventure. She screamed over the loud music. "Hey, Link! You think we can get one of my friends since we goin' to Great Adventure!?" She asked.

He gave her a funny look through the rear view mirror. J.R. cut in. "Naw. Them bitches ain't goin' nowhere." Toni just screwed her face at him. It turned her on in a way. It wasn't no secret he didn't like some of her friends too much. He might speak every now and then, but he didn't fuck with them like that.

They stopped in Jersey to pick up one of Link's girls. Toni was glad when J.R. didn't move to let her sit in the front. Link turned around to the back seat. "Darlene, that's my sister Toni. Toni that's Darlene."

"What's up." Toni mumbled.

"Hi." The girl replied.

They rode in silence, until Darlene started talking to J.R. She was trying to be nosy. She wanted to know if Toni and J.R. was a couple. "J.R., my girl Carol asked for you." Darlene leaned forward and said to him. J.R. paid her no mind.

She tapped him. "You heard me?"

He answered her nonchalantly. "Yeah, I heard. But I don't care. You don't know? I don't pay ya' chicks no mind."

"Why you so shady?" She asked him. He just kept smoking his weed and bopping his head to the music. He was a funny character. For the most part all he cared about, what came first in his life was—his drugs, money, and the streets. Everything else came secondary. But he liked Toni. He couldn't understand what it was or why, but he liked her. He didn't know if he would ever pressure her. It would depend on how he felt at the time.

By the end of the afternoon the crew was high and drunk. Toni had a hand full of stuffed animals. All sizes. J.R. had a pocket full of numbers he had collected from girls. For a nigga that don't give a fuck about chicks, he sure was racking up on them numbers. Toni had collected a few herself. Whenever Link turned his back. Link didn't play that shit. He told Toni stick with them and don't be talking to no nigga's. He said she would make him have to pop some cat. He didn't see, but better believe J.R. saw. He couldn't help it, he kept his eye on her all day. What she thought Link didn't see J.R. did. They all took pictures, which they had to beg J.R. to get in. Finally he gave in and posed in a couple. Darlene stuck up under Link all day. And he hates that! If she only knew.

On the ride home Darlene got to take the front seat. She was in her glory. Toni got in the back with J.R. and she fell right to sleep. When she woke up J.R. was behind the wheel and Link and Darlene had disappeared. She jumped up out of the slouched position she had fallen asleep in. "Where's my brother, J.R.?" She asked

"He asked me to drop you off. I was 'bout to wake you up and ask where you lived"? She tried to get her thoughts together. Here she was alone with him. No way she was going to let him go that quick. Before she knew it she opened her mouth and words were coming out. "I'm hungry. Can you stop to get me something to eat before you drop me?" She asked him.

"Okay." He replied. Surprisingly to her, he didn't have a problem with her request. "Where you wanna go? You know I don't be eating in the streets too much. I don't know where shit to eat at."

"You don't know anything. We can go right to the village to French Toast." He turned around and looked at her like she was crazy. She knew it was too good to be true. She knew the shadyness was going to come sooner or later.

"The what?" He asked her

"Its right on Sixth Ave." She answered.

She was open. She tried to hold her composure the whole ride there. She felt like she was on a date. She wanted him to come home with her. She wanted to sleep with him. "You slut!" she thought to herself. She laughed a little laugh out loud, but he didn't pay her no mind. He just smoked his weed and listened to his music. His beeper and cell was going off the hook! He just looked at the numbers that came up on both of them and ignored them. Until finally, when they parked in front of the restaurant, he sat in the car while she got out. He was beefing with somebody on the cell phone. She could tell it was a girl. She didn't care, though. He was with her. She didn't care that he had mad bitches either. She knew his style and she didn't give a fuck, she was going to get with him. And tonight was her big opportunity. Her brother had warned her, and still she insisted. She knew his style, but she had it in her mind that she would change all that. Yeah, he had a baby mama, a few at that. But so, she thought. And she knew he was in the streets, but that's all she ever had fucked with. Even though she said she was trying to get away from that life style since she got her record deal. Shit was getting deep in the street and nigga's weren't playing the game right. But none of that mattered at this point. She was a street bitch, no matter what.

He sat across from her while she ate and watched her yap on her cell phone. Now, who the hell could she be talking to this time of night, he thought to himself. Bitches is crazy he said to himself. He was attracted to her, though. But to J.R. chicks was chicks and that was that. She was smart though. Even when she didn't think he was checking her out, he was. And he knew she was smart, street smart. He was getting into her slowly, but surely. Plus her being an up and coming artist didn't hurt, either. He also knew she could be dangerous. He knew he could end up falling for her and that wasn't good. Toni was loyal to her men, he knew that. She was thugged out and he liked that. He knew she would have his back, if anything.

The phone rang off the hook in the morning. Toni was in a deep sleep and tried to ignore the ringing, but whoever it was on the other line wasn't giving up. She rolled over and snatched the phone of the base. Clearing her throat. "Hello."

"Yo! You ain't hear ya' phone ringing?"

"I was sleep. What's up?" She replied.

"Nothing. I need that stuff out the closet."

"Da' food or the paper plates?" She asked her brother. By this time she was out the bed and in her closet on her knees.

"Da' food. All of it. I'm gonna send Shorty there for it. A'ight?" He answered.

"Ok."

"Yo, did J.R. say where he was going last night? I can't find da' nigga' no where."

"Naw."

"A'ight call me when Shorty leaves." They hung up. She knew she had told a bold face lie to Link. But she didn't know what she should have told him. He threw her off with the question. She didn't know if J.R. wanted her to tell his business. She bagged up everything nice and tight and walked over to J.R. She stood over him. He had such a peaceful look on his face. He was sleeping like a baby. She didn't want to wake him, but she knew she had to. She wished he could stay forever. She tapped his bare back softly. He didn't budge. She bent down in his ear.

"Hey...Hey." She whispered in his ear

He rolled over opening his sleepy eyes. "What time is it?" He asked. "Eleven-thirty." She answered.

He rolled back over. "Wake me up at one-o-clock. Ya' heard?" She was satisfied with his answer. He wanted to stay longer. Yes!

When the bell rang, Toni went and retrieved the bag she had fixed for Link earlier. She knew it was Shorty. She opened the door and handed the bag to Shorty and closed the door. She didn't bother with Shorty on a personal level. She dealt with Shorty when she had to, and usually it would be something concerning her brother.

After they ate the breakfast Toni had prepared, J.R. got in the shower and got dressed. Toni got in the shower as he stepped out. Bare ass. By the time she came out the shower he had his Timberlands laced and was half way out the door. He lit his blunt and dialed a number on his cell phone.

"Yo, what up?" He asked the person on the other end of the phone. "Man, whateva'. I don't want to hear that shit. One!" He hung up on the person. He turned to Toni, who was sitting on her bed reading mail.

"Hit me later, a'ight?" He said to her.

"A'ight." She answered like it wasn't nothing.

He walked out and she just sat on the bed and tried to make sense of what just happened. Before Toni left the house J.R. called her about three times. Asking her if she had spoke to her brother. All of a sudden, he can't find Link. He knew he just wanted to speak to her. He had a problem with communication. But that was all right with her, she understood his language and she knew how to read in between the lines.

She was on the phone doing interviews most of the afternoon. Her car was supposed to get to her house at four-thirty to take her to her photo shoot. She couldn't stop thinking about J.R. It wasn't until she went under her bed to look for her other shoe, when she realized he had left his beeper. It must have dropped when he took his pants off last night. She thought she heard something vibrating, but she wasn't sure. She held it for a minute or two. Then she pressed the button. It was on overflow. Naw, she thought to herself. She stuck the pager in her pocketbook and picked up the phone to dial his number. She realized that's why he probably called her, so his number could show on her caller ID. He knew he didn't leave it with her when he left.

His phone must have rang four or five times before he picked up. "Who's dis?" He said. His music was blasting in the background.

"It's me, Toni."

"Oh, what up?" He asked as he lowered his music.

"Nothing, you left your pager here."

He paused like he was looking for it. "OH, shit! I sure did. No wonder my shit ain't been going off, I don't got the shit. How long you gon' be home?

"I'm gettin' ready to break out now." She answered

"A'ight... Where you going, around the way?" He asked.

"Naw, a photo shoot in the city. In da' village. If you want you can come and get it from there."

"A'ight, just hit my phone when you get up there. I got to take care of something." The car people clicked through on the other line just as he hung up. The car was downstairs and it had already picked up Stacy.

After the photo shoot Toni cleaned the makeup off her face and changed her clothes, she kept looking out the tall loft window to see if she saw J.R. She hadn't mentioned to Stacy that he had stayed the night or that she was going to be taking the car home by herself if he had showed up like he said he would. When she looked at the number on her cell phone and saw it was him she got a warm feeling. Like when they were making love the night before.

"Hello" She answered.

"What up?" He asked.

He had no idea he was taking her home. She came to that conclusion on her own. "Nothing. Just finished. You coming up or you want me to come down?" She asked. All of a sudden she got too scared to ask for a ride home. Not that she needed it.

"I'm not comin' up there. Who up there?" He said and asked in the same breath.

"Nobody, but staff...oh and Stacy." She replied.

"Naw, come down." He said kind of agitated.

"A'ight. I'm coming down." She hung up and gathered her stuff. She told Stacy she would call her when she got home and that the car would be there in ten minutes to get her. She figured all he could do was say no and she would just take the car with Stacy back to Brooklyn. When she got downstairs he was on his cell and counting money. He made a hand gesture telling her to come in the car. When he pulled off she felt relieved. He must of known he was taking her home.

As the days, weeks, and months went by, Toni and J.R.'s relationship grew. So did Toni's career. The streets got more hectic as Link and J.R.'s money grew larger. Toni was on tour by now and was on the road more than she was at home. J.R. didn't mind. The way he saw it was at least his girl was doing something with her life at least she was somebody. Don't get it wrong, he was still a street nigga', he was still fucking! But everybody knew she was his girl and nobody was coming close to that.

While Toni was away, war was at its peak in the streets. Nobody didn't know where it came from. It just came about. She spent most of her days worrying about J.R. After every show she would go straight to her hotel and call home to check on J.R. He had keys to her place and his own side of the closet. And in the same closet he had his stash. He kept a good amount of his drugs and money there also. So did her brother. She never really thought much of it. That was her brother and she was going to be there for him no matter what. And in J.R.'s case, it just happened.

She was on tour for two and a half months and was going home in the morning. She couldn't wait. She told her brother to pick her up. Tomorrow couldn't come fast enough. She wanted to party with her friends, even though her friends alternated coming on the road. She just laid in the bed counting down the hours. In all reality, she was trying to forget about the drama she had to face when she got home. She had been hearing a lot of rumors about J.R. She didn't want to bring it back up to him again. Last time she said something about it, it caused a big ole' argument, so she decided to just chill. She had to catch herself. She knew that bullshit came with fuckin' with street niggas. But it's been ten months since she started fucking with him and feelings were taking over. Somehow she had convinced herself to do her, like he had suggested in one of his angry outbursts. She was gonna go home in the morning and live her life as it came. She wasn't gonna stress J.R.

Back @ Home

Link was rushing to make it to the bridge. He knew it was no way he could make it to Harlem to pick up weed and get to the airport in time. But he was determined. And just as he got to the 125th St. exit he remembered he had to stop at the diamond district to pick up her watch. He had ordered it the week before. Damn! He thought to himself. He put his foot to the gas and copped his weed. He took the streets downtown to the district. He smiled as he looked at the iced out Rolex. You couldn't see the band it was so many diamonds. It was platinum with diamond band and face. The last row of diamonds were pink. On the back it was engraved. "U Da' best! luv u 4 life. Link" The jeweler had argued with him about it not fitting. Link told him "Make it happen...like Nike"! And he did just that. It was written in a circle around the back of the watch.

When he got to the airport, Toni was standing outside signing an autograph. She looked at him with her hands on her hips shaking her head. He looked at his watch. He was a half an hour late. She jumped in the truck and kissed him on the cheek. "What up my dunn!!" She asked excited.

He wiped his face off. "Yo, man!"

"Don't even try it nigga'! You don't miss ya' little Sis?"

"Yeah, but I don't know where ya' lips been, man!" He said joking.

"Whateva' nigga'. What's going on? How you been?" She asked hyped.

"Man you act like you didn't call me almost everyday." He replied.

"So! It's not the same as seeing you." She continued with the questions. "Are you takin' me to eat? Oh! Are you goin' with me to the awards Saturday? You told me you would think 'bout it last week."

"Man! If you don't shut ya' trap for a minute... Where you want to eat? And don't tell me Carmines, I hate that place. And I really don't feel like going to the city."

"Man, come on. I just got back. I been craven Carmines. Please. And don't try to avoid my question about the awards. I want all ya' ta' come."

He looked out the side of his eye and twisted his mouth. "I bet you do!" He replied.

She knew he was talking about J.R. "I do. How it's gon' look I'm nominated and my big brother not there?"

He paused for a minute. "A'ight, big head. I'll make da' flight reservations tomorrow." He said.

"For real! Don't front, Link."

"Man, what I said? Don't stress me."

The whole ride to the city she talked his head off about the tour. Toni and Link were the closest out of the five. Her sister Katlynn lived in Florida with her husband and two kids. Her other two sisters lived in Brooklyn with their kids. Her and her sister Rose was tight too. She would go on the road with her every now and then. She offered all of them to come to the awards, but they couldn't. She didn't expect them to anyway, except Rose. But Rose started a new job and couldn't take off. She needed her brother there, for support. Their parents died a year and a half ago in a car accident. They didn't talk about it much.

When they got in the restaurant there was a wait and during the wait it seemed like every black person recognized Toni. Link was high he didn't pay it no mind. He knew his sister was famous, more than she did. He forgot the watch in the car. On his way back to the garage, J.R. called him. He knew he wanted to ask if Link had spoken to Toni. Link knew he wanted to ask too. But...he didn't and Link didn't bother to volunteer. He did tell him he was in the city taking Toni out to eat. When he came back Toni was sitting at a table already. He sat down and put the box, wrapped in silver shiny paper, on the table.

She looked up. "What's dat'?"

"Man, stop askin' so many questions and open da' box." He replied. He didn't have to tell her twice. She snatched the box off the table and ripped the paper off. Her stomach was doing flips. Link was kind of nervous too. He didn't know why, he just was. Her mouth dropped to the floor as the watch shined off her face. "Oh shit!" She whispered. "Oh, my God...It's beautiful." She said with amazement.

"You like it?" He asked as he reached over the table and took off her old gold Rolex to replace it with the new one.

"What?...Like it? Da' shit is off da' hook! Thanx... Man thanx!" She answered

"You ain't got to thank me.. You deserve it."

She just watched the street lights bounce off her watch as they drove to Brooklyn. She couldn't believe it. She could have copped it herself if she really wanted to, but it felt different somebody else giving it to her. It felt good, her brother giving it to her. She rather him giving it to her than a nigga' too. They said their good-byes and he promised he would make him and his friends' flights in the morning. She said thank you again for the watch. He said he had to take care of something and would call and check on her later.

When she got upstairs her machine was full. She undressed while listening to her messages. They had to be recent, cause she checked her messages daily while she was away. They had called to let her know the tour bus would reach in the morning and her bags a be dropped off as soon as it reaches. J.R. was on the machine a few times, but only left a message twice. Good. She thought to herself. That gave her a reason to call him, to see what he wanted. She ran a hot bath while J.R.'s phone rang.

She could hear a girl in the background when he picked up. "YO!" He answered. Talking loud over the music.

"Hey, what up?" She asked, trying to focus on what was going on in the background.

"Oh, what da' deal?" He asked, looking at his watch checking the time. He was kind of salty not hearing from her sooner. But he couldn't tell her that, it wouldn't had been him if he did.

"Nothin'. Where you?"

"In da' streets." He answered, sounding like he was moving away from the noise...and the girl that was talking in the background.

"I know that. Where I meant?"

"In Bk." He answered

She noticed his shade. "A'ight. Call me when you get a chance or somethin'." She hung up.

She poured a glass of champagne and soaked in the tub. She yapped on the phone with her friends and drank. By the time she finished, she was wrinkled like a new born.

She missed him. She couldn't fool herself. She was horny and she needed him. She wondered where and what he was doing. She had a gut feeling he was with someone else. Riding around, in his brand new car, that was in her name. That thought made her sick to her stomach.

The clock read 4:39AM when she answered the phone. It was a collect call from J.R. He was locked up. She had to pick up the car since it was in her name. She didn't know for what. He couldn't talk for long. She jumped up and threw some sweats on. She was still kind of tipsy. Oh my God! She thought. She didn't know what to do. Should she call Link? Naw, she would wait until she found out what was what. She started crying. She wished he would have put down his guards and came over.

When she got to the station, she signed for his belongings and showed her license for the car. He had not gone to Central Booking yet and she could see him a little in the back cell. A young cop recognized her and told her on the low what had happened. Apparently he ran a light and got stopped. When they checked the car he had weed and a large amount of money on him. He told them his girlfriend was a rapper and it belonged to her. Him and the cop exchanged words and they arrested him. They didn't find the stash box. Thank God! She thought. She could have imagined what might have been in there.

She went home and waited for a phone call. But never got it, until early afternoon. She went to court, paid his bail and they went home. They drove in silence. Half way home she broke the silence.

"I think I'm pregnant, J.R." She said staring straight in front of her.

"What?" He asked

"What you mean what? I think I'm pregnant." She replied.

"When da' fuck you was going to tell me? When you went into labor!"

"No. I was waiting for the right time."

"And what made you think this was it?"

"I don't know. If you would have came over yesterday...I mean I had planned to tell you last night, but you was too busy to come over. I guess." She said rolling her eyes.

"Man, listen."

"Man listen what!. I come home from tour and you running da' street with some bitch!! So you listen muthafucka!!" She said defensively.

"What da' fuck you talkin' bout? That's what I be talkin' bout wit' you chicks!"

"You know what I'm talkin' bout'! So what you sayin, you wasn't wit' no bitch when you got arrested?" She asked looking dead smack at him.

"YO! Tell ya' fuckin' friends keep my name out de' mouth for I pop one of them!!"

"My friends nothin'! Stop using them for an excuse. Da' cop told me a bitch was with you and when she showed i.d. they let her go. Let me catch a bitch in this car and you gon see... Fuck wit' me if you want. You fuckin' crab!! As a matter of fact I want dis' mothafucka out my name. You disrespectful fucker!!" She shouted.

He pulled over on Flatbush and jumped out. "What?! Fuck you!! That's my word.... Fuck you!!!" He shouted and slammed the door. She watched as he hailed down a cab and disappeared. She crawled over into the driver's seat from the passenger side and pulled off. She mumbled to herself all the way home. Fuck him, I don't need his sorry ass anyway!! She thought to herself. She drove down the Ave. to show any thirsty bitches, who might want him, she was back. If she only knew who was in the car last night.

It had been five days since J.R. got out the car and she hadn't spoken to him. She was leaving today to go to the awards. Her brother had kept his word, he was meeting her at the airport. Him and three of his friends. Never once did she bother to ask if J.R. was going. She had intended to stand her ground. Even though she did take the car on the Ave. and left the key in the Laundromat for him. Oh, by the way the pregnancy was a false alarm.

The limo got to her house ten minutes late and she still had to pick up Stacy and Shelly. Her friends had to draw straws to see who would go, being she could only take two of them.

When she pulled up to Stacy's building the kids ran to the limo asking for dollars. After she passed out twenty dollars in singles they pulled off. She fell into depression as they approached the airport. She wished J.R. was going.

Link and them was standing outside waiting. She didn't roll with no security this trip. She had her brother and them, she didn't need it.

The Awards

Even though the awards were Sunday, Toni had to go out to L.A. early to do radio and for meetings. She had to get something to wear too. She felt good rolling with her people. She wished her brother would get out the streets. She wanted him to roll with her all the time.

They dropped their bags at their rooms and went straight to Rodeo Drive. Link and his boys must have brought ten to fifteen thousand a piece with them. J.R. called Link's phone about five times since they had landed. He was beefing about some shit that was happening back at home, but Link ain't want to hear it. He just kept telling him how much fun he was having and how he should have joined the rest of them out there. And of course being the stubborn person he was, he declined the offer. He claimed somebody had to be home taking care of business. Deep inside he wanted to be there...but his pride. He was going to make it his business to watch the awards though...no matter what.

"Girl, don't be nervous." Stacy said while she helped Toni get dressed.

"For real. Ya' makeup look bangin'! That makeup artist is no joke." Shelly insisted.

Toni looked at her watch. "Where is da' damn hairdresser!"

"Girl, calm down. She probably on her way. Look, this is ya' day. You gon' win dat' shit....and if you don't at least you was nominated. And we gon' party our asses off no matter what!" Stacy shouted slapping Toni five. "Now stand up and let me look at you." She continued. She just stared at her friend. She looked da bomb!! They all did. Of course they was boosting the whole time during their shopping spree. They only paid for 20% of the stuff they got.

After Toni's hair was done, they all met in the lobby of the hotel. They saw everybody. Every rapper, singer, actor. That's when Toni really realized who she was. People were snapping pictures of her, other artists were shaking her hand and saying hello, and fans were mobbing her as her and her entourage got in the stretch limo.

"Man, girl! I guess you are the shit. I don't know what de' see in ya' ass!" Link said to her in a playful way.

"Whateva' nigga'!" She replied, laughing.

"You done blew up Shorty!" Dex said smiling.

Dex was one of Link's good friends. They all grew up together. He was a loyal cat. She always checked for him. He was a little on the crazy tip, but he didn't take no shit. And he didn't think twice about poppin' a nigga'.

Now Trips, both of them, was just as crazy! But they were fine as hell! Everybody called both of them Trips. It was three of them, they were triplets. Everybody around the way just referred to them as Trips. People would just ask, "Which one?" And you would have to describe which one you were talking about. The third brother got killed years ago, on the Ave. So when people look at them and say," Oh, they're twins." They would reply, "No, we're triplets."

She looked around the limo at her friends. They had no idea how nervous she was. Trips, the shorter one, kept rubbing her leg to comfort her. He knew she was nervous and stressed. He knew she wanted J.R. to be there, but at the same time J.R. was his man. He couldn't get in the middle of it.

As soon as the limo pulled up the commotion started. She had her publicist pulling at her, the people from the awards tugging at her, press calling her name. She pulled her brother in about every picture she took. And the ones she didn't take with Link or herself, she pulled Dex, Trips (both of them) Stacy and Shelly. The guys didn't want to participate in any photos. They couldn't have a cat pointing at them in magazines saying I copped coke from them. She walked the red carpet into the theater with her people. Once in the theater, the usher directed them to their seats. She was surprised to see where they were sitting. She really didn't realize who she was. They were sitting in the second row in the middle. All eyes were on them as they sat down. People were wondering more so who was the guys with her. People never saw them a day in their lives. The guys were clean cut and iced out and that raised the eyebrows of everybody in the industry.

About an hour into the awards, it was time for Toni's category. She grabbed her brother's leg. She looked straight at the stage.

All she heard was, "And the nominees are...". Her mind and ears went blank from there. Until she heard, "And the winner is Big

Toni!" Her mouth dropped. Her heart dropped. She hugged her brother and jumped up. Before she knew it she was on stage in front of a screaming crowd. She smiled and leaned closer to the mic. "Thank you. I don't know what to say. First of all I would like to thank my Lord and Savior, Jesus Christ. Without Him none of this would be possible. I wanna thank my fans all of you." She pointed to the balcony of the arena. "My friends, so many I can't name all of you, but you know who you are." She pointed to her crew in the audience and then into the camera. "My mother and father, I wish you both was here, God bless y'all soul. My sisters no matter what I love ya'. Umm... my label, radio, J.R., what up!. And last but not least...my brother. You're my friend...You're everything to me, without you I don't know what I would do. I love you. You're my other half, I love you Link. Thank you." She held up her award and walked off the stage. She won one more before the evening was over.

After taking millions of pictures they went to the after party. Her butterflies were gone. She was feeling the champagne she had drank in the limo on the way there. They were standing at the bar ordering more champagne when she felt someone's hand on her shoulder. When she turned around she saw the face of an unfamiliar man, a big man at that. "Hello, how are you? Big Man wanted to know if you would like to join him for a glass of champagne."

She looked at him with confusion. "Where is he drinking? And why he can't ask me himself?" She asked with her hand on her hip and with her sassy attitude.

He smiled at her wit. "He's over in the back. And it was too crowded for him to walk over here." He replied

"Well, I walked over here...Tell him I said thank you, but I rather wait until he can ask me himself...And plus I got my family wit' me." She answered with a smile.

He reached out his hand and shook hers. "Okay, nice meeting you. I'll tell him." He walked away and disappeared into the crowd.

Link turned to her. "What dat' nigga' want?" He asked.

"Big Man sent him to ask if I wanted to have a drink of champagne with him." She answered.

"And what you say?"

"Told him I was with my peeps and why he can't ask himself."
He smiled at his sister. "You crazy."

Within minutes she felt another tap on her shoulder. When she turned around she was face to face with Big Man himself. The Biggest artist, record company CEO, and nigga' in the rap world. He had the same huge guy, who approached her minutes ago, with him. He reached over her and shook Link's and the rest of the guys' hands. "Hey, what up. I'm Big Man, nice to meet you." They all shook hands and then he turned back to Toni with a smile, showing his platinum and diamond teeth.

"And what up wit' you, Shorty? Now what was you tellin' my man?"

"You know what I told him. That's why you over here now." She replied with a smile.

He laughed. "Yeah, you right. So?"

"So what?"

"So I'm over here...will you AND ya' crew join me and mine's for a drink. Ya' know to celebrate us winning."

She turned to her people to see what they wanted to do. She turned back to him with a smile, really feeling her drinks now.

"A'ight. Let's go."

They all moved through the crowded club. Once in the double booth area, which was packed, they drank, laughed, and politicked. Link and Big Man talked a lot. Big man liked Link's style. He reminded him of himself before getting in the record game. Link checked for him too. To Link he seemed like a regular nigga' on the street. The two departed with promises to stay in touch. And so did Toni and Big Man.

Toni woke up to pounding on her hotel door. Her head was spinning from the night before. The message light on the phone was blinking and the clock read 2:30PM! She jumped out the bed and walked to the door.

"Who is it!" She shouted.

"Umm... The front desk ma'm. You have a package...It's marked urgent." The tiny voice said on the other side of the door.

She wrapped a towel around her naked body and cracked the

door. The voice fit the young lady that stood on the other side of the door. She was holding the largest floral arrangement Toni had ever saw. And she had a long gold box sticking out her jacket pocket. The tiny young girl smiled as if she knew before hand who was behind the door. "Hello. I have a package for you...as you can see. May I come in and set it on your desk?"

Toni opened the door wider and let her in. "Sure, come in."

The hotel attendant put the flowers on the desk. And handed Toni the gold box with a card. She let the girl out and read the card. She knew it was from her brother. The card read. "I had to leave earlier than expected. But I had a ball last night, hopefully we'll hook up soon. Here's something for you. Call me later. Big Man!"

She opened the gold box. "Oh shit!" She shouted. It was a platinum Tennis Bracelet. It had to be three carats. It took her a minute, but she got it on her wrist and the safety lock snapped. She thought she was dreaming. "Now that's a real nigga'" she said to herself, smiling.

She was the first one in the lobby at 9:45 later that night. They were on the red eye. The flight left at 11:00PM and got into New York at 7:20AM. That was good for her. She was going to sleep on the plane. She didn't mention the bracelet or flowers to anybody. She was going to let them see for themselves.

When they got on the plane Link switched his seat with Trips, so he could sit closer to Toni. Once they got good in the air Link started to talk to Toni.

"You know I'm proud of you, right?" He whispered in her ear.

She looked at him with a weird look. "What?"

"I'm proud of you...You know with the music and everything. I want you to keep it up, don't get distracted. Man, you got a chance to make it and to go places a lot of people wish de' could. You know how many people wish de' could be in ya' shoes? I want you to know I got ya' back no matter what."

She looked at him and smiled. "You act like you goin' somewhere or something."

"Naw, I just want you to know ... that ...look. I'm in da' streets. You know that, so I won't always be able to be with you like this weekend. But I got ya' back. I wish I could be by ya' side twenty-four-seven. But I can't, and I know that's what you want....But I can't. Maybe after I do what I got to do in the streets I can rock like that. That all, Kid!" And reached and kissed her on her cheek. She felt a warm feeling inside. She never heard her brother talk like that to her before. Except when she was a kid and would come in the house crying from a fall or something. That was the closest he came to being mushy. She slept on his shoulder the whole flight. She fell asleep wishing she could get her brother out the streets. Even though that's the way he lived his whole teenage and adult life. She would figure a way.

Back Home

When Link got back, shit was crazy. Money was coming in faster than ever. He was copping triple the amount of drugs. Shit was at fast pace.

It was about a month and a half since they got back from the awards. And Toni was about to do her fourth video. Her life was just as hectic. So, when Link told her Shorty was coming to pick up a package and Shorty hadn't got there, she was stressed. Shorty is never late. She tried calling Link's phone and the machine came on. She left a message and beeped him. The phone rang twenty-four minutes later, she was watching the clock.

"Hello." She answered.

"Yo, what happened? You paged me 911 about ten times."

"Shorty never came and I have to be on the set. Remember I told you I had to do a video today." She said.

"What you mean didn't come?!" He screamed.

"Like I said, didn't come."

He paused for a minute. "Shit! I got to do something with that shit...in a hour." He continued

"What you want me to do? Wait longer." She asked

"Naw." He replied, aggravated.

She paused for thought. "Where you at?"

"Uptown....Where your video at?"

"Today, we shootin' at a sound stage in Queens. Why?"

"You think you can meet me and drop it... I'll meet you downtown. I should be back in BK by then. I'll meet you at the gas station before you get on the bridge, on Flatbush Ave."

"A'ight. But make sure you there, I'm runnin' late already."

"Bet. That's why I love ya'!"

They hung up and she retrieved the six kilos of cocaine and went down to the limo, which was waiting for an hour. Of course when she got to the gas station Link wasn't there, but he pulled up not too long after her. She passed him the package and pulled off.

She sat back in the limo by herself. She thought about her brother and how much he had changed. How much he had adjusted to fit his environment. She didn't like it. He had dough, but he was looking more and more stressed everyday. He didn't go no where without his gun. He was always looking over his shoulder. He didn't think Toni noticed, but she did and she didn't like it. It gave her a cold feeling when she thought about it. The ringing of her cell phone broke her concentration.

"Hello." She answered the cell phone with a shallow voice.

"Hey! Are you in the car yet? Wait til you see the set. It's the bomb! You're gonna love it!" Lisa, Toni's new manager, said.

"Yeah, I'm in da' car I'm on my way now." She replied. Lisa noticed she wasn't sounding right. "Are you Okay?" She asked.

"Yeah, I'm straight."

"Oh! I almost forgot... Guess what?"

"What?"

"You're on that Big Man Click tour! I got the phone call about an hour ago. And they agreed to the numbers we told them, so you're looking at a lot of money and a lot more record sells." She said, with hopes of cheering Toni up.

"Word? Dat's hot...Dat's hot." She replied. "Are my friends there yet? She asked.

"Yes. They're waiting for you in your dressing room." She answered.

"A'ight tell them I'll be there in about fifteen minutes." She hung up the phone.

She knew that Big Man had a lot to do with her getting on that tour, not that she wasn't hot or nothing. But he had a lot to do with the tour. It was his shit and he really called the shots! She wondered if her brother knew. He had to know something. Him and Big Man was talking on the phone almost everyday. Link even went out of town to meet him to hang out. Big Man was trying to make Link see how he could use the industry to get out the street.

When she pulled in front of the sound stage, she saw Dex's truck double parked. She walked over to the heavily tinted truck. The windows were so tinted she couldn't see inside. She tapped on the window. When the window rolled down she was surprised to see J.R.

"Oh, where is Dex?" She asked, trying not to look so surprised.

He took a pull of his weed. "I don't know, I guess in there talking to Shelly." He said with an attitude

"You know you don't have to be like that all the time." She replied.

"Like what?! You asked me a question and I answered you."

"J.R., I never did nothin' to you... Why do you got to always act like that with me. I bet you don't act like that with them chicken head bitches you be fuckin' wit'!"

He smiled. He felt good. She had made him feel like she still cared. "Yo, what you talkin' bout'? What chicken head bitches? And just for da' record da' day you kicked me out ya' crib and gave me everything I had there, you fucked up with me." He said looking straight in her face.

"Come on, you know what that was about." She said.

"You talk 'bout me wit' chicken head bitches? You better stick wit' dem corny ass rappin' niggas!" He replied. He made a gesture with his head telling her to look over her shoulder, were there was a group of guys standing talking. It was Big Man and some of his crew. He rolled the window up in her face and turned the music on full blast.

What was he doing here?!!! She thought to herself. It was nothing left for her to do but to walk away. Even though J.R. wished she would have stayed and begged for him to roll the window back down.

She walked over to Big Man with a curious smile. "Hey, what up? What you doin' here?"

He hugged her and whispered in her ear. "What, it's a problem? I came to support you."

They all walked into the sound stage. She knew J.R. saw him hug her. In a way she was happy.

After Toni finished taping, her and Big Man, along with their crew, went to get drinks. In between autographs and shaking hands, Toni and Big Man talked about the tour. He just kept saying. "Da' shit gon' be off da' hook!"

For some reason Toni felt like her and Big Man was some type of couple. All the magazines thought so too, the public thought so, and J.R. thought so.

"Look Darlene, I told you don't call me wit' da' bullshit!! I'm takin' care of my business I don't need ta' hear da' bullshit!!"

"I don't give a fuck Link! Don't give me dat' bullshit! I'm tired of you and ya' bitches!! Man, fuck you!! And come get da' little bit of shit ya' got in my house!!!" She shouted on the other end of the phone."

He looked at his cell phone with a frown. "What!!! You can throw dat' shit away!!! I don't want it!! And as a matter of fact bring all dat' shit I bought you to da' Ave. and leave it wit' Trips, he up der' now!!!" He hung up on her and shut the power off. He knew she would keep calling. He was changing the number anyway. His blood was boiling. His friends had warned him about her from the start, but he didn't listen. During the whole time he's been messing with her, it was always a fight about something. He dug in his pocket and pulled out the receipt he had just got an hour ago from the travel agent. He shook his head. He couldn't believe he just went and paid down on a cruise for him and Darlene. What perfect timing. He sat in the car and thought for a minute. He turned the power to his cell phone on and started dialing Toni's cell.

"Hello." She answered on the other end.

"What up? What ya' schedule look like in about four weeks?" He asked.

"When...The beginning of next month?"

"Yeah."

"I got that week off. Why?" She asked

"You want to go away wit' me?"

"Where?"

"Look big head stop askin' so many questions. Ya' wanna go or not?"

"Hell yeah! Oh...wait I think Big Man wanted to go away that week too."

"Fuck it he could roll too. I'll call him now and tell him the info. A'ight?"

"Bet! Thanx! I love ya'"

"Yeah, me too."

They hung up and Toni just smiled. She was happy. Her life was going as good as it could. Just when she got deep into her thought there was a knock at the door.

"Who!!" She shouted

"Twenty-minutes to show time, Toni!!" A voice shouted on the other side of the door.

She got up and started to get ready to go on stage.

Four Weeks Later

All Toni could think about was going away in two days. She went straight from the stage to her dressing room. She wanted to get back to the hotel early tonight. She had to start packing her stuff to send back to N.Y., since her and Big Man was going to meet Link in Miami, that's where the cruise ship was docking. She ran all over the arena looking for Shelly. Shelly had her cell phone and she had beeped Link before she went on stage.

"You saw Shelly?" She asked one of Big Man's people.

"Yeah, she's in catering gettin' you some grub." He answered. She walked on the other side to catering to see if she saw her.

"Shelly! I need my cell."

Shelly walked out of catering with three plates of food in her hand. "I was just comin' back to da' room to bring you ya' food."

"Thanks. Did my brother ever call back?" She asked as she helped her with the plates of food,

"Naw. And I paged him three more times like you said, But he never called back. I even stood outside for twenty-minutes, just in case da' reception was bad." She answered. "Damn! I need him to go to da' diamond district and pick my ring up for me tomorrow... Dat's right he said he had to go take care of something and it would probably take a few hours. But that was earlier. Remind me to page Trips when we get back to da' hotel."

"A'ight." Shelly replied.

Toni kept paging Link. She even paged Trips, both of them and still didn't get no response. She knew they probably was with bitches they had met from Jersey. "Don't worry. You know ya' brother. He probably running around trying to take care of last minute shit before he break out." Big Man said to her, trying to comfort her.

"Yeah...But why he ain't call back to tell me that?"

"Listen ya' worrying ya'self for nothin', I'm sure. Stop stressin'. I'm goin' to a meetin'. You straight?" He said.

"Yeah." She answered

Big Man walked out the room. He also paged Link and got no answer. He didn't think much of it until now. Him being a street nigga' himself he knew the possibilities. He also knew Toni was from the streets, so she knew the possibilities too. But he also knew that it probably was nothing.

Toni told Shelly to page Link one more time while she went to get dressed. Within ten minutes, Shelly was walking in the dressing room with the phone.

"Here." Shelly said, handing Toni the phone. "I couldn't hear da' reception is messed up. I think it was your sister from Florida. I saw a 305 area code." She continued

Toni snatched the phone. "Shit! Dat' must have been Link. He said he was getting to Miami a day early." She started pulling up the number to redial. She anxiously waited as the phone rang on the other end. She was telling herself she was going to curse him out for not calling her right back.

"Hello." A woman's voice answered on the other end of her cell phone.

Toni paused for a minute before answering. "Hello...can I speak to Link please." She asked.

"Who's......Toni?" The shallow voice asked on the other end.

"Yeah....Katlynn? Where Link at?" She asked.

All she heard was sobbing on the other end. No reply to her question. Just crying. And then the phone dropped. At that point, when her sister dropped the phone, Toni knew. She knew shit wasn't right.

Katlynn's husband picked the phone up. "Hey Toni how you?" He asked her in his same old modest voice.

"Sam.... what's goin' on?" She asked with tears filling her eyes. She knew. She knew what was going on. She got a lump in her throat, as if she swallowed an apple. Her friend Shelly just stood and watched as she dropped to the floor.

"NO!!! NO!!! NO!!! It can't be Sam! We goin' away tomorrow! I'm tellin' you it's a mistake! I'm tellin' you he wouldn't do this to me!!!" Toni yelled into the phone as she sat on her knees rocking back and forth. Shelly knew then. She knew Link was gone. Shelly ran out the room to get Big Man. So distorted herself, Shelly didn't even think about Toni sitting in the middle of the floor. All she knew was she wouldn't be able to handle Toni by herself. She ran down the hallway to the other side of the venue to Big Man's dressing room. When she reached she had tears in her eyes.

"I need to speak to Big Man." She told the security outside the door.

"He's in a meeting. He said nobody is to come in." He replied.

"LOOK! This is a fuckin' emergency! Now go in there and tell him Shelly said to come out here!!" She shouted.

"Look Shelly I can't...." He tried to reply.

She cut him off. "No you look! Toni needs him NOW!!!" He went into the room. Shelly paced back and forth waiting. When Big Man came out all she could do is look at him and cry. He looked at her with his fore head wrinkled up. "What happened girl?" He asked.

"Somethin' happened to Link! Toni's freakin' out...you got to get down there to her room man. I don't know what to say I can't handle her myself." She replied sobbing. But by the time she finished her sentence he was running off to her room.

When he got there he found Toni in the corner with her hand over her mouth rocking back and forth. She looked like she was spaced out or something. She just stared, no blinking or nothing. He walked over and bent down in front of her. "Come on baby get up." He tried to get her out the corner.

But she just stared and cried like he wasn't even there. She felt shallow, like her insides were snatched out. The walls were closing in on her. Her life had just taken a drastic turn. She started to wonder. Who, what, where...why and how?

"Where was his friends!?" "Why!!!?...Huh... Why would somebody want to do this!?" She asked out loud.

Big Man just held her in his arms tight. "Oh...I'm so sorry Toni." He said, while his own tears ran down his face. Him and Link had grown so close. He wish he could have gotten him out the streets sooner. But it was too late.

She pulled up from inside of his arms. "Do you know that was my other half? When we was young he used to always take care of me. I would come in the house crying from fallin' or somethin' and he would wipe my tears and bandage me up. He had my back! I don't have my mother or father, he was da' closest...." She couldn't finish her sentence. She couldn't do nothing but cry. The lump got bigger in her throat and she got smaller inside. Then she thought about her sisters and his friends. She thought about who would be able to tell her something. She stood up and picked up her cell phone. "I need to walk." She told Big Man and she left out the room.

He didn't want her walking around by herself at a time like this, but he knew he couldn't stop her. He told them to let the crowd know she wouldn't be performing tonight and he went back to his dressing room to sit with his own thoughts. He knew how close they were. He knew that this was going to be a hard on her.

Saying Goodbye

Toni had sat in her house without eating for two days. The phone rang, she ignored it. She turned everyone away. She would just listen to people speak through the answering machine. It wasn't until she heard Dex's voice on the machine, she picked up.

"Yeah.. I'm here." She said as her hands shook, holding the phone. "Toni... Toni what happened? Are you all right?" He asked. "Oh... Dex please tell me what happened?" She started to cry.

"Please don't do that...you gon' make me cry Toni... I don't know what happened. The boys came and picked up me and J.R. two days before Link got killed. We in here together. I've been tryin' to get info. from the streets but it's been hard."

"What?? You're locked up? I... Why?" She asked astonished. "You mean you didn't know? You don't know what's goin' on?" He asked.

"No.. I haven't spoken to anybody since I came back. I haven't even been outside. You're the first person I've spoken to. I'm not answering my phone." She replied. "OH, my God Toni. Look I can't really talk on this phone, but you gotta watch out, you hear. They gonna be comin' for you soon. They had a secret indictment on ya' brother and us. Somebody talkin' and your name is in the middle. I saw J.R. today. He's worried about you. I couldn't talk to him long 'cause they separated us. But he told me they knew about da' closet... Look I gotta go I'm gonna call you tonight. Try to be there, okay. I love you, girl." His line clicked off. She just stood there with the phone in her hand, not paying the off the hook busy signal no mind.

They gave her just enough time to bury Link and there they was. The FEDS. They picked her up the day after his funeral. They had her on conspiracy charges. They knew she was once in a relationship with J.R. and he kept his drugs and money in her home for a period of time. They had her on phone conversations with Link and J.R. The phone conversations with Link was more incriminating than the ones with J.R., but Link was gone so they connected her to J.R. She wished she never had fucked with him. She should've listened to her brother when he warned her.

****

She sat in the hard wood chair, just staring. The lawyers went back and forth and it was like she wasn't even in the room. She couldn't believe how her life took such a turn. She wished her brother was there. Warm tears rolled down her face. She knew the press probably thought her tears were tears of fear. But they wasn't. They were tears for her brother. If he was still living she would have done twenty-five years for him if she had to, as long as they were down for each other. She thought about the baby she was carrying for Big Man, and how she hoped this didn't hurt his career. She had just finished an album so she was straight with her career for a minute. But she didn't want to have her baby in jail. Her thoughts was broken when she saw Shorty.

Where da' fuck did she come from!! She thought to herself. That bitch! She shouted in her mind as Shorty took the stand. She knew something wasn't right when she never showed up to her house that day and nobody hadn't really seen or heard from her. The bitch was snitching the whole time.

Toni looked behind her, to where Big Man was sitting, and winked her eye. A small tear ran down as her eyelid opened back up. He knew her pain. He knew he wasn't going to be able to hold her every night like he wanted to. He wanted to be there for her, but he too had a life he had to tend to. He just hoped that she never would think he could ever shit on her. Cause when the smoke clears and when it's all said and done......The one person, Toni knew, she could count on was gone.

Time to Love Me

It was the same old dreadful ride up to the jail. Same thing, single baby mothers with their crying babies. I just daydreamed the whole way there. When I got there the room was crowded with inmates and visitors. Digger and me sat across from one another. I had the only stressed look on my face.

"So, what did the lawyer say?"

"What da' fuck do they always say? I'm gonna see what I can workout, Ms. Brown. All he wants is more money. All these judges and lawyers, they all play fucking golf and have lunch together. He's probably friends with the god damned D.A. Fucking germ!"

"Well, how much money do we have left?"

"Not that much. You been locked down for five months and we've already given that fuck boy lawyer almost fifteen thousand dollars! He knows he can get you off this charge. He just wanna' drain some more money out before he does it."

Digger put his hands in his face for a few seconds and then looked up at me with a funny look. It was building up. I could tell. "Shit! This man told me he could have me out in three months or less, it's motherfucking five going on six! I go to court next Friday, I better walk."

"Well, the greedy fuck wants five thousand more before you go back to court".

"Give it to him. If you got to pawn my watch and bracelet. Just give it to him."

"Naw, I don't think we should pawn both. I'll pawn your watch and my chain. And if anything I'll take from what we got left over in the stash. I paid up the bills for another two months, so we don't have to worry 'bout that. My aunt paid for Destiny's ticket down South."

"When is she leaving?"

"In two weeks."

"Damn! I need to see my baby before she breaks out."

"I wish you let me bring her here just one time. One time isn't gonna hurt, Digger."

"Hell na! I don't want my baby to see me in this place. She's too young to understand. That's alright though, I'm gonna get out before she leaves."

Just as we were getting into our conversation an officer walked over and tapped Digger on the shoulder.

"Time's up Mr. Wilson."

Digger turned to the officer with a warm smile (as warm as he could conjure up) and replied. "Alright"

"He's new?"

"Naw, he works upstairs. He just started working the visiting room. He's a cool muthafucka' though. Well, I got to go. Call that lawyer and tell him you're gonna get him the money. And don't take from the stash, that's your money for that school you wanted to go to."

I paused for a few seconds. I guess I was stuck. "Naw, it's okay. I can do that anytime. It's not that important."

The officer yelled from the corner of the visiting room.

"Okay Wilson, time to break it up."

Digger reached over and kissed me softly on the lips and told me he had to go and that he loved me. I told him I loved him back. And before I knew it he disappeared behind that heavy steel door.

On the way to Sabrina's house I passed the playground and saw a little girl playing. It made me think about Destiny and her future. It made me think about life period.

Now my friend Sabrina is one of those motherly friends in a sense. You know one of those Afro-centric types. You can tell by her apartment what kind of person she is. I mean don't get me wrong her place is clean and shit, it's just so Afro-centric (as Afro-centric as her financial status would allow her).

When I got to the door I could smell the scent of her favorite China Musk incense and fried chicken cooking. She opened the door with her same jolly smile.

"What's up, Sassy? You're just in time for lunch."

"Girl, I can't eat. I'm too stressed."

"So what's up wit' Diggs?"

"What else? Stress. He's gettin' ready to flip out. He thinks I don't know, but I know him better than he thinks I do. I can't believe he's still in there for that bullshit."

"I tell you, they just do what they want to us, Sassy. Now it's common sense, if a motherfucker is locked up how da' hell is he supposed to make it to court for another case?"

"Brina, I'm just not ready to do another bid. I don't mind, but I'm just not ready. Shit, I need to see my man. Not for twenty minutes or in a room full of people. I need to see that mother fucker when I wake up, when I go ta' sleep. I don't understand why do de' put da' shit on da' street, knowing we have no way to survive, then wanna lock niggas up when de' use it for a source of survival."

Sabrina gave me a funny look.

"Look, Sabrina. I'm not tryin' ta' justify drug sellin', all I'm saying is that it's a set up. If our men have to go to jail for doing something they feel is right, cause I've come to the conclusion that most really don't see nothing wrong with it. Then there's a whole lot of mothafuckas' up in congress, the government, FBI, CIA, White House, and da' precincts that need to be in the cell next to our men! Tell me, you think dat' dem' mothafuckas' up in da' government don't know when ship loads of weed and coke sail in? Somethin' ain't right."

"And by da' time years go by of genocide and frustration our people's minds are all twisted and fucked up."

It seemed like within minutes I fell into one of those five second depressions. "I don't know. All I know is I need my baby daddy home." I broke out of my five second depression and sat up on the couch. "Chile, life a sure stress you out."

"Who you tellin' I can't remember the last time I had a good man in my life. I think I'm just slippin'. See, I know it's about how you think and where you put yourself."

I looked at her like she was crazy. I didn't know where she was going with this, but knowing Brina she was going somewhere. "What da' hell......."

She cut me off and looked me dead in my face I knew she was about to drop some science on me. "You know? What you think is what you attract. Dependin' on da' kind of places you go depends on the kind of people you gon' meet. If you go to the Shack, you gon' meet that no good ball ridin' ass!

Put yourself around a certain kind of men on a regular basis, that's the kind you always gon' end up with. You see dem' little basketball mothafucka's, they always, ninety percent of the time end up with them either model like or prissy acting freaks. All dem' athletes. You know why? For real, don't look at me like that. I'm gonna tell you why.

'Cause that's where 'dem smart ass freaks put themselves, that's where they go. They hang the places athletes hang and eat at restaurants athletes eat at. Where do you think they meet 'dem chicks? Not around da' way, where da' grew up at. See, I come to da' conclusion that most ball players come from da' ghetto. They have to."

"Why, Brina? Why do da' have to come from da' ghetto?"

"Because most of them do.... But anyway, they come from da' ghetto, but you always see dem' sportin' some half breed corny chick. That's 'cause that's all that's around dem'. Get it? If we just start going to the right places we would meet da' right kind of man. And if we started thinking a little more positive we'd attract more positive energy and men. And personally, I don't think the ball players that's from da' ghetto really be likin' dem' chicks."

"And how you figure that one, Sabrina."

She gave me a funny look. One of those looks that makes you feel like you're an ass. One of those looks that if it wasn't coming from your friend you would be busting the person's ass that was giving you the look.

"I'm not disagreein' with you, Brina. I'm just wonderin....." She cut me off again. "Please! How could a man from a certain environment, that's used to being around a certain kind of woman, want to be with the opposite. We have a certain strength, as black women, in da' ghetto. We know how to survive and have our man's back. We go and been through so much, which made us strong. How could you want to be with anything but us. Most come from single parent households or one with a step father. They grew up seeing de' mother struggle and survive. They know what a real women is. (Pausing). Just ain't no woman like that hanging where de' hang at, so I guess de' ain't got no other choice. I tell you one thing, though, I ain't going to da' Sugar Shack no fuckin' more. Can't even get a drink out dem' clowns! Askin' what somebody name is. My name is Thirstina from now on. I'm thirsty mothafucka'. Buy me a drink!!!"

I just laughed at her. "Girl you crazy!!!" I paused for a minute. "I saw this little girl in the park today.... it made me think about Destiny's future. I go through so much with Digger. I mean why shouldn't I. I love him."

"Can you see yourself without him? I mean do you think you'd ever break out on him?"

"That's scary. That's a scary thought. Yo, I got so much invested in him. Time, love, and a seed. I don' carried that man's drugs upstate when he couldn't get a hold of his vick, bagged up, fought bitches, pawned jewelry. Sometimes I think that I'm just stuck."

"Well, life's nothin' but a lesson. We learn from the things we go through in life. Just look at it like a lesson. One thing you can say is that you learned how to love. At least what you felt was love."

"Oh, shit!!! I got ta' go girl. I forgot I had ta' call the lawyer. And Destiny's at my aunt's house I got ta' take her some clothes. Call me later we all supposed to go out for drinks tonight. Alright?"

Brina looked at me like I was crazy. I knew that look. You didn't see it that often, but when you did, oh boy. "We all who?!"

"Oh, come on Brina. I know you still 'ain't mad at Peaches?"

Brina stood up and put her hands on her hips." And why ain't I? I'm tired of that bitch's attitude. She always acting like somebody got to kiss her ass. And when she's not waiting for you to kiss her ass she's walking around like the world revolves around her. That's my girl and everything and we go way back and shit, but I just can't have her in my space right now. She irritates the shit outta' me."

"Come on Sabrina, all of us is going to be there. Just ignore her. You know how she is."

"That's the problem. We always use the excuse, that's how she is. Just because she's like that don't make it right. Plus.... I don't want to have to punch her in her face again."

My eyes almost popped out of my face. "You hit her! I.....ain't nobody tell me you hit her. When.... why.... I mean how did that happen? What you just hit her?"

"Yeah. She kept yappin' and yappin' talkin' ta' me like I'm a damn child, so I just (balling her fist up to demonstrate) bopped her one good time."

"She didn't hit you back?"

"Yeah. And I just bopped her again. Even harder."

"Y'all is crazy. I'm out. I'll see you tonight right?"

"Whatever."

Later that evening Donnie was pacing back and forth in her living room talking to Peaches on the phone.

Donnie had the best crib out of all of us. Timmy hooked her up! She had a very nice well furnished four bedroom home. With no kids at that! What the fuck is she going to do with all that space and no kids! But she got it. She got to take a whole lot of shit from Timmy for everything she's got, but she's got it.

"Now, Peaches you know you two motherfuckers a be right back speaking. Speaking like you always do. So, you need to stop the shit, Peaches."

"Look girl, I don't even want to talk about it. I'm tired of that bitch's shit. And I might just talk to her again, ya' right. It just won't be happening tonight. It's time to grow up, all of us. I just don't feel like dealing with it."

"Look, I'm tired of the bullshit. I don't know why y'all bitches can't ignore each other. Y'all got issues that need to be addressed....... Wait a minute, girl I think I hear Timmy pulling up. I hear the music. I'm getting ready to get dressed. Call me if you change your mind. I'm gonna call you back."

She hung up the phone and sat on the couch. She started flicking through the channels with her face screwed up.

Timmy walked through the front door screaming out for Donnie. "Donnie! Donnie!"

He walked into the living room where Donnie was sitting flicking the channels and ignoring him. "Didn't you hear me calling you? What's up?"

She kept on ignoring him and flicking the channels.

"Oh, you wanna play stupid now. What the fuck is your problem now, Donnie?"

Donnie looked up from the television and smirked. "Excuse

me? What da' fuck is my problem? What the fuck is your problem? Why da' fuck did you have me waiting for two hours for you today? We both got cells. You could have called me at least."

"Look, obviously something came up if I didn't call you......"

She interrupted him and jumped off the couch and started to walk out the living room. "Something always comes up, mutha' fucka'!!!!" She left him standing in the middle of the living room looking stupid.

Later that evening I sat in the middle of my bedroom floor in a depression mode. Counting money and talking to myself. "Five fucking thousand dollars. And they call us criminals. This jerk wants five thousand dollars for what?"

The phone rang and broke my concentration. I jumped up. I knew it had to be Digga.

"Hello. Yes, I'll accept. What's up, boo? Nothin'. I was just sorting everything out for the lawyer. Me and the girls are going out for some drinks. Okay. Love you too."

I hung up the phone and plopped down on the bed. My eyes started to fill up with tears.

By the time I got to the restaurant the girls were sitting around the table with drinks and appetizers. Everybody was laughing and talking. You could tell there was some tension between Peaches and Brina.

"No! No! Now you know that's not how it happened, Donnie. Donnie was laughing so hard she couldn't get her words out. "Wait! Wait. Hold up, Sassy. How you gonna tell me how it went?" Donnie turned to Brina. "You remember how it went. Tell her she's bugging."

Brina gave her a funny look. "Look Chile, don't put me in y'all shit."

Donnie turned to Peaches looking for some support. "Come on Peaches. I got your back. Would you tell them that's not how it happened."

Peaches sarcastically replied, "Okay that's not how it happened." And she finished sipping her drink.

By this time I was a little tipsy, but I was still serious. I moved close to her face. "What the fuck is your problem, Peaches? Why you got...got to be so sarcastic? Huh? I mean... What? You don't want to talk about what we want to talk about? Why don't you suggest we talk... I mean won't you make a suggestion." By this time I was semi slurring.

Peaches smirked at me. "Sassy, I think you had too much to drink, girl."

I lost it! "No I don't think so, GIRL!" I took the rest of my drink to the head. "And anyway you know what they say. The truth comes out when you're drunk".

The girls just sat silently with blank looks on their faces. I jumped up. "That's it, let's talk truth. Better yet let's play truth, dare, consequences, promise, and repeat. And guess what? GIRL! You're first."

You could tell that Brina was getting a kick out of how I was acting. She elbowed Donnie and said, "Yeah that sounds like fun."

Donnie elbowed her back and gave her a look like a mother gives her child when they misbehave in public. Brina whispered to Donnie, "What? What I do wrong."

I was ready to break the silence. "Look everybody's always talking behind everybody's back. Won't y'all bitches start talking now."

Peaches started getting up from the table. "Look Sassy you had too much to drink and I have something to do. So, I guess I'll catch up with you all another time."

I jumped up and blocked her from getting up. "Wait a minute! Don't disrespect me. Don't...don't think you could just brush my ass off. You're not gonna treat me like I'm less than you. Everybody is so tired of that attitude."

She pushed pass me and if looks could kill we'd be dead and buried. "That's everybody's fucking problem!!!!!!" And she stormed out the restaurant.

The next morning I laid in my bed with a hangover. The phone rang and I crawled from up under the sheets to answer it. The motherfuckers had to wait right when I got the phone off the charger to hang up. The caller ID said out of area. It must have been Digger. Shit! I laid right in that spot, on the floor, and waited for the phone to ring back. I knew he would call right back, he always does that. But he didn't. I fell back to sleep wondering why he hadn't called back. And wondering what Peaches was thinking about at that moment. Knowing her arrogant ass, she wasn't thinking about shit, but herself. When I woke up I looked at the caller i.d., thinking maybe I slept through Digger's call. But he hadn't called back. I wondered why. Could something be wrong? It had to be. What part of the game is that? He usually calls everyday. Well the day isn't over yet, but still why wouldn't he call back? I got up and started packing Destiny's stuff for her trip. My aunt decided to go down south earlier than she had planned, so that left me rushing at the last minute. It wasn't like I had anything to do, besides waiting for Digger's call, what a life. That was just it. That's all my life is based on, Digger. I don't have a life. My life is Digger. I don't know why I'm stressing it, it's not like I'm going to change anything. Sometimes I'm not too sure if I even want a life. If I did get a life what would I do with it?

After I sent Destiny on her way, I stopped at a newsstand and picked up a paper. Don't ask me why. I found myself looking through the classifieds. I had a little computer skills and I could type pretty good. I used to book keep for Mr. Skippy at the number hole for a while. I didn't know what I was looking for. All I knew was I wanted to do something with myself.

Shit!! I forgot Digger's white T-shirts and commissary money. I was pretty sure he didn't need it, but I just felt like surprising him. I had a little extra money from taking some clothes back. I didn't mind spending it on him.

I just couldn't understand what the officer was telling me when I got to the jail. He must have been making a mistake.

"Could you check the name again?"

"Sure, but trust me.....see, somebody left money and a package for him earlier today."

"Oh. Thank you."

I left in a daze and confused state. Who could have came up here and left him a package? And why didn't he call back? I know it wasn't none of his friends, he doesn't even like them to come up. If anything, he would have made somebody give me the money and I would have brought it up to the jail. All the way home I wrecked my brains. 'Til I came to the conclusion that it was probably nothing.

"Girl, you can't be serious. See, you good."

"Well, what am I supposed to do? It's probably nothing."

"Yeah? Well I would have had to dig a little deeper to make sure it wasn't nothing. Catch my drift?"

I just looked at Donnie. She was convincing me. "Okay. Does your cousin's girlfriend still work at the jail?"

Donnie put a big smile on her face. "Now, that's what I'm talkin' 'bout girl!" She got up off the living room floor and got her cordless phone off the hook. She started dialing. "Hey, Tiff. What's going on? That's good. Look. I need a favor. I was wondering if you could check on something for me?"

That was the last thing I heard her say into the phone. I drifted away. I started thinking all types of shit. I couldn't believe I was condoning this.

My thinking was broken by Donnie's high pitch voice. Sassy! What the hell is wrong with you, girl? Did you hear anything I said?"

"Oh, no. I'm sorry, what happened?"

"I caught her on her cell, she was on her lunch break. She said she gonna check into it when she gets back on duty."

"Check on what? What you said to her?"

"Nothing, I gave her his name and she said she would check the records."

"She didn't need his I.D.#?"

"I asked. She said no. She said she would call back if she did. I told her what part he was in. She said if someone else has the same name as him, she would call back."

"Why am I getting a bad feeling? I mean, you know what they say."

She looked at me like I was stupid. "What?"

"When you go looking, you find shit that you don't want to."

"Girl, whatever!"

When the phone rang we both jumped. You would have thought Digger was her man.

"Well, answer it, Donnie!"

"I am...Hello. It's me Tiff. Who else would be answering my

phone?"

I sat staring at her with my heart in my stomach. I could tell by her facial expression, it wasn't good news on the other end of the phone. I stood up in her face whispering and making gestures for her to tell me what the girl was saying. She reached over and got a pencil and paper and started writing something down. She hung up the phone.

"What happened, Donnie what did she say? What was that you wrote down?"

She just looked at me with a funny look. Now, Donnie could be dramatic sometimes. But something was different this time. Her eyebrows lifted and her mouth frowned up.

"What, Donnie? What!"

She talked in low voice I never heard come from her before. It was like she was talking to herself. "That bitch." She got louder as she went on. "That dirty bitch!!!!"

She picked the phone back up and started dialing, like I wasn't there. "Bitch phone is busy." She kept pressing redial. I just stood there. "Donnie, what the fuck is going on? What happened?"

She put up her hand, to tell me to wait. "Chill. It's ringing.... Yeah... Don't Donnie me, you trifflin' bitch!!!... You know what the fuck I'm talkin' bout! How long you hoe bitch!!!? How long you been carrying on with Digger? Before he got locked up or what?"

I just flipped out. I snatched the phone out of Donnie's hand so fast and hard I scratched her hand. Didn't even notice the blood trickling down her hand.

"Who the fuck is this?!!" It was dead air on the other line I didn't know if the person had hung up or what. "I said who the hell is this!? Hello?" "Well, this is Digger's wife and the mother of his child, bitch! What the fuck are you to him?"

A whisper came from the other end. I could tell that it wasn't the person's real voice. But I could also tell that it was a familiar voice. I turned around and looked at Donnie, and her facial expression had let me know that I was right. I knew the voice....and knew the person that belonged to the voice. Very well! All morning, afternoon, and night Digger called. And all morning, afternoon, and night I ignored his calls. He caught me off guard when he had someone else call with him on the three way. I wasn't ready to talk to him. I just hung up the phone on him. The bitch wouldn't answer her phone or her door all day. Digger had a visit tomorrow. I planned on going up to the jail and talk to him face to face. I gathered all of the most recent pictures I could find of Destiny. I was going to leave them in his package box, cause that would be the closest he'll get to see her again. He fucked up big time! I souped myself up. I told myself that I wouldn't listen to no reasoning. I was just going to say what I had to say and leave. I didn't want to hear nothing he had to say. I souped myself up all day and night. I wasn't going to let him convince me or explain his side. There was no explanation. When the phone rang I ignored it until I heard Brina's voice.

"Sassy, you there? Donnie told me to talk into the machine cause you weren't answering your phone. Pick up girl it's me, Brina."

I jumped up and snatched the phone off the hook. "Hey, what's up?"

"You tell me. You spoke to her yet?"

"No. I guess Donnie told you what happened."

"What, she wasn't supposed to?"

"Naw, it ain't nothing. I guess she's taking it to heart, cause she went through it too. Even though it was three years ago."

"So?"

"So, what?"

"So what's next?"

"Nothing. As a matter of fact I have to go and get ready. I'm going up to the jail tomorrow and speak my piece. I'll call you when I get back and let you know what happened, okay?"

"A'ight. You sure you're okay?"

"Yes. Now I'll call you later. Bye."

I hung up and went straight to bed. I had a long day ahead of me.

When I got up in the morning I took my shower, gathered my i.d. and the pictures of Destiny. I jumped in my car and drove up to the jail. I didn't bother to take the van. I thought of what I would say all the way up there.

I got to the visiting room and did the regular procedure.

Something told me to look at the desk where the C.O.'s sat. There she was! She had the nerve to try and get a visit. I jumped up and walked over to her. Before you knew it I grabbed her by the arm. And looked her straight in her eyes. She thought she saw a ghost.

"You really must be out of you're fucking mind, Peaches!"

"Get off of me, Sassy." She said in a whisper.

I turned to the C.O. behind the desk. "Excuse me, officer. This young lady is trying to get a visit with someone that is my child's father and not to mention I was here first." I said in a proper kind of voice. Then I continued. "You can call Officer Tiffiny Ray. She's familiar with the situation." The officer picked the phone up and began to dial. In the meanwhile I turned to Peaches with a smile and calmly, slowly whispered in her face.

"Bitch, I'm going to break you're fucking face. I advise you break out and take your ass whipping at a later date and time....You know, save yourself the embarrassment,...Hoe BITCH!"

The officer saw me up in Peaches' face and came from behind the desk. He stood in between us and separated us. He pointed in Peaches' face.

"I'm sorry, but you're going to have to leave. You can't have a visit today."

She looked at him with a smirk on her face "What! How you gon' say that?"

I don't know what Tiffiny told that officer on the phone, but his whole attitude changed. In my favor.

After beefing and arguing Peaches left, popping shit. I sat while they pulled him down from Rec. I couldn't wait. Seeing Peaches up at the jail just put the icing on the cake. My ears rang with an echo when the officer called my name. I walked through the doors and sat at a table in the middle. Especially cause he always told me not to sit in the middle. He hates the middle. Fuck him! When he came through the doors with the other inmates, he looked around the room. Mostly towards the corners of the room, where I usually sat. He finally noticed me in the middle of the room. He walked over to me with a confused look on his face. I was trying to feel him out, to see if Peaches told him I knew. He just sat down with his eyebrows twisted. He didn't even say hello or nothing. He just looked at me and asked with attitude.

"Sassy why would you sit in the middle of the room? You know how I feel about the middle.....Don't you?"

I looked him dead in his sorry pitiful face and said in a whispered, but stern voice. "Yeah.....? Well why would you be fucking or needing a visit from my friend?"

His face just dropped. He had a look on his face I never saw in my life! And I had been with him basically all my life. He turned hot sauce red! At that point I knew I had the upper hand. I gave him time to answer. And of course it took him forever to answer. And of course when he did answer he had to say some stupid shit!

He tried to keep a serious face. "What the fuck you talking 'bout Sassy?"

"Don't act like you don't know what I'm talking about, nigga'. I know already, about you and Peaches. Whatever you consider y'all having I know already. And all I got to say is I don't want to have nothing to do with you no more. I left pictures of Destiny in your box and I would appreciate it if you would stay the fuck away from me! I'm going to leave all your paper work, for your case with the bitch Peaches, and she can handle your case...Oh, I'll leave your stash money with her too... Let her deal with that bullshit. I'm calling the phone company in the morning to change my number. I'm going to drop your stuff at her house or your mother's house. Good luck with your case and your life. You would make it easier for yourself if you don't come near me when you get out. Cause if I have to I will get a restraining order against you. Oh..... by the way FUCK YOU!!!."

I lost it. I had promised myself I wouldn't let him see me lose it, but I couldn't help it. He snatched my arm when I tried to get up. Before I knew it an officer walked over and pulled him off me.

"Excuse me, Mr. Wilson. Is there a problem over here? You're ready to end your visit?" He asked Digger.

"Naw. We straight."

I looked at him like he was crazy. "Naw, we ain't' straight. I'm ready to end this visit."

"No she's not officer. We a'ight. Everything is cool. We'll keep it down. Sorry 'bout that."

The officer walked back to the corner, but kept a close eye on us.

Digger held his face in his hands like he often does whenever he's thinking hard. I just sat across from him with my arms crossed and my face twisted. I knew everybody in the visiting room could tell I was hella mad. He looked up with the sad puppy dog look.

He said. "Sassy, you know I love you. You're coming up here flipping and you don't even know what is what."

"Yeah? I know one thing she ain't got no business coming on visits, leaving you commissary, or nothing. I knew some shit wasn't right by the way she's so defensive about you. And as a matter of fact it doesn't matter. I don't want to hear your side or her side. I'm gonna whip her ass I can tell you that!! Goodbye Digger."

"Wait Sassy, I'm not finished."

I looked at him with fire in my eyes. "Well Digger, I am. I'm finished. It's over."

I got up and walked off. I didn't look back and didn't care to. I could feel his eyes burning through my back while I stood and waited for the doors to open.

The tears finally came. My eyes watered up. I tried to hold them back. I got one of those apple feelings in my throat. I thought about how I lied and told him I was calling to change my number. It sounded good at the time. Maybe I will change it, I thought. It was time that I changed a lot of things.

For the next few weeks I sat in depression. I didn't eat, I didn't comb my hair, I didn't go outside. I barely brushed my teeth. I slept a whole two weeks away. It was like after I came home from the jail that day I zoned out. I came straight home packed up Digger's stuff, took all his money out the safe, and dropped it at his mother's house. Straight from there I went to Peaches' house and tried to ask her in a nice way, what she and Digger had. Of course she had to come out her face. And of course I had to bust her ass. I felt funny afterwards. I was in the street fighting like I was a teenager or something. With every punch, I thought about how she used to be in my house and the times she would play with Destiny. She probably had her eye on him back then.

I finally changed my number. Digger beat his case and came

home a month and a half later. I saw him the day after he came home and didn't speak. Me and Destiny was riding down the Parkway and he was at the light. I turned my music up and put my foot on the gas. He tried to follow me and catch my attention, but I didn't pay him no mind. He even tried to get his mother to call me, but I wasn't trying to hear it. I felt bad, cause his mother is really cool with me. I took Destiny to see her a couple of times.

I started a job in the city. I was content. About three months after he came home from jail I started hearing the rumors. The word on the street was Peaches was pregnant from Digger. I must admit at first I kind of caught feelings, but I got over it. Come to find out she was pregnant from some cat she had met at a party she went to out of town. She ended up getting rid of it. Bitch to selfish to be a mother. Donnie finally got pregnant. She made Timmy get out the street and open up his own business. She told him she would only have a baby if he would get out the game and marry her. I guess he was okay with that. Brina....Brina is just Brina. She still single and childless. She still think she's our mother. Brina is still and probably will always be a good friend. I'm still working everyday. Digger went back to jail and came out. He's sick over my new relationship. I think he's stressed, cause I'm engaged. Well, it's just a feeling.....He'll get over it!!!!!!

A Promise

9/14/999/14/99. Okay, here I am running through the airport, trying to catch a flight that I knew I wasn't going to be able to catch. But I had no other choice. When Dottie called crying hysterically, I really had no other choice. It's very rarely that a friend calls you and tells you they need you, when they know you live hundreds of miles away. All I knew was my friend was going through some shit and I had to go! I dropped my son over by my mother's house, stopped at the bank and ran to the airport. I had fifteen minutes to get to the gate. And just my luck the door was closing as soon as I got there.

"Wait! Wait!." I was running and screaming at the same time. "Please don't tell me it's too late."

"Well." The attendant said looking at his watch. "No. You made it just in time. Hurry hand me your ticket."

"Thank God. Thank you."

This morning when Dottie called I automatically knew I had to make this trip. She was messed up in the worst way. We've been friends for years. We've been through a lot together. So it was only right to go when she needed me. I had been in between jobs, so it wasn't like I had to take off from work or nothing. I just wondered what was the deal. I couldn't really understand what was going on, with all the crying and yelling. But I knew it had something to do with him. I mean let's be realistic, a lot of the times it has to do with "HIM". We're always putting and going through changes because of that certain man in our lives. So, now here I am sitting on a flight to Atlanta puzzled. I was so worried about getting to her I didn't think much about what was wrong with her. All I knew was she was hurt and angry.

See Dottie and David both are my friends. And have been for years. I hope I'm not going down here to be in the middle of some shit! My stomach started bubbling the closer we got to the ground. I didn't know if it was the landing itself or the fact that I was here and didn't know what to expect. Then it dawned on me, Dottie never behaved in such a way. So something really had to be the matter. Well, I stood up and took a deep breath. I daydreamed for a moment as I walked down the walkway of the plane. Whatever the problem was, I wasn't leaving Atlanta until it was fixed.

There she was. I hadn't seen Dottie in nine months. So I didn't know what to expect. I damned sure didn't expect to see her with a belly! What the hell.... She never once mentioned to me about being pregnant. I didn't know what to say. Her eyes, her eyes were so red from crying. Once she took off her sunglasses, I knew it was serious. They were so sad, her eyes. And kind of shallow. You know your eyes tell a lot. Your eyes are the key to your soul. I tried to put on a smile as I approached her, but it broke down to tears as soon as I reached the spot she was standing in. She hugged me so tight. A hug you would never want to receive from a friend. The kind of hug that had a lot of drama and hurt behind it. And still I felt like it was a hug of relief. Like she was happy to finally have somebody to hug. Like she's been waiting for this moment. For a quick second I thought about what would have happened if I didn't come. My friend probably would have crawled in a corner and cried herself to death.

We rode to her house without much conversation. I didn't know what to say or how to say it. She just cried and I just rubbed her shoulders and told her it was going to be all right. And she kept saying no it's not. I wish she would tell me what the problem was. "Buttons, how long have we known each other?"

"For.... I don't know since we were about nine or ten."

"I need you now more than ever. More than the time I got pregnant at eighteen and I knew my mother would kill me. God rest her soul. And I know you're probably wondering what's going on. But it's so hard for me to deal with it."

"Deal with it. Deal with what, Dottie?" We pulled into her driveway. She didn't answer me. It was like I didn't even ask her nothing. I was so wrapped up in our conversation I didn't even pay attention to the house. Dottie used to write me letters about this house. Her little palace. Shit! Compared to where we come from this shit is like the white house! It was everything she said it was and then some. "Dottie." I whispered in amazement. "Girl... You.... wasn't lying." She still didn't speak. The windows were so high and the drapes looked like somebody's wedding gown.

It took a lot of hustling to get this motherfucker. Her man Dave always promised Dottie some shit like this. He always did good by her. He was a street cat, but he always did good by her. They've been together since we were sixteen years old. Now we're twenty nine. David thirty-nine. All our birthdays in September.

I remember the day we met David. It was the last day of school. He and his friend Sammy was driving past our school. Sammy was my ex. God bless his soul. He was killed three years ago. Shot eleven times and robbed. They left him in front of our house in his car. But, anyway you couldn't tell me and Dottie we wasn't hot shit when they pulled up on the side of us. We were young, but we were mature for our age. We both had older sisters so we picked up a couple of things along the way. David was driving and Sammy was in the passenger seat. Sammy tried hard as hell to get us in that car. Talking about taking us home. Our mothers would have had a fit if they saw us getting out some grown men's car. They yapped and yapped. Driving slow to keep up with us. Then it had to take Sammy to push the issue. "Come on now. Well if we can't give you young ladies a ride home, maybe we can pick you up tomorrow and give you a ride."

I stopped and walked over to the car. "When was the last time you've been in school? Today is the last day of school you know? It ain't hard to tell it's been a long time. Which probably means you two are too old to be following us home."

Yeah, well guess who we snuck around the corner to meet on the first morning of school. Sammy and David. We got in the car like we were professionals. We were about to turn seventeen in a couple of weeks and we were hot shit! Couldn't tell us nothing when we pulled up in front of the school in our new clothes. When our mothers gave us shopping money for school, Sammy and David told us to put it away for a rainy day. They took us shopping. We told our mothers that we caught a good sale. My sister wasn't stupid. She knew the deal. Not only did she know the deal, she knew Sammy and David. They was all in the same circle. My sister was a big sister, but she was cool. She just always told me to be careful and come to her before making any serious moves. They couldn't take us when they saw us getting out of that Benz! A Benz back then! Was like the shit!

But who would have known that it was the beginning of a long life for us. See, Dottie was more of the laid back type. So, she never really saw the life David lived. I mean we knew but in the beginning we never saw. We had to be in the house at a certain time, so we didn't bear witness to all the girls and shit.

But anyway, that afternoon after school they were outside waiting for us. They just wouldn't give up! And we didn't insist that they did. Through the years we went through some crazy shit with them two, but we also had our good times.

Dottie left home before I did. David set her up nice. I've never known them two to be apart. Except in the very beginning of their relationship. They had a big fight and she left and stayed with me. That only lasted about two weeks before he came and got her. So I couldn't imagine things getting this bad between them two that I would have to fly out here.

She showed me to the guest bedrooms. She said I could sleep in which ever one of them I wanted. She said I could stay in the room with her if I wanted to also. When I asked where David was she just brushed me off. She said he wasn't around. After I took a shower and we went to the supermarket to get a few things, I felt it was a good time to start a conversation with Dottie about why I was here; being that she barely spoke to me in the car on the way to the store. What the fuck was up with her. I tried to figure it out, but I just kept getting stuck. Something's gotta give. I walked in the kitchen where I found her singing and cooking. This was the happiest I've seen her since I got off the plane.

"Dottie?"

"Yeah."

"What's up with you, girl?"

She was talking to me like it was nothing. Like I lived across the street or something. Like I didn't just fly all the way from N.Y.

"What you mean what's up with me?"

"I mean, when you called me you was hysterical. You haven't said anything to me yet. I'm confused. And where's David?"

"David isn't around right now. I thought I told you that already. And I'm gonna talk to you. When the time is right."

"Well when was you going to tell me you were having a baby? I mean I've spoken to you almost every week and not one time have you mentioned you were pregnant."

She stopped what she was doing and turned to me with a serious look. "There's a lot of things I haven't mentioned to you. Now, are you ready to eat?"

I decided to leave it be. "Yeah. I'm starving girl."

After dinner we laughed and talked about old times. It started getting late. I was wondering where David was. But she was acting shady everytime I asked for him.

"Dottie, did you kick David out? Did you two have a fight or something?"

"No. No to all of the above."

"I know you may not be ready to talk yet, but.... . It's very weird to me."

"Very weird for me too." And she just left it at that.

I didn't know. I didn't know what to think. What is a person to think in my situation? Now I knew I couldn't bust my brains trying to figure out what was what. But I knew something serious was up. I have never known things to be this shady with David and Dottie.

We fell asleep in the living room. In the morning I noticed, on my way to the bathroom, that none of the guest rooms were furnished for a baby. I mean Dottie was at the end of her pregnancy and there was no sign in this house that a baby was about to enter the home.

I wasn't being nosy or nothing. And David still hadn't come home yet. I called home to check on Lil' Sammy, my son. Everything was fine at home. It's sad to say it wasn't fine here. When I went back down stairs I found Dottie sitting in the middle of the living room floor holding her stomach and crying.

"Dottie? What's the matter? Is it time?"

"Oh, God! I can't take it buttons!! Why! I've never done nothing to anybody. I just...." She was a wreck.

"Dottie calm down. I'm gonna call the ambulance." I was panicking. I couldn't find the phone, she was hysterical, and I didn't know what to do. I knew I had to get her to the hospital.

"Buttons!!!!!!!!" Dottie screamed at the top of her lungs.

I dropped the phone and ran out the kitchen.

"Dottie! It's going to be okay. Just breathe." Now I knew when I was in labor nobody couldn't tell me shit about breathing. So why in the hell I was trying to tell her that shit.

Dottie grabbed my arm and pulled me close up on her and just held on to me. I could feel her shaking." Buttons, I'm gonna die. I'm gonna die!!!" She started yelling.

"Dottie, no you're not. Just calm down. I'm going to call the ambulance. Did your water break?"

"No! I'm gonna die. I'm trying to tell you I'm going to die." She was crying and screaming at the top of her lungs. Her face was wet from the tears and the snot. She had turned red.

"What am I supposed to do? How could I even bring a child into this shit?" She grabbed me and hugged me so tight. She just held me and wouldn't let go. She cried so hard she made me cry. "Buttons I have never been with no other man in my life besides David. I never even thought about looking at another man let alone sleeping with another man. How could he do this to me?!!!!!!!"

"Dottie..... David cheated on you?"

She didn't say anything. She finally let go of me and sat sobbing.

"Dottie...... David cheated on you? I mean.... how do you know? Are you sure?"

She looked up at me with tears falling down her face. She looked at me with a look that was so unfamiliar to me. The saddest look I've ever seen in my life. "Buttons. Why me? I just wanted to live my life and be happy. I don't deserve this!"

"And you're right Dottie you don't......"

Then she just cut me off. And what she said I don't think I will ever forget it. She paralyzed me for just them few seconds. I mean my whole body numbed up as her words so innocently rolled off of her tongue. "I'm sick, Buttons. I have only been with David all my life and still I end up with AIDS. This is not the way life is supposed to be for me!!!"

Oh my God! I thought to myself. Oh, shit!!! I just couldn't say it. I couldn't say nothing. I could only cry. I was blank. It was like one half of me was taken away. From that point on I wasn't whole anymore. My best friend, like my sister..... .

I got this feeling in my stomach. A nasty feeling. What was scary was I hadn't had this feeling since I walked outside and found Sammy's body. And before then I had never had this feeling. I waited..... I wanted to know how to deal with this, but I wasn't ready.

That night I couldn't sleep. How could I? In the next room from me was my best friend, someone that was like my sister, someone who just told me she was dying. How am I supposed to sleep? I sat up and cried silently. I held myself so tight and just cried. I couldn't breathe. I felt as if it was me. That's how close and tight we are. It was like I was dying. In a way.... I was.

In the morning I was awakened by Dottie screaming my name from the kitchen. I jumped up and ran down the stairs. Ever since last night I've been paranoid. I don't know what to expect. I'm walking on pins and needles.

"Damn, Buttons. I just was calling to let you know breakfast was ready."

"Oh. I didn't know. I just heard you screaming out my name. I thought something was the matter." I sat down at the breakfast nook. Out the corner of my eye I noticed all of these little and big bottles. They were medicine bottles. She caught me. I didn't even realize that I was staring.

"It's my medication, Buttons."

She caught me off guard. "Uhh?"

"I said, it's my medication. Honestly, I'm starting to think that the shit over there in them bottles makes me worst. It's breaking down my immune system, man. But, my body's gotten so used to it."

"But, Dottie... you... you don't look..."

"Look like what? Like I have AIDS?"

"I mean... yeah. You don't look sick."

"It's called AIDS, Buttons. Don't be scared to say it. And don't worry you can't catch it by sitting too close to me or by kissing me on the cheek. Don't worry you're safe."

"I know. I know."

"So, we're straight. Right?"

"Yeah."

The next days I nursed Dottie. It seemed like as soon as she revealed her sickness, she got worse. Those few days lead to a few weeks. Then one day in the middle of the night I was awakened by her screams.

"Buttons!!! Oh, My God!!!! Shit!!!! Buttons, it's time!!!!!!!!!"

I ran in Dottie's bedroom, where she was laying in a fetal position. "Okay, Calm down. Breathe...."

She cut me off yelling at the top of her lungs. "Calm down!!!! Fucking breathe? Ain't that much breathing in the world! Oh, Buttons I can't do this. I change my mind."

"Baby, it's a little too late for that. Don't you think? Come on let's get to the hospital or do you want me to call an ambu...."

"No! I want to go on my own. They ask too many questions. My doctor's number is in the drawer over there. Call him, let him know I'm on my way."

On the way to the hospital Dottie begged and pleaded with me. She made me promise that I would take care of the baby. And when she passed I would adopt.

"Buttons. When we get to the hospital go to the second floor and go see David. Let him know what's going on. The doctors say he can't hear all the time. He comes and goes. But I believe he hears."

When I finally found David's room, my heart started beating rapidly. I stood outside the door for a minute or two, before walking in. I didn't know what I was about to see. I just stared at him. He didn't look the same. He looked like he had aged double and his hair looked thin. There was a funny smell in the room, I couldn't take it. I backed out the room in a daze.

When I got back upstairs I sat in the waiting room daydreaming. I couldn't believe how he looked. I started to wonder if I would be able to handle Dottie looking like that. I couldn't watch my best friend die slowly. I cried, silently. My thoughts were broken by the doctor.

"Excuse me. Hello, I'm Dr. Bell."

"Oh, I'm sorry. How are you? I'm Buttons. Dottie's best friend." I wondered if he could tell I was nervous. I knew he was going to talk to me about her sickness.

"Well, she's given birth to a seven pound six ounce baby girl. They're both in Intensive Care Unit."

"Why did something go wrong... What happened?"

"Well you're aware of her condition?"

"Yes."

"Well, the delivery weakened her. Besides the cancer, she has a few other medical problems. We like to keep an eye on babies that have the possibility of being HIV positive.

On my way to see the baby I cried. I didn't know why I was crying, all I knew was I couldn't stop crying. And Dottie hadn't mentioned no cancer. My God! I screamed in my head. I stared through the nursery glass.

She was so pretty. Usually you can't tell which parent a baby looks like right away. But she had features. She looked like Dottie and David. She looked like an angel. I don't know what I expected her to look like. I mean was she supposed to come out looking like she was HIV positive? What was the next move? What was I supposed to do now? And what about David? This was too much for me. I had forgotten about my life back at home and forgotten about my own baby back at home. All I could concentrate on was Dottie and her situation. And now that the baby is here, I'm sure my life is going to be even more distant.

Today they came home. All of them. David, Dottie, and the baby. To calm down my nervousness and in between anxiety attacks, I cleaned constantly. Since the day I left the hospital all I did was clean Dottie's house. I don't know why. It was clean already. I don't know, I've known the both of them for years and still I felt like I didn't. I didn't know how to be towards them now. I know it may sound crazy, but I just don't know how to act around them. I wanted to know so much. I had so many unanswered questions. Like the number one question... . Where did he get that shit from and when? Like, how could he do this to my friend. He knew with no doubt in his mind that she was not sleeping with nobody but him. At least he could have given her the respect to wear a condom when he was fucking other bitches! My whole outlook on him had changed. At the same time I felt sorry for him, though. At first I wanted to kill him. But how could you want to kill someone who is already dying, slowly at that? I wondered how many other women he had given it to. And where is the person that had given it to him. I wondered if he really knew who had given it to him. Is the bitch still alive? I'm sorry, but I can't help but to call her a bitch. Bitch probably knew she had it, too. After a while of thinking about it I had to realize that I was being a little unfair, but I guess I was angry. Wouldn't you be? I tried to be a little more compassionate for the other parties involved. But it was so hard. I mean true, maybe the girl who gave it to him didn't know she had it. Maybe even she too was an innocent victim, like Dottie. I don't know all I knew was my friend was dying and nothing can change or fix that.

Later on when I had gotten up in the middle of the night, to pee, I peeped in Dottie's room, the door was opened. I noticed that David wasn't in the room. I saw Dottie sitting in the rocking chair I had picked up yesterday. She was rocking the baby and singing. Just like nothing was the matter. Like she wasn't going to die.

The next day I over slept. I jumped up and looked at my watch. 12:45! Damn, I was supposed to catch my baby's phone call. I ran down stairs to the kitchen after I saw Dottie wasn't in her room.

"Dottie? Dottie, are you in here?"

My heart started pumping fast. I don't know why. I guess I was just paranoid. Nobody was here. Where the hell could they be. I didn't know what to think. I'm sure if something happened I would have known. I stood in the middle of the kitchen, stuck. I felt like I was acting like I was their mother or something. Like I was responsible for them. Just at the end of my thought I heard the key in the back door. It was Dottie and David. They had a lot of bags like they went shopping or something. Dottie had the baby in one of those carrying things that straps to your chest. David was holding a whole bunch of bags.

"Hey, girl. What's up?"

"What's up? Where were you? I woke up looking for you guys. I got worried."

"I'm sorry. We had to run a few errands and pick up a few things."

"Yeah, well I could have done that for you. Why didn't you

wake me up? You could have stayed in and got some rest."

"That's all right. I needed to get some air anyway. Buttons... you don't have to worry about me. Whatever is gonna happen is gonna happen. I can't stop living. Don't worry about me. You'll know when it's time to worry, trust me." She reached over and kissed me on my cheek.

It changed my whole mood. She made me feel better, more comfortable. "So, what you guys got here." I started looking through the bags.

She snatched the bag out my hand. "Oh no you don't. You always been nosy, girl. We got a surprise in there for you. Hold your horses. Won't you go out and help David with the rest of the bags while I go lay the baby down."

"It's more?!"

"Yeah, we got carried away. I haven't been shopping in so long I couldn't help it. I'm gonna go up and lay the baby down."

When she went up stairs I paused before going outside. I haven't been left alone with David yet. I don't know how to handle him. When I got out back he was still unloading the car. They sure did some serious shopping. There were all types of bags from all types of stores.

"Hey, David what's up? You need some help?"

"Hey, Buttons. Yeah. You know your friend once she starts she can't stop."

We carried the bags in the house with limited conversation. I guess he picked up on my vibe. By the time we brought in the last load of bags, Dottie was back in the kitchen making lunch.

Dottie turned to David and gave him a funny look. "So, David. Did you talk to Buttons about what we talked about?"

You can tell that she caught him off guard. "Uh?"

"You heard me, David. Did you talk to buttons?"

"No."

"Well, what are you waiting for?"

"You.... I was waiting for you."

Why were they doing this to me? That's all I could ask myself. I mean it was like it didn't bother them. It was like Dottie had no resentment towards David. She had no hatred towards this man that's taken her life from her. I just didn't get it. I've known them both almost all my life and I had a little bit of hatred in my heart towards him. I was very hurt. All of a sudden I started getting hot flashes and my mouth started getting dry. What the hell could they be talking about?

"Well, Buttons, since David is having problems with his vocal cords today.... Look we feel like you are the only person we can trust with Angel. We know you have your life back at home, but... we need you Buttons. We decided to, if you agreed, to leave you the house and the money we have saved...". She paused. "And Angel. We know you could raise her. You could bring little Sammy down here. They have a great school system."

It was a lot for me to swallow. I didn't know what to say. I knew they could tell by the look on my face they caught me off guard. What was I supposed to say? She talked like I was supposed to give an answer right then and there. But then it wasn't like they had forever to wait for an answer.

I looked up from my plate, finally, and looked in her eyes. All I saw was my friend, how I once knew her. "Well, it's something to think about." After I said what I said I felt like an idiot. How do you say something like that when your friend, who's dying, makes a request like that. She just left it at that. "Okay. Let me know."

For about a week I thought about what Dottie had asked me. I tried to think with an open mind. At this point, I thought, I really didn't have much of a choice. I was all she really had. Her and her sister hadn't talked in years. The morning I came to the decision to accept her offer....David died. In his sleep. Dottie laid next to him for hours before calling an ambulance. After the funeral she sat in her rocking chair and rocked and rocked and rocked. I took care of Angel, Dottie's daughter.

One night, about a month after David's death, Dottie called me into her room. She sat in her rocking chair with her eyes closed. She had a glow about her.

"Buttons, thank you."

"For what Dottie? You know I don't mind."

She was much weaker now. "Yeah, but you didn't have to do what you did. You didn't have to stay with me or Angel." She took a deep breath. I could tell it was a struggle for her to breathe. "I'm not going to be here much longer.... I saw my mother last night, that's how I know. But, I wanted to let you know that I will be with you every step of the way...I'll be looking over you guys." Tears began to run down her face. "Please let my daughter know how much I loved her. Let her know that it's not my fault that I'm not here to see her grow up. Buttons... as much as I'm not ready to leave this earth, I know I have no other choice. I had so many plans and dreams that I'll never get to accomplish. But I've learned to deal with the hand that has been given to me. I can't waste no more time wondering why and asking why. I don't want anymore of that medication. It just makes me feel worst. I want to spend my last days with my daughter. Everything is set up the way I explained last week. I....just wanted to make sure you knew that I loved you." She closed her eyes and went to sleep.

I covered her with a blanket and whispered in her ear. "I love you too, best friend."

One year and five days later

I sat in the living room crying all morning it seemed. Today made a year Dottie had been gone. I thought about the conversation we had in her room last year, five days before she passed, in her sleep. I heard the back door slam. I hurried and wiped my eyes. My son came running in the living room.

"Ma! Ma! Ma!"

"What! What's the matter?"

"I think I saw aunt Dottie."

"How many times I have to tell you, baby. Aunt Dottie is gone. She's in heaven. It's just your imagination."

"No! No! I saw her. She was looking for Angel."

"What? What makes you say that? She told you that?"

"No."

"Then how you know that?"

"I can just tell. I felt it."

I picked him up and hugged him. "Oh, baby...you have a good imagination and there's nothing wrong with that. Come on let's go see if Angel is woke."

I carried him up the stairs and into Angel's room. I must admit I was kind of scared. You know what they say about children, they say they can see spirits. I thought maybe Dottie was coming to get Angel, you know maybe it was her time. I really need to get that out of my mind. Especially since the doctors can't find nothing wrong with her. They can't understand how she's not HIV Positive. Look... I don't wanna know why and I don't care why. I just pray it stays that way.

God is good. Ain't he?

Forbidden Fruit

The club was packed. It was hot and weed smoke filled the air. You could barely move. So Lace and her friends decided to stand in one spot, until they spotted Darren and his crew. They walked over to the bar where they were standing.

Now Darren was Lace's stepbrother and her daughter's father's friend. And he didn't really like her hanging on the club scene, especially when he's there with his friends. Her friend Mekka liked Darren, but never really got no where with him. Lace's baby's father happened to be out tonight with Darren and the rest of the crew. They weren't really a couple no more. You know how it is with baby daddies and baby mothers. One day they alright and lovie dovie then the next they beefing and at each others' throat.... Well, that's Lace and her baby daddy. But anyway, Darren ain't feel like they bullshit tonight. Lace wasn't thinking about Freddy, her baby's daddy. Darren screwed his face when he saw Lace and her friends.

"Yo, what you doin' in here?" He asked Lace pouring her some champagne in a glass. "It's Mekka's birthday." She answered. And walked away before he started his shit.

She went over to the rest of the guys and spoke. The crew looked at her like a little sister, so it was nothing but love when she went over. She didn't speak to Freddy. It was too many ballin' nigga's in the club and she wasn't thinking about her tired ass baby daddy! She decided to stay over at the bar with the guys while her friends went downstairs to the bathroom. The whole time she could feel Freddy's eyes on her every now and then. She couldn't front, she felt a little flattered. But it wasn't him she had her eyes on. She felt a funny feeling inside when she looked at Jason. Their eyes would connect every opportunity they could get, without nobody else noticing. She knew, just like he knew, they had no business. But she couldn't help it. She didn't know what it was for him, but for her it was for real. He was the forbidden fruit. If her stepbrother ever knew, if anyone ever knew, all hell would break loose.

But as the night went on and the more weed and champagne she drank...the more she wanted him. She hadn't been with him in a long time, actually since the first time. She only had been with him once and that was over four months ago. But they would talk on the phone and see each other around the way. He came to her job a week before to bring her some money to get her daughter some things. But they hadn't been intimate with each other. She peeped the girls in his face and his big smile everytime one came over like he was the president or something. He saw the guys after her too. She made sure of that. And why wouldn't they want her? He thought. She was a pretty girl.

She had light brown eyes to match her brown streaked shoulder length hair. She had a nice shape and she knew how to treat a man. Freddy knew that. That's why he really couldn't stand the thought of her being with somebody else. But he had worn out his welcome with her. He had dogged her out to the point where she couldn't be dogged no more. He fucked up her credit, like most street guys and irresponsible men can do. He loved her, don't get it twisted, but he didn't know how To love. And that was the problem. It didn't take long before Freddy started flipping out. He just couldn't take Lace doin' her thing. She didn't bother him the whole night. She even stayed out his way. But he had smoked too much purple haze and drank too much Hennessy. Lace was standing across the bar, talking to a kid she had met a few weeks ago from Jersey, when Freddy walked over to her and grabbed her arm.

"Yo! Come here for a minute." He shouted in her ear over the music. She looked at him like he was crazy. "What!?"

"What!? What? What? You heard me come here! I don't give a fuck about dat' bitch ass nigga'!" He shouted, pointing to the guy from Jersey. By that time, Darren had come over to where they were standing.

"Pardon us son." Darren said to the guy while pulling Lace and Freddy away.

"Naw, man. Fuck him! Ya' sister tryin to play me in front of that nigga."

"Man, Freddy I saw you go over there starting. Usually I be breaking on Lace but you startin' this time. Let's just go back over here and drink." Darren pulled him back to the spot where they were standing all night. Lace went over to the guy from Jersey and apologized. And of course Freddy was giving her the evil eye from across the bar. For a person who didn't care about her and who had so many other women...I don't know he just made it hard to believe sometimes.

She was turned off with him. All night bitches in his face and not once did she act a fool, like he knew she could. She went and found Mekka and told her what happened. Shit, Mekka was just as turned off. She was trying to get with guy from Jersey's friend. The guys offered to take them to get some breakfast and they accepted. They went and said bye to their other friends, who was no where near ready to leave. They told the guys they would meet them back at the bar. Lace figured it was nothing else for her to do, since Jason had left out the club with some chicken head.

Lace stopped to tell Darren she was breaking out. Just as she was walking towards the door, Freddy came behind her and grabbed her by the neck and pulled her back. "Bitch you runnin' round here wit' niggas...Where my daughter at!!?" And he punched her in her mouth. She picked up a glass and hit him in his head. Blood started gushing out of his head.

Darren had seen it all coming. He couldn't get over to the two in time. The bouncers had pulled Freddy and Lace apart. Blood was coming from her mouth and blood was pouring from his head. Mekka and the guys was pushed outside by the bouncers. The bouncers was tussling with Freddy. Darren and his friends snatched Freddy and Lace from the bouncers and walked them outside. By this time blood was on all of them. The police was outside at the corner, so they walked the other way to get to the car. Mekka looked at Lace and just shook her head.

"What, Mekka?" She asked, barely being able to talk.

"Girl ya' mouth." She whispered as they walked behind the guys. Lace stopped and looked at her reflection in a store front. She liked to die! Her upper lip was split. He must have hit her with his ring, she thought. She just stood there. "That muthafucker!" She thought to herself. She looked down the block where Freddy was walking with the guys. She saw Darren and Freddy arguing. She saw Darren pointing up the block in her direction shaking his head. She turned back to the store front and looked at her face. How would she work like this? She couldn't. And she was going no where near Freddy.

Darren kept calling up the block to Lace, but she walked in the other direction. She would find her own way to her car. Mekka followed behind her. A horn honked at the girls as they crossed the street. It was the guys from Jersey. They stopped to talk to them. They offered to take the girls to their car, so they got in. "I think you need to go to a hospital, Lace" Mekka suggested.

"I know." She replied

"What happened anyway?" Mekka asked.

"I don't know. Ya' was in front of me walking out and he just came from behind." She answered, looking at her mouth in the mirror. The guy from Jersey just looked and shook his head. He didn't understand how some man would act like that over a girl if he wasn't with her. They dropped them to Lace's car and said good night. He told Lace he would call and check on her tomorrow.

After Lace got her lip stitched up she dropped Mekka home. "Lace, you sure you don't want to stay here instead of going home?" Mekka pleaded with her before she got out the car.

"Naw, I'm all right. They gave me enough pain killers to last me 'til I fill my prescription. I'm straight, boo. I'll call you when I get up."

Mekka got out and went up stairs. Lace stopped at the store to buy water and a can of soup. She knew by the afternoon her lip would be worse and she would barely be able to eat solids. As soon as she walked through her door, the phone rang. Instantly she knew it was Freddy. She shut her machine off and refused to answer the phone. But it kept ringing. Finally she answered it. "Hello." She could hardly talk.

"Yo, what happened?"

"I'm sure you heard. That was fast...You finished at the hotel that quick?"

"What? Man listen...What you talkin' 'bout Lace? I just called to check on you. Darren said he was trying to call ya' cell and da' machine came on. Did you go to the hospital?" He asked.

"Yeah." She answered him with a little attitude.

"Well,...What happened!?" He shouted through the phone.

"I got fuckin' six stitches in my lip!" She shouted back. She had popped a pain killer so it was a little easier for her to talk.

"Get da' fuck outta' here! You okay, you need anything?" He asked.

"Yeah....You. I need you, Jason."

There was a pause before he answered." Lace...Man... A'ight. I'm gon' come through. Where my girl?" He asked.

"She at my mother's. You really comin'? You know how you do? And where's dat' girl you left the club with?" She asked. "Man, shut up! I got to go meet ya' brother to get something. Then I'm gonna come through. What time is it?...3:45 in da' morning. I'll be there by 4:15 or so." He hung up. She knew he wasn't coming. She didn't even know why she bothered. Nothing couldn't come out of it.

Jason was her baby's father's friend and Darren's friend. She had no business feeling the way that she did. But she couldn't help it. She knew Jason first, that was her excuse, even though they was always just cool. Sometimes she wished she would've had a baby from him instead of Freddy. She was too far into her feelings for him to just walk away. He didn't know how she felt. He just thought that she liked the excitement of sneaking. He knew she was a good girl, Freddy just didn't know what he was missing out on.

When Jason knocked at the door, Lace jumped up. She didn't expect him to really come. She opened the door with a slight smile. She couldn't fully smile because of the stitches. "Hey, I thought you wasn't gonna come." "Yeah, yeah, yeah." He pulled her close to him and lifted her chin. "Damn, he did a number on you this time, huh?" He kissed her softly on her cheek and then her neck. Chills ran down her body. He made her feel good, he made her feel wanted. He slowly removed her night gown and began kissing her body.

She also made him feel good. If it was any other girl and under any other circumstances, she would definitely be his main girl...at least one of them. He tried to stay away from her but it couldn't be helped. They were from the same circle first of all, so he had to see her. He figured if he didn't see her by themselves he would be a'ight. But he liked the way she did what she did to him. She made him feel good and not too many of the girls did. There was a few but not too many.

Lace... Well Lace loved him. She didn't know why or how. She didn't even know if she should tell him. For now she figured she would keep it to herself. And he figured he wouldn't let it go on for too long, it couldn't.

Boom! Boom!! Boom!! Lace heard banging on the door and jumped up. Jason smoked a blunt before he went to sleep so he was knocked out. She tip-toed out to the front and peeped through the peep hole. It was Freddy banging on the door. Her stomach turned into a knot. She ran back to the bedroom and shook Jason.

"Jason...Jason get up!" She whispered.

He slowly opened his eyes. "What up?"

"Freddy's at my front door banging it down."

He sat up. "What! What he said?"

"Nothin' he's just banging on the door. Did you park out front?"

"Naw... Naw. I took my car to Darren before I came here. I took a cab....Go see what he wants." "What!! Are you buggin'? Why would I do that?" She asked.

"Don't open da' door just ask him what he wants." He got up and slipped his boxers on. "I'm goin' ta' take a shower." He left her sitting on the bed. She got up and walked back out to the door. He was still standing outside her door. He walked back to the door and started banging again.

Boom! Boom! "I know ya' fuckin' in der'! What ya' got one of ya' nigga's in der hoe!? You better not have dem' clowns around my daughter!!" He shouted outside the door. "Get da' fuck away from my door, Freddy!!!" She shouted back through the door, as much as her swollen lip would let her. "Fuck you, Lace! You hoe bitch!!" He yelled and walked away.

Jason came out the bathroom butt naked. She wished he was hers. "What happened, what did he say?" Jason asked "I was a hoe bitch and I probably was in here wit' one of my nigga's. I don't understand, I don't even have a lot of nigga's."

"Whateva' Lace. I don't know who you think ya' talkin' to."

"I got you... That's all I got and want. But ain't it a pity I can't have you and you don't want me how I want you." She walked into the kitchen and started to cook them breakfast. He followed her. "Lace you know how our shit is man. If shit was any different it would be easier for us..." "Oh...but it's easy to come and fuck me every now and then, right!! It's easy enough for you not to spend time with me!!" She shouted.

He just stood in the kitchen and smiled at her.

"What da' fuck is so funny?" She asked him.

"You. You are crazy. You don't want me, Lace."

"What does that supposed to mean?" She asked.

"What I said? You don't want me, Lace. You may think you do, but you don't."

"Okay since you know everything." She rolled her eyes and kept cooking. He walked behind her and wrapped his arms around her. She wanted to melt. She felt how he really felt, through his hug. She felt how he really felt without him even speaking. His hug told her that he wanted her too. His hug told her how much he really did care even when she thinks he doesn't.

Two Weeks Later

Two weeks had passed and not once did Jason pick up the phone, on his own, to call Lace. She had given up on him. It was the same old shit. Promises that wasn't kept. She was on her way to the doctor to get her stitches out. She was tempted to pick up the phone and call him, like every day since she last saw him. But she wouldn't, she wasn't gonna do it this time. "Just let it go" she told herself.

Then the phone rang, just as she was walking out the door.

It was him. "Why?" She asked herself when she looked at the caller ID and saw his number.

"What." She asked as soon as she picked up.

"Hey. What's goin' on?" Jason asked.

"Nothin'. What ya' dick is hard? Oh, that's right you must have known I got my stitches out today...What you want some brain now that my mouth is back in effect?" She spoke sarcastically. "Look...What ya' doin' dis' weekend?" He ignored her attitude.

"Why you wanna know?"

"Do you got somethin' to do?"

"No..."

He cut her off. "A'ight. See if ya' mother a watch the baby. I'll be at ya' house at 10 tonight. Bye." He hung up. Should she or shouldn't she? She played with the pros and cons. And of course she couldn't help but to give in. Just like before.

She made arrangements with her mother to take the baby. She packed the baby bag and dropped her off after she left the doctor. She went and got some scented candles and a bottle to travel with. All through the day she prayed he didn't stand her up, like he had done other times. Once it hit 10:30 she picked up the phone and beeped Jason. She paced back and forth with anxiety. It was Friday and he probably was with Darren and them. She called Darren's cell. "Yo!" He answered

"Yo, what up? What you doin'? She asked listening to the background.

"Chillin' where you at?"

"The crib. Where you?"

"At the Honey Comb Hide-Out wit' these nigga's."

"Oh...What ya' doin' tonight?"

"I'm chillin'. This nigga' Jason must be goin ta' hit somethin'. He in here wit new kicks and smellin' all good and shit!" He said clowning Jason. She could hear everybody laughing in the background, including Jason. That mothafucker is hanging and I'm waiting for him, she thought.

"Alright then... I'll hit you later." She said.

"Yo, what's wrong wit' you?" He asked.

She could tell he had walked away from the crowd. "Nothin' I'm a'ight." She replied.

"A'ight then hit me later, maybe we can get somethin' to eat or somethin'."

"A'ight." She hung up the phone and started to take her clothes off. She was pissed! Made her waste baby-sitting not to mention her time. Just as she got her pants off the phone rang. She looked at the caller ID and it was Jason. "10:00 huh?"

"Man, I'll be there in ten minutes. I had to take care of somethin' over there. Don't start. You took da' baby to ya' moms already?"

"Yeah. I been did that earlier."

"Alright, listen for da' horn." She jumped up and put her clothes back on and fixed herself back up. It was no time before she heard his horn. She grabbed her stuff and ran out her apartment. She jumped in the truck smiling. He took all the regular streets. She figured he would take back streets, but he didn't and she didn't bother to ask why. She just sat back and enjoyed being with him...besides in the bed. He sat his hand on her leg. Giving her that warm feeling. That feeling that she felt the last time she saw him and he wrapped his arm around her in her kitchen. She noticed they was going through the city, then through the tunnel. Once they got in New Jersey she knew they were probably going to a hotel.

"Where we goin', boo?" She asked.

"Atlantic City... For da' whole weekend."

She smiled with satisfaction. "Say word. Stop playin'!"

"I'm not playin. Why, you got to get the baby?"

"Naw. I just didn't think...you know."

"You don't got no confidence in me?" He asked

"No I don't. Should I?" She questioned.

"Yeah you should."

"Why is that?"

"Cause things gonna be different between us from now on."

"Is dat' so?"

"Yeah dat's so."

She just laid back in the seat sipping her drink out of a plastic cup. She was soaking up everything he was saying. And of course she believed him as usual. When they got there he sent her inside to check in the hotel while he parked the car. He told her he had already made reservations for a suite. She waited for him in the lobby when she noticed a familiar face in the crowded lobby. They made eye contact and he took a double look. Her heart started pounding as he walked closer in her direction. He walked over with a smile plastered across his face. "What you doin' here?" He asked.

She didn't even think before talking. "What else would I be doin' here... gamblin'." She replied.

He laughed. "Yeah, who you wit'?"

"Oh... My nigga's. I see you not wit' yours." She pointed across the room to where he had left a young lady standing.

"Well, you wasn't tryin' to fuck wit' a nigga'. I guess you don't fuck wit' Jersey cats, huh?"

"Whateva nigga'. Do you." She walked away and left him standing by himself. He just looked at her and shook his head. He wished he was here with her instead of the chick he had brought with him.

As soon as they got in the room Jason asked about the kid from Jersey. "Yo, who was that you was talkin' to."

"Oh, that's the nigga I was talkin' to when Freddy started flippin."

"Oh." He left it alone.

She was unpacking her toiletries when she felt his arms unbutton her pants from behind. They dropped and she stepped out of them. She thought briefly about Freddy and how he would feel if he knew what was happening, what was about to happen. One of her baby's father's best friends. Before she knew it he had her on the bed kissing all over her. He kissed her belly button, but stopped right over her bush. He never went down on her, so she didn't expect to get no head. But he tricked her ass this time. That was it. She knew he must have checked for her, he gave her some head. Couldn't tell her no different.

She went downstairs to gamble. Jason said he had to make some phone calls and he would. He sat on the bed and thought about what was going down. He went up in her raw. He was open and there was no way he could let her even get a hint. He joined her downstairs after taking a shower. He dialed Freddy's number, he had to check on some business he was supposed to take care of for him. Jason felt guilty calling him after just banging his baby mother out.

"What up Freddy?"

"What da' deal? Where you at?"

"Out in da' world. Did you take care of that?"

"Yeah. I just left. Everything is straight. I'm sittin' outside Lace's crib. I know she up to some shit."

He knew why his friend was bugging out. He had just witnessed why less than an hour ago.

"Yo, kid why you starting shit?" Jason asked.

"Man, I know she fuckin' wit' somebody, I just don't know who. That crack head nigga', Charlie off da' Ave., told me he seen some nigga' creepin' in her crib a couple of weeks ago. He said he thought the kid looked familiar. I hit him off every now and then to keep a eye out on her place." Jason couldn't believe what he was hearing. He laughed. "Nigga' you crazy. I'm gonna be out of pocket for the weekend. I'll hit you up when I surface." He hung up. He knew he was the kid Charlie saw creeping with Lace. Nobody else went to her crib. At least as far as he knew. He started wondering if she was fucking somebody else besides him. After toying with his mind he convinced himself she wasn't.

He went down in the casino. He spotted her at a five dollar slot machine. He just looked at her. She was so pretty. He wondered how Freddy could diss her. She was perfect. Good job, faithful, pretty, and good sex. But how far could it go. It wasn't like he could sport her. He wanted to be able to ride with her in his passenger seat. He walked over to her and kissed her cheek.

"Any luck?" He asked

Holding up a huge plastic cup full of coins, she smiled. "Yeah. But I keep putting them back into the machine." She noticed something was strange about him. He tried to let her see his thoughts. He knew he had to break it off. But how? Should he just back away slowly and hope that she doesn't realize? He thought of several ways, but still couldn't come up with anything concrete. Fuck it, he thought. He figured he would just go with the flow.

Back In B.K.

Freddy was sitting in front of Lace's apartment smoking a blunt. He was destined to catch her. They weren't together no more, but that wasn't going to stop him. His excuse was their daughter. *He claimed*, she was running the streets not taking care of his daughter. Which is bullshit. Freddy didn't even check for his child. He would give Lace money every now and then, but not on a regular basis. He didn't even spend time with his daughter. It was only in his jealous rage would he care about the whereabouts of their child. Lace got used to Freddy's objection to his responsibilities. She would take care of her baby with or without him, she has no other choice. And Freddy knows he can contribute to his daughter's life, he just refuses. It's not like he doesn't have the money, he's holding more than ever. His street career is at a high. He kept looking at his platinum, diamond faced Rolex, which he had just copped the day before, and he can't cop a coat for his daughter. What type of shit is that?

He had been sitting in front of her crib for a couple of hours and still no sign of her. He started his car and went to Bed-Sty to check some girl he had met at the club the week before. He didn't know why he was going, one thing he didn't do was mingle with a lot with girls. He had mad chicks he was fucking or had fucked, but he wasn't good with approaching chicks. They seemed to find their way to him. He debated if he should stop by his stash crib to drop off the $63,000 he had in a plastic bag, sitting on the back seat. He decided not to. He figured he would only be over in the Sty for a minute. When he reached the girl's block he slowed down. He rolled down the window and looked for the building number. "566...566." He mumbled to himself. He stopped the truck in front of the building marked 566, rather the board that covered the windows of the building.

The building she had directed him to was an abandoned three story house. He picked up his cell and started dialing the girl's number. Maybe he had the wrong address he thought. Just as he finished dialing the girl's cell, he caught someone's shadow out the corner of his eye. He dropped the phone and reached under his seat for his gun. He cocked it back and started the car, but out of nowhere a dark tinted Oldsmobile jumped out and blocked him in. Two men, with their face's covered, jumped out with burners in their hand. There was enough space between Freddy's car and the car that was parked in front of him, to inch up and push his way out. But not without slamming repeatedly into the Oldsmobile that had double parked on the side of his truck. "Yo, motha' fucka' get out da' whip!!! Nigga' get outta' da' whip fo' I push ya' wig back!!!!" One of the guys screamed. The guys hadn't noticed the burner in Freddy's hand. The other masked man jumped over the hood of his truck and stood on the passenger side of Freddy's truck with a 45. pointed at him.

"Nigga' ya heard what he said!!! Get da' fuck out and give us all ya' shit, BITCH!!!!"

Freddy raised his hand, the one that was holding the cocked back glock, and pointed it to the guy's chest. Before the man, standing on the outside of the truck, could react Freddy pulled the trigger, twice. He flew back several feet, falling to the ground. For a few seconds, Freddy had forgotten about the other guy, until he heard a loud pop and bullets started piercing through the truck. Freddy fired back immediately. Not even paying attention to if he was hit or not.

People started running out of their houses. Not much could be seen with all the smoke and quick burst of fire that came from Freddy and the guy's guns. After the noise seized and the smoke cleared, Freddy noticed he had caught the guy in the side and upper part of his chest. He jumped back into the Oldsmobile and skidded off. Freddy followed behind him, until he noticed a burning feeling in his leg and arm. He turned off the block he was driving on and headed towards the other direction, away from the sirens. By the time Freddy got to a pay phone to call Darren, he was weak and soaked with blood. He knew it was a possibility the bullet hit a blood vessel or something.

Darren's cell phone rang out. And just when Freddy was getting ready to give up hope for an answer on the other end of the line Darren answered. "Yo!"

Freddy paused for a second before responding. "Son... I need you to come and get me... I just got hit up."

"What? What you mean hit up?"

"Nigga's just tried to smoke me...Dunn!   I'm over here on Flushing Ave. down the block from dat' gas station." He struggled to talk. The pain started to over come him.

"Stay on the phone with me, I'm on my way on dat' side son. Where you hit at?" Darren asked speeding through the streets to get to his friend. "I think just my leg and arm, but I'm not sure now. My whole body is numb. Look, I got to hang up now... Hurry up.."

Freddy slid to the ground. He didn't realize the blood coming from his chest before. He wasn't sure if it came from him touching his chest after touching his leg or arm wound. But his chest began to burn like fire. His breaths got shorter and shorter. He was hit in his chest also, besides the leg and arm wounds. And the bullet didn't exit. He closed his eyes and tried to hold on to his breath...his life..he tried to hold on to his life.

Jason was in the middle of giving Lace a back shot when his cell phone and beeper started going off at the same time. He didn't bother to look over at the number.

Lace moaned with pleasure. "Please don't stop." She begged. "This is supposed to be my weekend...Please Jason don't stop." She pleaded.

"Oh...Don't worry baby I'm not. You feel too good to me, Lace." Jason whispered in her ear. Him whispering in her ear made her even hotter. They made love all through the night. It wasn't until Lace dropped into a deep, exhausting, sleep Jason decided to check his pager and cell, while Lace slept. He immediately dialed Darren's cell. Darren never paged him 911, unless it's really an emergency. He got the machine instantly, he knew his phone had to be shut off or his battery had died. He saw a little envelope at the top of his phone so he knew Darren must have left a message. He checked his messages. Before he could hear the whole message he hung the phone up and started shaking Lace.

"Yo..Yo, Lace! Get up, we got to go!!" He shouted while throwing his clothes on. Lace rolled over and sat up, still drained from the constant sex they had just had an hour ago. "What..happened?"

"Get dressed we got to go. Hurry up! Come on come on!" She jumped up and got dressed. She knew something serious was going on.

She never saw him like this before. He had a weird aura about him. She didn't bother to ask any more she just followed his instructions.

He broke the silence once the got on the highway. "Lace we can't do dis' shit no more.. I mean we can't fuck wit' each other no more."

"What you fuckin' talkin 'bout, Jason!? You always playin' some type of fuckin' game wit' me! I don't understand you. You think I'm some type of joke!.."

"LOOK LACE! Your baby father is my fuckin' man!!! If the situation was different then it would have been alright, but it's not!!! And we can't change dat'!"

Tears ran down her face. She felt played. "OH..Is dat' so? You always comin' to some fuckin' conclusion after you finish fuckin' my brains out!! Dat's all I'm worth to you is pussy!! Freddy has nothin' to do wit' it and you know it!!" He hadn't told her about Freddy getting shot. He didn't know how. He felt guilty.

"Lace...Freddy got shot up tonight..Dat's why we're on our way back. Your baby's father, my nigga' got shot da' fuck up tonight and I wasn't around! I was busy...fuckin' his baby's motha'!" His words rung in her ears. She had never felt guilty about their affair until now. She felt like she was at her lowest point. He made her feel like trash. She didn't know why or how, but he did. It took seconds before the actual news had hit her brains. Her body ran hot.

"What you mean shot up? What...What you talkin' bout? Where?" She asked barely being able to digest what was going on.

"I don't know everything yet. Darren is at the hospital wit' him now. I do know this is it between me and you. It's over Lace, I'm sorry but dat's just how it's got to be, baby."

At The Hospital

Lace paced back and forth with her arms crossed. All she could think about was her daughter. He was a lousy father, but at least he was a living lousy father. She couldn't understand why it was taking so long for the doctors to come out the operating room. Darren sat in the corner with his hands in his face. At a time like this men usually are at their worst. Jason stood up against the wall with a twisted face and red eyes. He had a million and one thoughts going through his head. He thought to himself, "Why wasn't he there?" He felt guilty about fucking Lace. He looked around the waiting area at everyone and wondered what they would say if they knew he was fucking one of his best friends' baby mother, who was in an operating room fighting for his life. Then he looked over at Lace and started thinking about the passionate sex they had shared just a few hours ago. Just a few hours ago he had realized that he actually loved her. But Freddy getting shot would change everything. The doctor appeared from the operating room. Removing his gloves and cap. Everyone stayed stuck in their places, afraid of what they were about to hear.

"Who's Lace?" The doctor asked

A shaken Lace raised her hand. "Me." Her voice cracked.

He walked over to her and reached his hand out. "Hello, I'm doctor Dice. Freddy managed to squeeze you're name out before he went under anesthesia."

"How is he?" She asked scared of what his reply may have been.

"Well, he's unconscious now..."

Lace interrupted him. "What you mean? He's in a coma?" She asked with a blank look.

"No, he just hasn't woken up yet. Hopefully his vitals won't change. He's under heavy observation. He insisted on seeing you." He pointed in the direction where Freddy was.

Lace looked at Darren and Jason, then turned and followed the doctor. Lace took a deep breath before entering the room. She looked around for the doctor, but he was no where to be found. She walked slowly into the room. There were beeping noises coming from the many machines he was hooked up to. He had a tube down his throat and little wires connected all over. She walked over to him and stared at his weak looking body.

"Oh, my god." She whispered to herself. "Damn, Freddy, what have you done this time?" She pulled a chair up to the bed and sat down, holding on to his hand. She cried a silent, but deep cry. She pulled up her chair and leaned over into his ear.

"Why did you ask for me? Out of all the people, why me? Why? And what happened?" She began to cry harder and louder. She wondered off into thought. "What if I didn't make it here on time? I wouldn't have forgiven myself...And he wouldn't have either. Please just wake up...I'll be there for you." She knew she could not leave his side. At this point it didn't matter what he had done to her in the past. The beatings didn't matter, the abandonment of his responsibilities to his child didn't matter,..... Jason didn't even matter at that point.

It had been two weeks since Freddy had been home. Lace had kept her word to Freddy. She was more than there for him. He had moved back in with her. She took a leave of absence from her job to take care of him. Darren agreed to pay her bills. Freddy slept most of the day, high off of his painkillers. He was slowly getting it together, very slowly. His friends would stop by every day, sometimes two, three times. She could barely look into Jason's face when he came over. She couldn't handle how passive he was when he came over. He acted like they were never intimate. She never got the slightest feeling that he had missed her or even gave thought to them.

Lace was in the kitchen doing her daily routine, cooking and washing dishes from last night's dinner. Freddy was in the bedroom lying down in pain. He was trying to deal with the pain without using the pain medication. "Freddy, I think you should take one of those pain pills." She shouted from the kitchen.

"Naw. I'm straight. I gotta get used to not taking them shits." He replied.

" A'ight, suit ya'self."

He pulled himself up straight in the bed and worked his way to sit up on the edge of the king size bed. He reached for the breathing toy the doctor had sent home with him. He wrapped his lips around the contraption and began blowing into it. He tried to make the ball inside of the plastic toy reach the top with every breath, but he was unsuccessful. He got frustrated and sat it back on the night stand. He pulled himself up slowly off the bed and stood up. He walked, like a toddler taking its first steps, into the kitchen. He stared at Lace's back as she stood over the stove cooking. He loved her, no doubt 'bout that. But he also was obsessed with her and that wasn't good. The two just didn't mix well. She always had his back, he knew that, but he just couldn't do good by her. She turned around, feeling his eyes burning through her back. "What's the matter with you?" She asked as she took the pot of grits off the stove and stirred them.

"Nothin'. Just looking at you cook. He answered.

"You okay?"

"Yeah. I figured I would walk around a bit. The doctors said I need to walk around a little everyday. I should've started a few days ago. I was gonna go outside for some fresh air today, but it's rainy. Maybe it' a stop. Told the nigga' Jason to come by and get me. Nigga' always late." He turned and slowly walked back to the bedroom.

She turned cold inside at the mention of his name.

Lace had a gut feeling, that Freddy was gonna flip the script soon as he got better and didn't need her to baby him. But for some reason she still did whatever she had to for him. She broke her neck for him. She was feeling a little guilty about her and Jason's little thing. Why? She didn't even know why. After all the bullshit Freddy did to her.

After breakfast Laced helped Freddy get washed and dressed. There was a long and uncomfortable silence between the two while she helped him get his *over sized* jeans on. She could never understand why he had to always buy his pants so big! Was it to make him appear to be bigger than what he was? She just didn't get it. He broke the silence. "You know Lace, I really appreciate your help through all of this shit." She just simply smiled. She knew this tone he was caring, She knew him all too well. He stopped her from pulling his left pants leg up.

"You heard me, Lace?" He questioned

"Yeah, I heard you. It's nothin' don't worry 'bout it."

"I mean....You didn't have to look out like you are and shit.
"He continued as if she didn't even reply a minute ago.
"I said it ain't nothin' Freddy."
"Well..." He started, but was interrupted by the phone.
Ring, Ring...
Lace ran to the phone. "Yeah, hello."
"Hey, you. What up? Is Freddy there?..."Before she could reply he continued in one breath. "How's my little girl? I miss ya'. *Both* of ya'. There was a lot of bad shit that was said that night we came from Atlantic City...I'm sorry kid maybe we can talk about it one day."
"Hey, what up Dunn. Hold on here he is." She took a deep breath and passed the phone to Freddy. Her heart was beating a thousand beats a minute. She felt wobbly inside. Just in those few seconds she regained that feeling for him. That feeling she could never understand its depth. Nor could she understand the meaning of it. All she knew it was love. Love in the worst way. He had said the *both of ya'*. He had admitted to missing her too. But was this one of his games? No way could he'd been stressed like she had been, not being able to see him or be with him. Just when shit was looking up for them, the bullshit with Freddy had to happen. She knew Freddy was about to pull the Willy Bo Bo on her. She had been checking his pager everytime she got a chance. They say seek and you shall find? Well she was seeking and she was finding, too! She thought it was kind of bugged out for a motherfucker to be all hurt the fuck up and still worrying about getting a new god damn pager, with the same number as the old one he had lost in the shoot out. She noticed a lot of late night pages, with code 01. Like a motherfucker thought they was the #1 bitch in his life. While she was playing fucking ER, some bitch was somewhere out there thinking she was A number motherfucking One! Oh, you wanna know how she was so sure it was another female calling? Well, she decided to call the number back one night, while Freddy was knocked out on pain medication. Now Lace ain't no new jack, so she knew to call the operator and request that the *operator* put the call through because she couldn't get through dialing it herself. Lace knew that would block her number. And dialing *67 didn't work the first trip around. Anyhow,

before the phone could get a full ring in a female voice picked up on the other end.

"Hello." The young voice on the other end answered.

"Yeah, somebody paged me?" Lace asked. In a calm voice.

"What? Who dis'? I paged somebody, but it wasn't you."

"Excuse me? I'm looking right at my pager and this is the number on my pager."

"Well, I paged my baby daddy, and you sure ain't him.!" And the girl slammed down the phone. Lace just stood with the phone in her hand, puzzled.

"Baby daddy" she whispered to herself. "Who the fuck is that?" She asked herself. She knew how chicks could get defensive and shit when another woman calls them about a man. She knew that girls made all types of shit up to seem like they have the upper hand, so she just took it as that. But that wasn't enough for her. She had to repeat the operator routine again, that was after Freddy's pager went off again....three times in the row, once again with that annoying code 01 again.

Before the phone could fully ring, the same voice picked up on the other end, "Freddy?"

"Miss I don't know who you trying to reach, but you keep reaching my pager. Who are you looking for?" Lace asked in a friendly tone. Niceness would get her further she figured.

"What da' fuck..."

Lace cut her off, killing her with kindness again. "Excuse me, but I'm not calling beefing or nothing. I don't know your child's father. I just got this pager a few days ago and I've been getting a lot of weird pages. So,...." The girl cut her off. Calming down and taking notice of what Lace had just mentioned, about the weird pages. She also chose to use the nice guy approach to get as much info. as she could. Just what Lace expected,

"Oh, I'm sorry. I thought you was some chick answering my man's pager." The girl on the other end replied, in an about face tone.

"Oh, chile please, no. I'm married with two kids."

The girl took a sigh of relief. "Oh, I'm pregnant now, my first. Eight and a half months... Ummm you said you've been getting weird pages, I mean I feel funny asking...but have any other women besides me...you know... been paging looking for somebody named Freddy?"

"Oh, don't feel funny, I understand. But naw, all guys. A couple of guys, that's all. I think something's wrong with the frequency lines or something. I'm gonna go get a new pager tomorrow."

"Oh, okay. Sorry 'bout my attitude at first. Thanks a lot.... What's ya' name? I'm Mo, Monique."

"Oh, girl it's no problem. Been there before. My name is Tammy."

"Okay, good night Tammy."

"Okay, Mo. Get some sleep. You gonna need it when labor time comes." They both of them laughed and hung up.

She just stared at Freddy while he slept comfortable in her bed. At first she thought the girl could have been playing games. Like Lace was. But knowing Freddy she wasn't.

By the time she came out of her thoughts, Jason was standing in her living room waiting for Freddy. All of a sudden she grew a hate for him too. She knew he had to know about this girl, Mo. Him and Freddy was tight, of course he knew.

"Hey, you." Jason spoke with a friendly type tone. Freddy was in the bathroom.

"Hey, my mother fuckin' ass. You phony fucker." She replied in a calm but stern tone.

"What's up wit' all dat', Lace?"

"Oh, you never give up, huh? First my heart, then my trust. Me and you supposed to have something special no matter what, J. Even if we're just friends or if we're fuckin'."

He just stood confused. Then Freddy appeared out of the bathroom with a big smile on his face.

"Yo, son, what up!" That was Freddy all hyped up. Jason went over and slapped him five. Lace stood looking, turned off! She had promised herself she would keep her cool.

"So, what you got to do today, Big Fred?" Jason asked, as if him and Lace's conversation never took place.

"Oh, I need to go check on some dough, go on da' Ave. to check some other shit, and I wanna run Uptown."

Why he said that! Uptown? Lace knew what that was about. He was gonna go check the pregnant chick out. The chick with the 212 area code and the 01 pager code. She knew she had promised herself she was gonna keep her cool, but god damn not today she wasn't!

She walked over to the closet and pulled all of Freddy shit out, in a rage!

"Yeah, mother fucker take this shit wit' ya' sorry black ass!" Then she walked to the night stand and snatched all his medicine and his little breathing toy. "Don't forget this shit, bitch ass nigga'!!!! Take all ya' shit!!!!!!"

Jason stood with a blank look on his face, to match Freddy's look.

Freddy picked up his stuff that she threw to the floor. "Yo, what da' fuck is wrong wit' ya' ass?!"

"What?!!! You still trying to play somebody? After my ass took you in, took care of ya' temporary cripple ass, took off of work to tend to you!!!!!! Motherfucker you would want to get up out my space before I open up a can of whoop ass on you!!!!!!"

"YO, You's a dumb ass fuck, Lace!!!! You be flippin' for no reason!!" He shouted.

By this time he was in her face and she was in his. And she wasn't backing down, she held her ground. Jason finally grabbed her.

"And you, motherfucker!!" She shouted and turned her anger "You better take your motherfuckin' hands off me!!!! Both of you nigga's better get the fuck out my space!!!! Freddy take ya' ass Uptown to ya' young ass baby mama!! What's her name again? Mo...Monique, is it? You dirty bitch. You could lay up in my bed, have me nurse you back to good health, but you couldn't be real enough with me to tell me you had some bitch eight and a half months pregnant?!"

Both Freddy and Jason stood speechless. Freddy could feel the wrinkles in his forehead getting more visible by the second. The confused look. He knew that wrinkles in the forehead spelled out confusion and he didn't want that.

"Lace..." Freddy attempted.

Lace walked back over to him and stared him right in the eye. "Lace" "What, motherfucker! What, Freddy? What you got to say this time?... Nothin'!! Now get ya' sorry cripple ass up out my shit!! Oh, yeah you don't got to worry about giving me shit for ya' child. You don't even got to worry about me asking for shit. For as I'm concerned you don't even exist. We don't need no part time baby daddy 'round here no way! Now get the fuck out, I said. And take all ya' shit!!!! You and ya' sorry ass friend!!!!!!"

She walked away and went into the bathroom. Before he could get to the bathroom to explain she had slammed and locked the door.

It took Freddy and Jason three trips to collect the stuff. Rather it took Jason three trips. Freddy stayed down stairs in the car after the first trip. He was too weak to carry stuff up and down. On the last trip up, Jason tried to talk to Lace, but she didn't want to hear it. She dismissed all conversation with him.

"Look, Lace...." Jason tried to explain.

"Look, Jason. You're full of shit just like ya' tired ass friend sitting downstairs. You knew about that bitch all the time and you didn't say shit to me. You just let me be a fool and shit. You stood by and watched me play myself. That nigga' could have went Uptown and laid up in that bitch's shit and got better!! I was a fool for you too. I'm a fool period. I don't know why I expected you to say shit to me, when you yourself was playing me!! Now take the rest of this shit out of here and close the door behind you, please." By this time her eyes were teary and her throat was cracking.

He did just that. He collected the last of Freddy's stuff and headed towards the door. Lace just stood with her back turned to him, staring out the window.

He stopped at the door, with his back turned to her also, full of guilt. He whispered. "I still love you kid. No matter what you think."

The door closed and her tears fell. She felt like an idiot. Like some type of toy. How could everybody know and not her.

The ride Uptown was silent and full of tension. The most activity between Jason and Freddy was the passing of the Backwood full of Haze.

"Yo, son you sure you should be smoking weed this soon? Jason questioned.

"Man, what you think? Shit after that shit that happened fuck if I'm supposed to, I need to!! Man I don't know how this shit happened."

"Look, you brought that shit on ya'self kid."

"How you figured?" He asked taking deep pulls of the blunt.

"Cause you should of told her. If you would have told her you wouldn't be going through this shit."

He chuckled. "Yeah, 'a'ight! What da' fuck eva'. Turn right here, on 116th. It's the beige building on ya' left."

Jason did as Freddy directed. The block and building looked familiar to Jason. He couldn't place it off hand.

Freddy reached in his pockets and pulled out a set of keys.

"It's on the first floor, so we ain't got to do all that walking and shit." He told Jason.

Jason helped him out the truck and over to the building. He noticed the keys he had pulled out was to the building.

Jason laughed. "Nigga' you got keys to the girl crib? What you livin' some type of double life." Freddy didn't reply. When they got into the apartment, Freddy pushed some buttons on the security system and told Jason to go straight and make a right into the living room. Jason looked around the place

"Damn, Freddy this shit is hooked the fuck up! You wouldn't think this shit looked like this from the outside...not that the building is fucked up or nothin'. Just that the neighborhood and shit. How many bedrooms?

Freddy flopped down on the plush leather love seat next to Jason.

"Three." He replied.

Jason noticed the big poster size picture of Freddy and a Spanish girl, encased in an expensive frame, hanging on the opposite wall. She was a young well-shaped girl. She looked familiar, but he couldn't place her face. He didn't let his mind give it much thought.

"You can smoke in here?" Jason asked. "Yeah, this my shit."

Jason lit another blunt. "So, that's ya' baby mother?"

"Yeah. dat's my shorty."

"What she Spanish?"

"Dominican. She cool peeps, I just can't take her on a regular. You know constantly. I fuck wit' her like dat', but I can't be coming home to her every night and shit. Naw, not the kid." He took a toke of the weed and passed it.

Jason took a pull and sat it in the ashtray. "I know what you mean, son. That's how I felt 'bout my Jersey shorty. Shorty was hot! Body was off the meat rack! Head was straight! But somethin' 'bout her made me not want to be up under her. Shit, I can't even lay next to a chick all through the night 'til the sun come up. Unless she's my shorty, shorty. But, not no bitch I'm fuckin'."

Freddy struggled to get himself up. While Jason's puzzled mind went back to Freddy's Dominican shorty, staring him in the face. He tried, once again, to place her face somewhere in his memory. But, Freddy had something else in mind. He knew he couldn't let Jason sit and remember where he knew Mo from.

"Yo, let's go bring all dat' shit in before my pain killer kick in". That was Freddy, already half way out the door. Soon after Jason was on his heels and his thought was history.

Freddy used the fact he had not too long ago took a pain killer and that he was feeling tired.

Jason gave him dap and walked toward the door. "A'ight you 'ain't got ta' tell a nigga' twice. Hit me up later I'm goin ta' da' crib."

Freddy slowly walked over to Jason at the door. "A'ight...what crib you going to?"

"Jersey, probably. Shorty at work still. I can go and smoke wit' out her ass all followin' and shit. I'm gon' probably sleep there tonight. Take her to da' movies, make her feel special."

By this time they were in the hallway. "Yeah, I might do that shit too."

By the time Jason foot hit the gas, Freddy was on the phone paging Mo off the hook. After about forty minutes she returned the page.

"Freddy?" Her puzzled voice asked on the other end.

"Who da' fuck else would be paging you from here?"

"Nobody, you just caught me off guard. I 'ain't hear from you and shit. Look, I be there in a minute. I gotta go."

"What?! What you rushing for?"

"I'm not rushin' I'm at the repair shop. That fuckin' lemon you brought me keep breakin' down and shit."

He felt a since of relief, knowing her whereabouts. Whether she was telling the truth or not.

"Don't worry 'bout it. I'm gonna cop you another whip next week. Yo, hurry up I'm hungry." He hung up the phone before she could get her reply in.

Jason dialed Freddy to make sure he was still where he had left him, well over an hour ago. After getting confirmation from Freddy, he looked at his watch. It had been thirty-two minutes since he pulled in front of Lace's place. He was still undecided about calling her.

He said fuck it and picked up his cell and dialed her number. The phone rang out until the machine came on. He dialed it two more times until she picked up.

"Hello."

"Why you didn't pick up the phone a minute ago?" Jason asked on the other end.

"What? Yo, what you want? I'm busy."

"What? Busy doing what?"

"None of your biz, that's what." She replied.

Jason heard a man's voice in the background. "Who da' fuck is dat'?" He snapped.

"Look, I got company. I'll hit you another time." And she hung up.

Jason sat downstairs until he saw an unfamiliar cat come out her building. Then he remembered that the guy was the one from the club the night Lace and Freddy got into it. Jason had noticed Lace talking to him before he left out the club.

He watched him walk to the corner and jump in a 600Benz coup. Before he could drive off, Jason was out his whip and at Lace's door, knocking.

Lace opened the door. "What the fuck are you doing here Jason?"

"Man shut up!" He pushed his way in the door. "Why da' fuck you had that nigga' up in ya' crib!?"

"You better leave me the fuck alone." She picked up the empty champagne bottle up off the coffee table and took it into the kitchen.

"Oh, you just was having you a big ole' party, huh?"

"Sure was." She replied sarcastically.

"Yeah, a'ight. Don't let me bust you upside your head." He replied. He started taking off his boots and jeans.

"May I ask what are you doing?" She walked over to him and asked.

"Taking my shit off. What it look like?"

"I see. But why?"

"Cause I'm staying here tonight."

"What!?" She laughed. "No you're not! How you know my company ain't coming back."

"I don't know and I don't give a fuck either."

"Look Jason, I don't have time to play your games no more. I'm moving on ya' heard!"

"Ain't no such thing when it comes to us. Ain't no moving on! So shut up and come here."

Lace stood looking at him. She promised herself she wouldn't give in to him or tell him about the baby. She said she was just going to take care of it without anybody knowing. But she couldn't. She couldn't do neither.

"I'm pregnant, Jason." She blurted out.

He sat back up on the bed. "What?"

"You heard me...I'm pregnant."

"Wait... By who? Freddy or......"

She cut him off. "You. If that's what you were gonna ask."

"You sure...."

She interrupted him again. "Sure what?! If it's yours or if I'm pregnant?"

"You sure you pregnant, I meant."

"Hell yeah! But I already made a doctor's appointment."

"For what!?"

"To take care of it. What you think, I'm going to keep it?"

"Yeah!! Why wouldn't you?"

"Why wouldn't I? You got a lot of nerve. You the one who always got an excuse when it comes to us."

"Well, ain't' no excuse for my seed. "

"You bugging. What we gonna tell people?"

"All of a sudden you worrying about people."

"I don't know, Jason. I already have a baby and...."

He cut her off. "And what? I take care of mines! What you tryin' ta' play me?"

She kneeled on her knees and put her head in his lap. "I'm scared you're gonna play me."

He rubbed her head. "Naw, you don't gotta worry about that. It's different now, you talking about my seed."

Seven Months Later

Jason had moved Lace and her daughter out to New Jersey, on the low. Lace hadn't seen Freddy in about six months. She heard about his baby being born. She hadn't really seen Mekka. Mekka knew she was pregnant, but didn't know the whole story. Darren didn't officially know, but he knew. He stayed out of it. Jason spent most his days in the street hustling. Lace played the "House Wife" role. She was due next month and couldn't wait to drop her load.

She knew sooner or later she was going to have to face Freddy. Even with all the bullshit he put her through she still worried about how he was going to feel.

Jason was by the projects waiting for Freddy. He promised Lace he would take her to the movies and he was already an hour late. Freddy was late and holding him up. Just as he was dialing him, Freddy knocked on the window.

Freddy jumped in the truck with a big shopping bag. "What up?"

"Nothin'. What took you so long?"

"Had shit to do."

"What you think I don't got shit to do?"

"Yeah, I'm sure you do....Look the dough is a little short...."

Jason cut him off. "Again? Come on man this the third time."

"Well, I think you should be givin' me da' Wiz for a little cheaper anyway."

"Yeah, oh really? Don't you think I'm lookin' out already?"

"Not like you can. As a matter of fact, considering you've been fucking my baby moms behind my back....."

"What!?"

"Nigga' you heard me. Oh, what you thought I wasn't going to find out?!

"Bitch pregnant too, I heard. As a matter of fact, I think I'm gonna keep this dough right here." Freddy pulled out a glock and pointed it at Jason.

Jason pulled his gun out from his waist and pointed back at Freddy.

"Boy, you must be crazy!!" Jason shouted.

"Naw, you must be fuckin' crazy, to think you was gonna play me like dat'!!"

Bang, bang, bang, bang, bang, bang. Shots fired inside the truck.... and blood splattered the window and doors.

Both Freddy and Jason lay in the truck barely breathing. Holding on to life.

Darren turned the corner minutes later, noticing Jason's truck. He pulled behind the truck and jumped out. He noticed the shattered glass from the windows.

"What da' fuck! Yo! Somebody call an ambulance!!!!"

He noticed the shopping bag full of money and took it before the police came.

Lace fell asleep on the couch. The phone woke her. She looked at the clock, 9:34pm.

"Hello." She answered.

"Yo, it's Darren....You satisfied! Huh? Why couldn't you just chill? Why you had to cause all this trouble between Jason and Freddy?!"

"What!?"

"Look, you need to get down to Brooklyn Hospital. Ya' baby father.... Both of them are clinging on to their lives!!!!" He slammed the pay phone down.

Lace grabbed her chest and jumped up. She ran out the house and into her car, a Benz truck Jason had just bought her a few days ago.

Monique ran to the nurse's desk in tears holding her baby on her hip. "I'm looking for Fredrick Noles..."

Darren turned around when he heard Freddy's government name. He took a double look.

Monique continued. "I'm his child's mother."

Darren walked over to the desk. "Monique? What you doin' here.....?"

"Darren where's Freddy?....what happened....What's going on??!"

"How you know....?"

Freddy's mother came through the doors. Monique ran over to her crying.

"They won't tell me nothin' " Monique told his mother. His mother walked over to Darren. "What happened to my baby?"

Darren hugged her. "Ma, I'm not sure. I found him and Jason shot up in Jason's truck..."

She broke down. "Jason too! Oh my Lord!!. I tell you boys about that life!! Who did this?!"

Darren pulled her to the side away from Monique. "They did it to each other.... I took both their guns out their hands before the police came."

She stood in confusion. "What are you telling me, boy?" She whispered.

Just then, the doctor and Lace appeared. "Hello. I'm doctor Frost. Who's here for Fredrick Noles and Jason Drake?"

"We are!" Everyone said at the same time.

"I'm Fredrick's mother."

"I'm his child's mother."

"I'm Jason's child's mother." Lace said and then paused before continuing. "And his wife."

Everybody's mouth dropped open.

The doctor continued. "Well, I don't have any good news for you. Both are in comas.....and we don't know what to expect." A nurse walked over to the crowd. "Doctor, we need you right away."

"Excuse me, I'll be right back. And he disappeared behind the swinging doors.

Darren pulled Lace to the side. "Wife? What are you talking about?"

"We got married three months ago...." He cut her off. "I could just punch you in your face!" He shouted, in a whisper tone. He walked away, leaving her alone and crying.

Freddy's mother walked over to Darren. "What is Lace talking about, Darren?"

The doctor came back out, saving Darren from explaining.

"Who is Lace and Darren?" Dr. Frost asked.

Lace and Darren stepped up. "We are." They answered. "Well, Mr. Drake has woken up and he's insisting on seeing you. Usually we wouldn't allow it so soon, but he's insisting."

"Wait what about my boy?" Freddy's mother asked the Dr.

"I'm sorry ma'm there has been no changes with Mr. Noles." She hugged tightly to Monique and they cried hard.

Lace and Darren stood side by side in front of Jason's bed. He looked so bloated and helpless. Much worst than Freddy when he got shot. Lace walked closer to Jason. "J, can you hear me?" Jason's eyes opened slowly. "Lace?..Where's Darren?" he spoke weakly.

"I'm right her son." Darren answered.

"Look, I'm not gonna make it..." Lace cut him off. "Shh, don't say that....." He cut her back off. "Look, Lace there's no time. I didn't want you two to think we got into it over you, Lace. Freddy tried to rob me. Darren take a hundred g's out and give the rest of the dough to ya' sister. Lace, I love you. You always been my ride or die chick. And Darren you my nigga' for life. I saw my moms and pops and they said I'm straight." He closed his eyes and the flat line on the machine appeared.

Doctors and nurses swarmed the room pushing the two out. Lace fell to her knees outside the room, "No!!!! Please God don't do this to me!!!!"

Darren picked his sister up and headed towards the double doors to join Monique and Freddy's mother. Before they could get threw the doors Darren heard Freddy's mother and Monique's cries. "Not my boy!!!! Jesus please don't take my boy!!!! Why my boy?!!! Why did you have to take my boy!!!!?"

Jason and Freddy's wakes were a day apart. So within two days Lace had to go to both her children's fathers funeral's. It was too much for her. Too much for her pressure. Her blood pressure shot up the day Jason and Freddy passed. The time of death on both of their death certificates read the same thing.... 12:47AM.

And Lace lost her and Jason's baby, a week before her due date.

TRICKS

"Girl, I don't know why."

"Why what, Charlene?" Tricks asked.

"Why you keep putting up with that asshole." Charlene answered.

"Look not today, okay." Tricks replied in an annoying way. "Oh, really. Then when? After he kills your dumb ass?"

"You don't understand, nobody understands." Tricks answered, staring into the eyes of her friend of twenty-four years. See, Tricks just couldn't find a way to make her friends or anyone understand. (Not that there was a way.) And being she's been with him for so long somehow she felt she couldn't leave him. Even though he beat the shit out of her. I can remember when she first met Ticky (real name Howard Jones.) She was about fourteen or fifteen.

Boy, Mamma Pots was hella stressed. Mamma Pots, havin' that name since anyone could remember, was labeled that 'cause of her skills in the kitchen'. Boy could she burn some pots and chase a smoke detector out of a house! Well anyway, Mamma Pots could not understand how her little baby could get in the mix with this kind of boy. But still Mamma loved her granddaughter. So she put up with Tricks' choice of a man, so to speak. Now, Ticky was always that hip street guy. And always had dough. And at the same time he was very sweet. That's probably the reason Mamma Pots lifted off him.

See, Tricks is from what some people call the ghetto. I personally feel ghetto is a mental thing. But Tricks always found a way to keep herself together. She's always been a smart girl. And she also had a heartbreaking and hard life. Tricks was brought up by her Grandmother since she was four years old. Both parents passed when she was four. And when Ticky came along, I have to admit she changed. She was more loose with her feelings and personality. She smiled more. Ticky just moved in her life so fast. I remember the day she went out with Ticky for the first time.

She had to convince Mamma. She begged like a poor little girl. Still Mamma was not trying to hear it. I guess Mamma saw something

Tricks didn't. Maybe Mamma saw the future. I think she knew that underneath all that sweetness lay a very unhappy, abusive son of a bitch! But nevertheless, Tricks didn't see it. So what else was she to do once Mamma Pots kept denying Tricks pleas and requests? What else? She pulled a stunt and snuck out. Man! I don't know what the fuck was on that stupid ass child's mind. She thought she was in love. She just knew she was in love.

She called it love at first sight. I know one motherfuckin' thing she was calling for God and Mamma Pots when shots flew in Ticky's brand new whip as they left the movie theater. I don't know if it was that incident that drew Tricks closer to that loony tune, but ever since that night you can't even begin to get that child away from Ticky. Tricks snuck back into the house that night while Mamma Pots was still asleep. Successfully too. At least that's what she thought.

Mamma knew Tricks snuck out and not only did she know she snuck out, but she knew what went on that night. Tricks later found out about Mamma knowing from a letter she had left Tricks when she passed away. It's so funny when you come from a certain environment things are so different and certain things are looked at differently. See, where we're from it's never looked at like domestic violence or an abusive relationship. Usually it's just "my boyfriend punched me in my eye, gave me a black eye 'cause I wasn't supposed to go out last night'." Or "me and my baby's father had an argument and he fucked me up." It's a sad thing. But all the drama that's in her life now could have been avoided, if she would have just listened. If she just wouldn't have been so gullible.

"You know Tricks you can come and stay at my place." "Thanks Charlene, but I'm gonna be okay." Tricks always had a way of convincing somebody she didn't need any help. She just always hid her pain and stress. Rather, ever since she started fucking with Ticky. I think she was just embarrassed. At first we didn't think nothing of the beatings. We just thought it was lovers' quarrels they were having. But when that motherfucker broke her arm and when she started having black eyes on a regular basis we knew something wasn't right.

I mean everybody almost everybody had their share of fights with their mates (I guess) but Tricks' shit was type outrageous. He was so jealous and so possessive. She had so many dreams when she was young. I always felt that she still had them dreams somewhere deep down inside. Tricks was an exceptional artist. I mean she could draw like a pro. From a young age she was drawing portraits of family members. So many dreams are built and made in the ghetto and them same dreams die in that ghetto. So many young people are scared to dream these days. And then you got the ones that let either a negative person or a negative vibe interrupt their dreams. The devil sure be working overtime.

"Tricks!" "Tricks!!"

"Yes!" She replied to Ticky as he came up the stairs.

"Yo, have you seen that motherfucker Sam around your old way?"

"No, why?"

"Don't go covering up for him, Tricks!"

"I'm not." Tricks often covered up for Sam, Ticky's little brother. Sam was eighteen and had kind of a mental problem. Sam always was doing some crazy shit. Ticky just couldn't understand his sickness. It always hurt Ticky more than anything.

See, Sam wasn't always like that. When Sam was ten years old he was molested by a janitor at his school. After that, Sam kind of bugged out and never snapped back. As Ticky started getting older or shall I say getting more caught up in the street and the hype he became less sympathetic and less caring about his brother. The day they found out what happened to Sam, Ticky and his homeboys went to the school to find the janitor, but before they could get to him the police got him. Ticky was steamin'.

They had found out that he wasn't the only one. There was four others boys he had molested. But the police getting to the school first didn't stop Ticky. He had some of his people upstate occasionally whip up on that nasty ass janitor. The beatings had gotten so bad that they ended up transferring the janitor. That was I think two months after he got one of his balls cut off and lost permanent sight in his right eye. They sure worked a number on him. But compared to what he did to Sam, I guess that wasn't nothing.

"That little motherfucker!" Ticky shouted throughout the

house.

"What the fuck did he do?" Tricks asked with a puzzled and concerned look on her face.

"What the fuck did he do?!" He replied.

"What could he have done so bad?"

"He set my mamma's living room on fucking fire!!!!"

"What!!!!!!!!!?"

"Yeah!!!!"

"Why.... I mean how, when?"

"This morning." He replied pacing back and forth. "I can just wring his little neck. You know how much I paid to do that god damned living room?"

"Yeah, a whole lot of money."

"I know that little motherfucker knows what he be doing. Ain't that much retarded in the world."

Tricks turned around with a puzzling look, a look of confusion. "What do you mean retarded?" She asked in a whisper.

"What do you mean what do I mean?"

"I mean, since when has Sam been retarded?" "He's not retarded he's....."

Cutting her off "OH, what the fuck are you his guidance counselor now?"

"It's not about me being his counselor."

"You know what, I can see it coming. I'm breaking out."

Ticky left out the house, leaving Tricks stressed out. You know she used to think it was a phase Ticky was going through, but as time went on she started to realize that it wasn't. Her hanging out privileges started getting very limited over the years. I remember one time Ticky didn't want her to go to a party. Tricks had been planning to go to this party for weeks. Well, Ticky busted that bubble real quick. Some how her friends convinced her to go.

Ticky heard she was in the club, no more than an hour after she got there. How? To this day nobody knows, but he found out. Man!! When he came through those club doors, it was like a fucking tornado hit. He took Tricks by her neck with one hand and shook the holy shit out of her like she was a quart of orange juice. Shook the poor child's clothes right off of her. I mean literally right off of her. He beat her like she stole something. Let him tell it she did, his heart. He just never knew how to deal with it. I think that's one of the nights Tricks and her friends got their asses kicked by Ticky. The next day Tricks' eyes were swollen so bad. Her eyes were so red they favored those big peppermint balls. Ticky told her he didn't want her in nobody's club. Clubs were for thirsty hoes and hungry pussy wanting men. But still he stayed in the clubs.

She stayed in the house for about a month or so. By this time she had kind of moved out of Mamma Pots' house. But it was still weird when Mamma Pots hadn't seen Tricks in a month. Tricks found a way to convince her that Ticky had sent her on a cruise for a month. She always felt bad about lying to her grandmother. But it would have hurt her heart if she knew what was going on.

So Mamma Pots was praising Ticky for giving her granddaughter such a gift, if she only knew. She never liked Ticky anyway so I don't think she really praised him that much. I think she just wanted Tricks to be happy, and she felt if she acted happy that would make Tricks happy. If she only knew that she was home looking like a swollen ball.

As the years went on Ticky became what you would call "big time." The house got bigger, the cars changed, Tricks jewelry got more glittery. Even her clothes closet became larger. She had every name brand you could imagine. I don't know for what, she couldn't go nowhere. She always ended up lending her clothes to one of her friends. And along with the material changes came more beatings. By this time I would say she was immune to "her situation" I like to call it. She also became distant from everyone at one point. All she had was that big house and all of those materialistic things. And all of Ticky's street stress turned into 'Tricks' stress'. Such a very sad thing. It's like living in a certain environment you get immune to certain things. Subconsciously you get angry and sometimes don't know how to deal with your anger, because you don't know why you're angry. I feel sometimes we as African-American women never take time out to truly love ourselves. We just go straight into loving someone else. I think we lost that many years ago. And along with that we lost our support system for one another. In Tricks' case I think she had a pretty good support system, she was just in denial about her situation.

Tricks sat in front of her well dressed vanity mirror, with ice and wet dressings. As she looked at herself in the mirror, tears slowly ran down her face burning the cuts and bruises on her face. She looked at what was supposed to be her temple, her body. Inside she tried, but couldn't understand how she had gotten to this point once again. I mean this was getting a little out of hand. She had realized she was really an abused woman. Society had always showed her that this only happened to poor white trash, middle class white families, or dysfunctional families. It never is supposed to happen this way to someone in her position, rather someone from her environment. What would Mamma Pots have said? she thought to herself.

Sometimes she wished Mamma Pots was here. How could she go around her friends like this, the few friends that she did have. Charlene would never let her live this down. At this point Tricks couldn't even remember what it was that triggered Ticky to do this. All she remembered was it started out as a beef about something he heard in the street. And she remembered that she fought back this time, something she had never done before. It was kind of scary, she didn't know what he could be thinking of now. New ways to start arguments because of his frustrations with her reaction this time. She didn't know, all she knew was she was tired of the bullshit. Another scary thing was that she had been tired of the bullshit before and still ended up with him. The slam of the front door broke her out of her long daydream. She jumped up startled. Tricks didn't know what to expect at this point, so she ran into the bathroom in their bedroom and locked the door. She could hear Ticky run up the stairs. Within seconds she thought of a million and one things that were about to happen. She could hear his footsteps racing into the bedroom. Ticky ran straight to their walk-in closet and retrieved a brown paper bag from the top of the closet. Tricks stood nervously behind the bathroom door clutching the knob. Just as fast as he ran into the bedroom he ran out. Tricks breathed a sigh of relief. She opened the door and peeked out to make sure the coast was clear. Limping back over to her vanity table she continued to look at her badly bruised face. "He didn't even check if I was all right."

She whispered to herself.

This has been the closest she has ever came to realizing 'her situation'. What is a person to do once they've reached this point. Call your friend? Run and hide? It's hard, cause she really doesn't know if she is ready or strong enough to leave him. She first has to deal with her new discovery. Her thoughts are once again broken this time by the telephone.

"Hello". She answered with a very jittery voice.

"Tricks"?

"Yes".

"It's Stan, are you okay"?

"Umm, yes".

"Are you sure".

"Yes".

"Where's Ticky? He was supposed to meet me at the corner of your block."

"He left a minute ago".

"Okay he must be on his way.... Oh, here he comes".

"Okay".

"Thanks, Tricks".

"Bye". Tricks hung up the phone returning to the same confused state she left before Stan called. Stan has been Ticky's friend for as long as Tricks could remember, so he knows about her 'situation'. He could always tell when something is going on with Tricks and Ticky. He has continuously tried to talk to Ticky about his problem. As much as he could without effecting their friendship. Stan knows what goes on inside of Ticky's home is not quite right, but he also knows a man's business behind closed doors in his home doesn't concern anybody else (at least that's what he feels). Shit, Stan has been there at some of their worst incidents. The first time Ticky broke Tricks' wrist Stan had to take her to the hospital. Stan felt embarrassed for Ticky, but what could he do? Ticky was his friend. Once again Tricks couldn't remember what had really triggered Ticky off. All she knew was she was caught in one of her "situations" and before she knew it she was screaming from severe pain from a throbbing wrist. Which she discovered was broke when she got to the hospital. Stan had been at their house when the fight broke out. He tried to stay out of it, but once Ticky left out of the house, leaving Tricks on the living room floor in unexplainable pain he had no other choice but to escort her to the hospital. Tricks finally came to terms with her reality. She had to leave him. But was she really ready to break out on Ticky? Just because she realized it was time to go didn't mean that she would be able to.

With a spirit of confidence she jumped to her feet and gathered a couple of her things. She had never even come close to leaving Ticky before, let alone really making moves to leave him. She thought as fast as she could, scared that Ticky may return and flip out. She removed all the jewelry that was given to her by Ticky. She just didn't want anything from him and didn't want any reason to see him again. So she might as well leave everything behind. After packing she went over to the phone and started dialing frantically.

"Hello, Charlene?"

"Tricks?"

Breaking down into a semi hesitant cry. "Yes."

"What's the matter?"

"Can I .....I need to come there for a while."

"Are you okay?"

"No." She replied in a more calmer tone. "Can I come by?"

"Sure, you know you can."

"I'll be there in a minute, listen out for me. Oh, and if Ticky calls looking for me before I get there tell him you haven't seen or spoke to me."

"Okay."

"As a matter of fact, when we hang up call me back and leave a message on the machine as if you're looking for me. That will make him think off the back you don't know where I am."

"Okay, no problem."

Two minutes after the girls hung up the phone rang. She just continued to get herself together, as she heard Charlene's voice on the machine.

"Hey, girl what's up? Where you at? Look, call me when you get this message"

She walked out of the room backwards, slowly looking at the

space she and Ticky once shared. She then remembered that she couldn't and didn't want to drive her car. She didn't want anything that had any connection to him. Plus it would be easy to find her at Charlene's if her car was parked outside of Charlene's house. She walked through the rather large house into the kitchen and called herself a taxi. As she sat outside and waited for her taxi, she drifted off into one of her daydreams of when she first met Ticky. He was so good to her. Showing no evidence of the monster that he had turned into. She remembered the good ol' days.

"Hey, Ma'm. You called for a taxi?"

"Oh, I'm sorry. Yes.... yes I did."

She stood up and looked back at the house one more time and got in the taxi and pulled away. By the time she gave the driver Charlene's address her body was paralyzed. She could not believe what she was doing. Returning came to her mind. But before you knew it she was in front of Charlene's house paying the driver. And Charlene was on the stoop waiting anxiously for Tricks. Tricks grabbed her bags, adjusted the sunglasses on her face (which she wore to cover her new scars) and walked towards the stoop.

"Why did you a take cab?" Charlene asked.

"Look I'll explain it, let's just go into the house." She replied pointing to the front door. Charlene followed her into the house and locked the door. The girls walked into the living room, Charlene with a puzzled look on her face and Tricks still hiding her beaten face behind her sunglasses and baseball cap. Charlene called Lil' Keith (Charlene's son who is extremely small for his age) over to her. He was 9 but could pass for 5 or 6.

"Go into your room and play your game, baby."

"Yes, mommy."

Lil' Keith ran into his room and the girls walked into Charlene's bedroom and closed the door. Charlene kind of knew what she had in store once Tricks had pulled her shades off. She first pulled her cap off, which revealed her bruised and cut forehead. Then off came the glasses.

"What the fuck.......!!!!!" screamed Charlene.

"I fought back this time."

"Oh my God, Tricks what did he beat you in your face with?"

"His hands."

"Yeah, but what da' fuck did he have in his hand when da' motherfucker hit you!"

Charlene would never have expected this, at least not now, so far down in their relationship. She kind of thought the serious beatings was over. And trust she had seen some of the serious beatings.

When Lil' Keith's daddy got killed and Charlene broke down; Tricks, like any friend would, helped plan the funeral. Charlene couldn't do anything, but cry and sleep. Tricks did all the running around for her. Well, that caused a problem with Ticky at some point. Ticky started feeling insecure about her not being home, knowing she was out most of the day helping Charlene. The night before the viewing of the body Tricks came home and started dinner, like usual. It seems no matter how tired Tricks was she would always follow the same pattern. Well, of course Ticky came home with an attitude from street stress. This was in the very beginning of their relationship. Tricks was still in her love form.

"I need you to do something for me in the morning, Tricks." Ticky said as he came in the kitchen.

"Well, hello to you too." She replied.

"Don't start, all right. I had a long stressful day."

"And I didn't?"

"I don't know, did you?" He answered with an attitude.

"Yes. But you wouldn't know. You never ask."

"Look don't fuck with me tonight."

"No, don't fuck with me tonight!" As fast as she got her words out was as fast as the punch came across her face. She didn't know if she should cry, hit back, or run out of the kitchen.

"Keep getting the flip lip with me." He screamed with no remorse. He walked out of the kitchen as if nothing ever happened, leaving Tricks standing startled with a the warm sensation and throbbing of Ticky's fist. It took her a minute to move and realize what Ticky had done to her. By morning Tricks' lip had swollen up. And of course Ticky wasn't there by the time she had awakened. How could she go to the funeral parlor full of people with her lip like this. She had thought that the time before when he had beaten her so bad (when she lied to Mamma Pots about Ticky sending her away) would have been the last time. She always thought it was like a phase or something he was going through. Until now. And she would always find a way to convince herself that "this would be the last time", until now.

"Tricks, I know you love Ticky and everything, but come on this doesn't make any sense."

"I know. Why do you think I came here? Charlene, I can't take it no more."

"What is Ticky gonna say?"

"I don't even care right now. I just have to think about myself now."

"Well you know I got your back, no matter what. And you can stay here as long as you want and need to."

"Are you sure? I mean I can go to a hotel 'til I sort myself out. I don't want to get you in the middle of me and Ticky's shit..." Charlene cutting her off. "Girl please! You're my best friend. And it won't be my first time in the middle you know that. I don' got my ass kicked right along with you, back in the day. Remember that night he came in that club and shook your clothes off. We all got a piece of him that night, so don't you worry about me getting in the middle."

Looking at his watch, "Yo, it's after eight, where the fuck is Tricks?" Stan reached in his pocket and handed Ticky his cell phone, "wanna try to call her again, for the tenth time?"

Dialing his home number, "You know what she's been acting real crazy lately. I don't know what type of funny business she's up to these days, but she would want to get her shit together." Stan could feel it coming on. He wanted to say something, offer his opinion, but he just wasn't up to the debate with Ticky. He figured that they had gotten into something earlier by the way Tricks sounded on the phone earlier. "You know what, drive me past my house for a minute." He said to Stan.

"Okay." Stan made a U-turn to go back towards Ticky and Tricks' house. "Did you two have a fight earlier?" Stan hadn't even realized what he had asked, by the time his words came out of his mouth.

"Why?"

"Cause when I called earlier, she sounded like she was crying or something."

"Oh." He answered with no desire to answer Stan's question. And Stan had no desire to be persistent about getting an answer. They pulled up to the front of the house. Tricks' car was parked where she had left it, in front of the garage.

"Her car is here. I'll be right back." Ticky got out the car, not knowing what to expect. He walked through the doors screaming for Tricks.

"Tricks! Tricks!" Once he didn't get an answer he started to get worried. I mean it wasn't like he didn't care for her at all. "Tricks! He called out as he went and checked upstairs. "Tricks!" He went straight to the bedroom. He looked at the bed to see if it had been slept in. He took a peep into the bathroom, but the bedroom and bathroom was in it's exact shape as when he left earlier.

"Where the fuck is she?" He whispered to himself. He stood in the middle of the bedroom floor for a minute, never thinking maybe she had left him this time. He more so thought she was out with another man. In the corner of his eye he saw one of Tricks' drawers open. Makes you wonder if she left it open on purpose. He went and looked inside of the drawer to discover that half of her things was gone. He ran into their walk-in closet to find some of the things missing out there also. Now he knew! Now he knew what was going on. His heart dropped like he had fell from a plane. He went into a state of confusion. He walked out of the closet and back to the same spot in the middle of the bedroom floor. He looked over his shoulder and saw Tricks' jewelry, left on her vanity table. He went and picked up the jewelry and held it as if it was a lost item he had been looking for.

Talking to himself, "Tricks, Tricks, Tricks."

He looked around for a letter, an excuse. Maybe she left a message on the answering machine. He checked the machine eagerly, only to hear Charlene's message from earlier. He started to think all types of things. How is she getting around if her car is still here? If she went somewhere far that she possibly could be on a plane at that very moment. Why did she leave her car and jewelry? Could she be gone for good? He picked up the phone and dialed Charlene.

"Hello."

"Yo, Charlene have you seen Tricks?"

"No. I was looking for her earlier. Did you check at the house?"

"Yeah, that's where I'm at. And she's not here." I'm starting to get worried. Ticky didn't know if he should mention his discoveries or not. He figured he wouldn't. Why should he tell her their business.

"I called the house and left her a message earlier, but she never got back to me."

"Well, if you speak to her before I do tell her I'm looking for her."

"Will do, bye."

The two hung up and Ticky left out of the house on his hunt to find Tricks. He ran outside and jumped back in the car.

"What happened" Stan asked.

"Take me around Tricks' old way."

"All right. On the Parkway or on the Ave.?"

"Both. Go to the Ave. first."

Stan pulled off and headed to the Ave.

"What happened? Did you speak to her?"

"Nah. I think she broke out on me."

"What? What you mean?"

"Some of her stuff is gone, she left all her jewelry on her vanity, and her car is still there."

"Did you try Charlene's?"

"Yeah. She hasn't spoken to her all day. She left a message on the machine for her from earlier."

"That's weird, Charlene not talking to her all day. I hope she's all right."

"What did she say to you earlier?"

"Nothin' she just sounded like she was crying or something. I asked her was she okay she said yeah."

"Damn! I think I really fucked up this time, man. We had another fight."

"How bad?"

"Real bad. She hit me back."

Stan rolled down the window and called a young boy over to the car. "Shorty, have you seen Tricks around here today?" The little boy nodded his head. "No, not today and I been out here all day."

Stan reached in his pocket and handed the boy ten dollars.

"Here. Tell ya' mother I said hello."

"Thanks, Stan."

Stan pulled off. Ticky sat quietly in the passenger seat. Stan never saw him like this when it came to Tricks. He guessed because Tricks never left him.

"Want me to go to the Parkway, now?"

"Yeah"

Charlene sat at the end of the bed looking at her friend resting peacefully. She thought to herself, she 's known this girl all her life. Since babies. She's seen her go through so much with Ticky. And finally she's left him. She just hoped and prayed that she would stick by her decision. Tricks began to wake up.

"Charlene?" She called out in a low mellow voice.

"Yeah, I'm right here."

"Man, that nap felt so good." She sat up and leaned her head on the head board.

"Good, you needed that. Ticky called."

"What did he say?"

"Nothing much. Just asked if I had seen you?"

"What did you say?"

"No. I told him I haven't seen or spoken to you all day. He sounded like he was really worried."

"Yeah, sure. He's not worried. He's just stressed cause I broke out."

"I don't know, Tricks he sounded kind of sincere."

"Oh, don't tell me he's got you fooled."

"No, it's just that he sounded kind of different this time."

"That's because I left this time."

"Yeah, maybe that's what it is."

"What else did he say? Did he mention my stuff being gone and my jewelry on the vanity?"

"No. He just said if I spoke to you to tell you he's looking for you."

Tricks climbed out of the bed and walked over to Charlene's full length mirror. She stood and stared at her face. Tears began to roll down her cheek. She touched her face softly as if she was holding a newborn.

"He really did a number on me this time, huh?"

"Yeah. It is kind of bad."

She began to take down the gauze Charlene had nursed before she laid down to take her nap.

"I think I'm gonna need some butterfly stitches."

Charlene got up off of the bed to look at her face.

"Ooohh, I think so too. It should have stopped bleeding by now. And it's kind of opened."

"It burns."

"Maybe we should go to the hospital, Tricks."

"Yeah, but I'm sure Ticky's lurking around looking for me."

"So we'll go to a hospital out of the way."

"Maybe we should wait until tomorrow."

"Now you're making excuses, Tricks."

"What about, Lil' Keith?"

"Ms. Hattie will keep an eye on him. He's in his bed sleep already. She'll come next door and watch him." Charlene went to the phone and started dialing. Tricks just stared in the mirror.

"Hello, Ms. Hattie? It's Charlene. Would you mind watching Lil' Keith for a couple of hours, please? Charlene hung up and started gathering her things. "Come on, Tricks, get ready Ms. Hattie will be here in ten minutes."

"Let's take a cab. I don't want Ticky to spot your car. You know just in case."

"Fine. Girl get out of that mirror and get ready."

"I used to be pretty."

"What are you talking about, Tricks?"

"Just what I said. I used to be pretty."

"You still are."

"Nah. Not like back in the days. Now I have permanent rings from black eyes. Scars on my body that will never go away. And the worst....... internal scars that will never heal. Not to mention the broken heart. How did I get so caught up like this? Love? Did I really think I was in love that much? It was so different in the beginning. He was so different in the beginning." Charlene held Tricks for a few seconds, so tight and so close they could feel each others heart beats. The bell rang breaking their connection. "That must be Ms. Hattie. You ready?"

"Yes."

"I'll call a cab."

Ticky sat in the middle of what used to be their living room floor. He looked like a child lost in an amusement park. Could this be for real, he thought to himself? He sat with a bottle of Crystal Champagne and takeout food from the soul food restaurant. See all the days of beating on Tricks he never thought it would end up like this. He didn't even realize how bad he hit her. And when he came close to realizing it was only after her scars started healing. I don't know maybe he thought she would stay forever. I personally never understood why he would want to beat on a person like Tricks. I bet that everyone who knows someone in an abusive relationship says the same thing. "Why would he hit a person like her?" You could never, probably, never understand why. I think that person really doesn't understand why he does it. He may think he has a legitimate reason to beat on a woman, but in all reality he doesn't. Why, 'cause the house wasn't clean? Not good enough for me. Good enough reason for you? Because she didn't cook what he wanted to eat that night? Not good enough for me. Good enough for you? Maybe because he's frustrated and stressed from work? Not good enough for me. What about you? How about, 'cause she wants to go back to school or wants to do some extra curricular activities to have fun. Damn sure 'ain't good enough for me. You?

What in the hell goes on in these men heads? How could they lay next to a woman they're supposed to love after beating them half to death? Why would they want to look at a bruised face and body? And what happens when that woman goes crazy and kills that man? Nobody can possibly understand how she feels either way.

The girls rode back from the hospital in silence. Both in their own world. Charlene busted out laughing, out of the blue.

"What da' hell is so funny?"

"Nothing"

"What!"

"Nothing..... It's just 'cause you reminded me of when we were kids and you fell out of the tree in the park."

"Oh, you try getting stitches in your forehead!"

"OUCH! Please stop! It hurts! Are you sure I don't need a butterfly stitch?!!!!"

"Oh, shut up."

Charlene started laughing even harder. "No, wait.. wait. This lady was sitting in the waiting room next to me, she thought you was a little girl!"

"Oh, yeah right."

"No for real", she turned to me and said. "They should really take it easy on that poor little girl."

Tricks started laughing "I know I was a funky mess!"

"Girl, I said I wasn't going to laugh until I saw you were okay."

"Thanks, Stinky!"

"Stinky?! You haven't called me that in years!"

"What you thought I would forget?"

The cab pulled up in front of Charlene's house.

"Girl, I'll pay for the cab. Put your money back." Tricks said.

The house was dark except the t.v. light shining from the living room. Ms. Hattie was on the couch sleep. Lil' Keith was in his bed. Charlene woke Ms. Hattie up and thanked her for staying with Lil' Keith. The girls relaxed and sat in the living room chatting. Something they haven't done in a very long time. Tricks' relationship with Ticky stopped and changed a lot of things within Tricks' life. They sat in front of Charlene's fireplace, which she bought the first week Big Keith (her son's father) bought the house. She just had to have that fireplace, so she bought it and her and Big Keith put it up.

"Girl I got some kind of memories in front of this fireplace."

"Do you miss him?"

"Every day."

"I know it's hard. You two loved each other so much."

"Yeah. I still love him. I can't see myself with anyone else."

" It'll probably take me a long time to be with another man too. I just can't trust no man. Ticky's really fucked that up, especially for anybody else."

"Do you really think it's over with you two?"

" Hell yeah! This is it this time. I swear."

The girls talked all night 'til they both fell asleep on the floor in front of the fireplace. It must have been around three in the morning when the phone rang, waking them up.

"If it's Ticky let me speak to him."

"Are you sure?"

"Yes."

Charlene answered the phone with a dry sleepy voice. "Hello. Yeah, hold on."

She handed the phone to Tricks and sat back on the floor.

"Hello."

"Tricks, what is your problem?"

"I don't have a problem"

"Why don't you come on home and stop playing."

"No. I'm not coming home, never."

"What!! If you don't bring your ass home I'm a' come over there and...!

Tricks cut him off in his tracks, nipped him right in the bud. "And do what!! Kick my ass? Fuck me up!!! Like you did yesterday morning, Ticky!? What, you're gonna come over here and give me more stitches in my head!!!!!!?"

"What, stitches?"

"The stitches I got in my forehead!"

"Listen Tricks, I'm..."   She interrupted him again "What? You're sorry? Not this time Ticky, not this time."

"Come on, let me just come and talk to you for a minute."

"No, I can't. I'm not ready to see you yet, Ticky."

" Then when?"

"I don't know when. I need time to think."

"Well, how much time?"

"I can't tell you that."

"You're gonna call me, you're sure?"

"When I'm comfortable enough, you know."

"Okay, I love you Tricks."

"Yeah, all right I'll talk to you. Goodbye."

She hung up the phone and took a deep breath. Rather a sigh of relief. She felt so independent and at the same time she felt like she lost her best friend. Like a major part of her life was taken away. She could not believe how Ticky was acting. She had never seen him act like that.

The days went on and she was adjusting to her "new" life. She looked at one bedrooms and studio apartments, even though Charlene had told her she could stay as long as she wanted she felt like she was wearing out her welcome. She hadn't spoken to Ticky since that night last week. Although she was very tempted on plenty of occasions to call him. She went to the house once to retrieve some more of her things. She didn't know if she wanted him to be there or not. But she was very pleased to see he wasn't. She wondered to herself if he even had been staying there. The house was so neat not a dish or a glass in the sink. The bed was made up just as it was when she left. The message light on the answer machine was blinking, she was so tempted to check. But she knew she didn't live there no more and nobody never really called her anyway. Only friend (real friend) she had was Charlene. Of course there was Tammy, Kim, and Brenda who doesn't know about her leaving Ticky.

She gathered the things she needed, looked around her old room and left the house. She had been saving money from day one. Whenever Ticky gave her money to shop or for whatever she would always save some if not most of it and sometimes all of it. She had enough money to live for a while. Then she never touched the money Mamma Pots left her. She figured she'd go to art school. This was the first time she has been away from Ticky and she had not gotten used to it yet. Charlene had to convince her to get a pager. She didn't feel she needed one, but Charlene had a few good points on why she needed one so she bought one. She sat in the cab on her way to her old neighborhood just thinking about her future, something she hadn't done much in her past. She figured she'd go around her old way since she hadn't been around there in a while. She got out of the cab right on the corner of the parkway. She went into the bodega store on the corner, a place she hadn't stepped into in a while.

"Hey, Rashed. How ya' been?" Tricks asked the Indian man.

"Oh, Tricks! Where you been girl, you don't love us no more? I seen your boyfriend yesterday."

"Really. I still love you guys, I just been busy."

"You looking good as ever. Like da' bomb baby!"

"You're crazy, you're still picking up slang from the kids, huh?"

"Well you know. What you need?"

"Just a pack of gum."

"Here it's on me."

"Thanks. I'll see you later."

"Don't be a stranger."

Tricks left the store with a little girl smile. She went a few blocks towards the soul food restaurant. She must have seen twenty people on her way to the soul food place. Everybody asking the same thing, "girl where you been?" You would think they hadn't seen her in years. The smell of the fried chicken, collard greens, mac and cheese, and sweet potato pie hit Tricks as soon as she walked in the restaurant. This was the closest she came to Mamma Pots' cooking.

"Hello, Tricks." A voice whispered softly in her ear. It sounded so familiar, but she couldn't quite place it. She turned around and looked. How could she not know who belonged to that soft voice, maybe because she hadn't heard that voice in that form often.

"Hey, what's up Ticky... How are you?"

"Fine."

"What are you doing here?"

"Getting us a bite to eat."

Us, she thought to herself. Who is us? But she figured it wasn't her place to ask anymore.

"Oh, I guess that's a stupid question to ask. What else would you be doing in here?"

"Well, I'm gonna go order now. I've been looking at the menu for the last ten minutes."

"Yeah, I don't know why you always do that. You always look at the menu for a long time and turn around and order the same thing...." They both said at the same time, "fried chicken, mac and cheese, and collard greens." They laughed and then out of the blue Tricks got a serious face.

"Yeah I guess some things just don't change, huh?" She said.

"I still didn't get that call, Tricks."

"Yeah, I know I've been busy."

"I guess I can accept that."

"Take care."

"You too."

The two departed. She got her food and waved bye once again as she walked out the restaurant. She spotted Ticky's car on the corner she was curious who "us" could have been. She knew she could have kept on going the direction she was going instead of being nosy, but she couldn't help it. So she walked pass the car and tried to look out the corner of her eye, but whoever was sitting in the passenger seat had the seat back too far. Like when a girl is sitting in her man's car (the way she used to have the seat when she was with Ticky). She kept on walking.

"YO, Tricks!" She heard from the direction of Ticky's car. She turned and look, she got a feeling of security for a moment. It was Stan. She walked back towards the car.

"What's up Stan?"

"Nothing much. Same shit different day. You saw Ticky?"

"Yeah I was just getting some food."

"You know he misses you?"

"Really? Well take care, I gotta' go."

"Okay, Tricks. For real, he really does. Just try and talk to him."

"Come on Stan, you know if nobody else don't how much I been through with him. I'm just not ready yet."

"I understand."

"Take care." She walked away feeling so good about herself. She's never seen Stan or any of his friends act like that, trying to come to Ticky's rescue. She realized, today was the first day she started loving "herself."

Charlene, Tricks, Tammy, Kim, and Brenda was sitting in Charlene's living room drinking and laughing. Something the girls haven't done in a long time. "So what's up are y'all going to the club tonight or what?" Tammy asked them.

"I know I am." Replied Kim.

"Me too. I need to hear some music." Brenda said.

"Well?" Tammy turned and said to Charlene.

"I don't care. You wanna go Tricks?" Charlene asked Tricks.

Tammy turned and looked at Charlene, "wait a minute, girl. You tryin' ta' get our asses killed?" "You remember the last time we all went out? We got beat up! Ticky won't be kicking my ass, at least not tonight."

Tricks took a sip of her drink and stood up to walk out the room. She turned around and looked at the girls who sat silent and said, "oh, you won't have to worry about that anymore." And walked into the kitchen. The girls didn't know about the break up. Charlene felt that it wasn't her place to tell Tricks' business.

"What she talking 'bout Charlene?" Tammy asked.

"Ask her."

Tammy yelled out to Tricks in the kitchen, "Tricks, come here for a minute! What you talking 'bout!?"

Tammy was the wild one out the crew. What some people would call "ghetto". But she's been like that all her life. Tricks came out the kitchen with a bowl of ice and another bottle of liquor. She sat back in her spot as if nothing ever happened or ever was said. Tricks knew that she was playing hardball with the girls.

"Why is that?" Tammy asked.

"Because I left him."

"What!!!!!!!!!!!!!!!!". The girls screamed.

"Yeah right!." Kim said.

"For real." Tricks said.

"Nah--." Brenda responded

"Since when?" Tammy asked her.

"It's been like three weeks or more."

"Get the fuck out of here!"

"Charlene, is she lying or what?"

"No. She's been staying here."

"So, I can go if I want to and I think that's what I need a little bit of music in my life."

"OOHH, I'm scared of you." Tammy said.

"So, how does it feel?" Brenda asked Tricks.

"How does what feel? Being on my own? Truthfully, It feels funny. Not to have to worry about him coming home wanting to fight. I can come and go as I please. I think about myself now. I think about my future. I've learned to live for me." The girls raised their drinks and made a toast to the start of Tricks' new life.

Tricks was really hyped about going out. She hadn't been out, at least to a club in so long. She tried on clothes for at least two hours. She had gained back a few of her pounds since she left Ticky. So now her shape really shows. She's hidden it for so many years. She found a skirt set she had gotten a couple of months ago. She knew when she bought it that she probably wouldn't get a chance to wear it, but she said fuck it. She looked at the dress for a minute or two, she wasn't too sure she still had some of the "Ticky" worries. She had to really realize that she didn't have to answer to him anymore. She tried the skirt on and looked in the mirror. She hadn't paid attention to herself in so long that she kind of surprised herself.

She whispered to herself, "you lookin' kinda' all right there girl."

Charlene came into the room and stood behind her. "You sure do."

Tricks jumped. "Chile! You scared the shit out of me! Where did you come from? I didn't hear you come back in."

"Tricks where did you get that suit from? That's hot! Girl you gonna turn some heads tonight!"

"I don't know if I'm gonna wear it, Charlene."

"What! You crazy? Why?"

"I don't know. I think it's too much."

"Too much of what?"

"I just feel funny. I guess I never expected to be able to wear this. When I bought it at the time I just didn't expect to ever wear it. I was basically dreaming."

"Well, it's reality now and you're gonna wear that outfit if I got to sew it to your skin!" Charlene demanded.

When Charlene and Tricks stepped out the house to meet the rest of the girls in front of Charlene's house, nobody in Kim's car expected to see Tricks looking the way she did. Tammy looked at Brenda with her mouth dropped wide open. Kim sat in amazement. They hadn't seen Tricks like this.

"Yo, look at her!" Tammy said.

"Where... what....." Brenda stuttered.

The girls got in the car like there was nothing wrong. They laughed all the way to the club, just like old days. They even stopped at the liquor store and got themselves a personal bottle to get a little buzz before they got to the club. They felt good, being together again like the old days. By the time they got to the club the girls were pissy drunk. This was a scene Tricks hadn't seen in a while, but it was still a familiar one. Some of the people were different, and the behavior of the party goers was a little different too. The girls parked in the lot and walked towards the club. Tricks saw a lot of people she hadn't seen in a long time. She noticed how some of them gave her that funny look. That "damn where have she been" look. Or that "shit I thought she was dead or something" look.

But it didn't bother her one bit, she had her a little buzz and she was feeling all right! She couldn't help but to notice the way the men were looking at her too. She hadn't seen them looks in so long, not since Ticky. That was kind of scary to her. She didn't know why, it just was. Maybe cause that was a long time ago, or maybe cause that was the kind of looks that attracted her to Ticky. The girls stood at the bar a little while before they worked the club. By the time One 'O clock came Kim was drunk, like always, so the girls had to sit in the bathroom with her while she threw her guts up. After twenty minutes of aiding Kim, everybody was ready to continue to party. As they were walking out the bathroom Tricks smelled something.... something..... something she couldn't quite make out, but was familiar with. Then came that voice. She knew that smell and that voice. She turned to look as they walked through the crowd, but her eye couldn't catch a familiar face to match that voice and smell. She continued to follow the girls through the crowd, when a tall dark skinned man came from behind and tapped her on the shoulder. She smelled the smell coming closer as he tapped her.

"LaToya?" The young man asked as he tapped Tricks.

Tricks turned around in confusion. She hadn't heard that name in years. "What?"

"LaToya... I mean Tricks. Is your name Tricks?" He replied and asked in the same breath.

"Ray?" She asked with a big smile.

"Yeah." He replied and hugged her.

"How you been? I haven't seen you in a long time."

"A lot of years is more like it. Ever since you stood me up in the park."

She smiled. "Oh, I'm sorry. You didn't forget that, huh?"

"How could I? You broke my heart. You made it bad for a lot women."

She smiled even harder more like a blush this time. "Oh, come on. Ray. You can't be for real."

"Yes, I am. So, who you here with? I heard you were damned near married."

"I came with my friends and I'm not close to being married. As a matter of fact I just broke up with my boyfriend."

"Oh, I see. You still going around breaking hearts."

"No. It's a little more deep than that."

He smiled. "So, can I take you out tomorrow night?" Ray asked.

"Well... I... I really haven't started dating yet, since I broke up with...."

He interrupted her. "So don't consider this a date, look at it like old friends hooking up and having fun. Besides you owe me...remember the park."

She took a long sigh. "Okay. Let me get a contact number."

Tricks not noticing Ticky watching from the corner of the club, she took Ray's number and hugged him goodbye. Ray was the last person she ever thought she would see. She hadn't seen him in years. Ray was her first boyfriend. She left him when she meet Ticky, dropped him like a hot potato! He really had a thing for her too. Little did she know, but she really did break his heart. He had plans for them, until Ticky came along.

Ticky stood at the corner of the bar surrounded by all his friends, maybe six or seven guys. He watched Tricks until she got to the bar with her friends, then he turned to Stan and whispered in his ear. "Did you see that?"

"Look don't start no shit." Stan replied.

"I'm not. I just was wondering if you saw what I saw. You know who that was right?"

"Yeah."

"She couldn't wait, damn."

"Just chill, Ticky."

Ticky started walking the girls' way when Stan pulled him back.

"Look Tick, don't go there tonight. Remember you two are not together." Ticky stepped back where he was standing before Stan pulled him. "Stan, I'm not going to start no shit. I just want to see if her and her friends want some champagne. When are y'all going to realize that I'm okay?" By this time the rest of Ticky's boys gathered around.

"What happened?" One of his friends asked.

"Nothing. He wants to go over there where Tricks is at." Stan answered.

"Oh no! Don't start that shit, Ticky!"

"Listen, I'm not even fucking with her on that level, tonight. Why can't we just be cool?"

Stan asked him. "Why can't you just send a bottle over to her."

Tricks still didn't notice Ticky in the club. But Tammy did. She spotted Ticky and his friends at the bar. From where her and the girls was standing it looked like a commotion. All she saw was Ticky looking in their direction and him and his friends exchanging words. She and the rest of the girls thought he was about to start trouble. Tricks got nervous. She thought to herself, maybe he saw her talking to Ray. She realized that it didn't matter. She and Ticky were no longer together. The girls convinced Tricks to ignore him. And Ticky's boys convinced him not to go over to her.

As it got late the girls got more drunk. It was a funny situation for Tricks, she never would have thought to be in a club with Ticky.

She started thinking about her past and how much time she lost in her life. She thought about the things she could have been doing in that time that was wasted. She would sneak and look in the direction of Ticky and his boys every now and then. Even though she wasn't with him any longer she still found herself curious about his whereabouts in the club. Ticky did his thing once he loosened up and drank a little. He too was a little curious about her doings and whereabouts that night. Her mind wandered off to back in the day when she used to go out with Ray. She couldn't even remember what actually happened with him. She just stopped talking to him. All she remembered was Ticky. Ticky came along and changed everything. Just put her life in an uproar! "Tricks! What da' fuck wrong with you?" Tammy screamed in Tricks ear so loud it broke her concentration.

"Shit girl you scared the hell out of me." Tricks didn't realize how visible her drifting was. "Tammy, you need not to be walking up on people like that."

"No, you need not to be spacin' off in a club like you on prozac or somethin'. And I saw you talking to Ray earlier. See you needed to stay with him. You would have been better off."

Tricks looked in the corner where Ray was standing surrounded by at least five or six women and three of his friends. Friends she didn't notice from around the way. "Yeah, sure. So I could have been stressed out about all of that." She said pointing in Ray's direction.

"Tricks, please. Give me a break. What you expect? And anyway that boy loved the hell out of you. Look I'm going to the bar and get me a drink before last call. You want something?"

"No. Last call ain't 'til another hour and a half."

"I know, but I see Stan over there by himself maybe I can rekindle our flame. You know?"

"Tammy, why do you play them games with Stan?"

"What! Girl please, see you later." Tammy was dating Stan, but Tammy was so.. so wild should I say. Maybe wild isn't a good description. She just was so out going. And Stan was so laid back. But they say opposites attract, cause Stan was on her love. Even broke up with the girl he was seeing to go with Tammy. And of course Tammy broke out on him. They would fuck around every now and then. Stan really liked Tammy. I think he might have even loved her. Tammy loved him, too. She's just too stubborn to admit it. Tricks woke up to Charlene cooking breakfast and talking loud on the phone about last night. "Girl, I don't think Tricks even knows."

Tricks walked in the kitchen. "Even knows what?"

"Good morning sleepy head, or should I say good afternoon. Here she goes now. Okay see you when you get here, bye-bye."

"Who was that?"

"Tammy's ass."

"Where did she disappear to last night?"

"Where else."

"With Stan?"

"Yup. That's where she's at now. He's about to drop her over here."

"Them two kill me. Poor Stan. Tammy just does what she wants with him and he lets her. That's love I guess. What was y'all talking about I didn't know."

"What?"

"On the phone when I first walked in. You said you didn't think I even knew. Even knew what?"

"OH! About Ray."

"What about Ray?"

"Besides that you should've never stopped fucking with him for Ticky?...." The phone rang interrupting Charlene. "Hello. Yeah, what's up? Okay, I'll tell her. Bye-bye." She hung up the phone and sat at the table with Tricks. "That was Ticky."

"What he want?"

"To let you know you got mail. He said he would drop it off on his way downtown."

"Now what was you saying about Ray?"

"Oh, girl you mean to tell me you really don't know? Chile, that boy is a fucking millionaire. He just went pro."

"What you talking 'bout?"

"What you mean what I'm talking 'bout? Which part you don't understand? Millionaire or Pro? The boy just got drafted out of college to the NBA."

"What! Why didn't he tell me?"

"Maybe he thought you knew already. Everybody else knows. Plus you're different, I think he doesn't even look at you like anybody else."

"I'm really not going out with him now."

"Why."

"Why? Because that's not much of a change from Ticky."

"How could you say that?"

"Easily. That life is just as fast as the life Ticky leads. Just legal money. Ray's going to have too many females, probably gonna get a big ass head and I'm not gonna deal with no more headaches or drama. None of the sort. Any form or fashion."

"How could you say that without giving that man a chance? I'm surprised he's willing to give you another chance. After all you're the one that shitted' on him."

"Look don't start with me, Charlene. However it went I'm not fucking with him now." Tricks felt a sense of disappointment, she felt she could have really went out with him. But she's too scared of things blowing up in her face. She remembered the days she was in love with Ray. At least she thought she was. At that age she really didn't know what she was. He did grow up to be handsome. She couldn't believe it. The NBA. She was proud of him but disappointed at the same time.

"Now, I don't know what kind of mental trip you on, Tricks, but you need to get it together. 'Ain't nothin' wrong with going out with Ray. That was your first love. All that other shit that comes along with that NBA shit don't matter! You were before all that." Tammy insisted.

In a way Tricks felt she was right. Her and Ray shared a special kind of young love. A love that at the time meant the world to her, and him. The kind of young love where you make future plans with one another and take oaths to stick with those plans.

"Look, Tammy, I know what I'm doing."

"And what is that?" Charlene interrupted. Tricks felt for a minute like she was backed up against the wall.

"I'm protecting myself. Thank You very much."

Within a split of a second Charlene became very serious and concerned with her friend's response. "From what, Tricks?"

"From pain. I can't afford any more pain in my life."

"So you just stop living? I'm sorry, Tricks it just doesn't work like that. I understand your pain, but you can't live the rest of your life miserable. There's some things you just got to let go. You can't go around blaming Ticky's mistakes and bad ways on other men. I know it maybe hard, but you've got to give other people a chance. You're still young, girl. Live your life, for you not for nobody else. And let me tell you nobody can't hurt you, unless you allow them to. And never blame nobody for no situation you're in."

The Start of a New Beginning

It was so hot outside Tricks had to open all the windows in her new apartment. That's right! Her new apartment. Tricks finally found herself her own place. Just her not her and Ticky, just her. She had finished her painting and cleaning. Tricks had to get used to her new independent life. She was loving it though. The walls were dry, her laquor floors were shining, her incense was burning, and she sat on her couch relaxed like she hadn't been in a long time. She looked around the living room, which was fully furnished, and smiled to herself. She felt so good to be able to light her incense, Ticky never let her light them. He hated them. He said they remind him of the train station or the corners of downtown. She always thought he just wanted to have something to complain about.

She didn't want to invite her girlfriends over until she was finished decorating the place. Saving all that money from Ticky was about the smartest thing she ever did when it came to him. And never spending the money Mamma Pots left her helped also. She always said she was saving it for a rainy day, well I guess it came. She had more than enough saved from Ticky to put down on her condo. She wanted to make sure she put down enough money, so her rent wouldn't be so much at the end of the month. She decorated her place so beautifully. Her bedroom painted a soft, but different blue. She personally hand painted the ceiling of light blue and white clouds. So fluffy and exact, with little white doves in and out of every cloud. She was truly an artist.

Her bathroom marbled floor with specs of gold. Wall paper black, gold, and pearl white with border to match. Very hard to believe when you walked into her place that she came from where she did. Her new home gave off more of a look that could make somebody think she was born into a family with money. That goes to show it doesn't matter what you come from it's all about your mental and your heart. She came from a lot of heartache, stress, drama, poverty, and at the same time a lot of love (Mamma Pots). She and Ticky had a very comfortable home also. But that came from his street money. This was from his money too, but it was hers. You know? Everything in the place was hers. She was so proud of herself. Of what she did with her new home, she couldn't wait for her friends to come over later that night.

The bell rang right at eight o' clock on the dot. Surprisingly the girls was on time, but you know how black folks are they just wanted to be nosy. She paused before opening the door. She felt a tingle in her stomach. She felt like a child awaiting the approval from her parents on her school project or something. This is the first time Tricks had made such a step. The first time she's made a step period without Ticky. She opened the door with a little girl look. The girls held balloons, bottles of champagne, and gifts. It was a big surprise to Tricks, she would have never expected this. Her facial expression changed instantly.

"Surprise!!!!" They all screamed from outside of the softly lit and floral candle scented apartment. "Well, are you gonna let us in or what?" Tammy asked with her bold and blunt voice. The girls walked in and looked around as if they were at a museum. The place was truly a sight to lay ya' eyes on. The night ran long with laughing and reminiscing on the past.

"So why won't you go out with Ray?" Kim asked in her humble way.

"Yeah, Bitch. What's da' problem?" Tammy jumped in. Tammy had a habit of calling people "bitch". She never means it in a disrespectful way, usually it's her friends she calls bitch. "It's been a while since you got bondage. You would want to christen this fab apartment!" The girls busted out laughing and in their own way agreed with Tammy.

"How you know I haven't already."

"Yeah fuckin' right, bitch!"

"I did. I went out with him the other night." Charlene turned and looked at her with a confusing look.

"Why didn't you tell us?

"I didn't think I had to and plus I didn't want to jinx myself." Then she began to tell the girls about last week, when she finally gave in to Ray's dinner date pleas.

Tricks had been working overtime in her new apartment when she decided to give Ray a call. She had run across his number unpacking. You know how you run across something while you're doing something else and that something takes your attention away from the original something you were doing? Well, that's what happened with Tricks. She was cleaning and unpacking when she ran across Ray's number on the same napkin he had written it on. She contemplated about calling. Stalled a little. She thought maybe she shouldn't cause he hadn't called her first. Shit he had her number too, she thought. She hadn't even looked at the number since the night she got it. It was really no interest to her at the time, but she started thinking a lot. She couldn't live the way she thought she could. She held the napkin in her hand for about ten minutes before really looking at the actual number itself. She picked the phone up and started dialing and clicked it right back to its off position.

She paced the floor and tried to understand why she couldn't bring herself to make the call. She didn't know what to say!! She's never been in this position before. All she knew was Ticky. And Ray, but Ray in the beginning. All her life she didn't know anyone else, but Ticky. What would she say to him? She didn't even realize he had given her his pager and house number. She couldn't even decide if she should page him or call his house. "Hey, this is Tricks. What's up?" She practiced over and over to herself numerous times. She decided to page him, being that he put a special code next to the pager number. She figured he should know it's her when he sees her page. If he calls right away he's been waiting for her call or he still had her in mind to remember the code he had given her almost over a month and a half ago. She dialed the pager number, happy with the decision to page him. It gave her more time to practice what to say while she waited for him to return the page, if he returned it.

"Hello. Welcome to the messaging service for Ray. This is Cindy, may I take your message please?

"Yes. Please give Tricks, T-R-I-C-K-S, a call at home if it's possible. Just calling to say what's up."

"Would you like to leave a number ma'm?"

Tricks didn't know if she should leave her number or not, being he had her number already. "Yes, 363-8979."

"Thank You. Have a nice day."

Tricks hung up the phone. With mixed feelings of relief and regret. The phone rang back before giving her enough time to deal with her feelings. She answered on the second ring never expecting it to be Ray. Besides she just paged him no more than five minutes prior. "Hello."

"Hey, Tricks!" A burst of energy came through the phone. it was that familiar voice from the club that night. It was Ray. Oh my God! She thought to herself. He called back! What was she to say? He didn't even give her time or a chance to think about what to say.

"Hey, Ray. What's up?"

"Nothing. Been waiting for you to call."

"Yeah, right. You had my number why didn't you call me?"

"I lost it, boo. I don't know what happened."

"That's a good one, Ray. But not that good."

"No, for real. I got a little twisted that night and when I woke up to call you the next day I couldn't find it." He planned to call her the next day that made her feel good.

"So, how ya' been?"

"Okay, I guess. When am I going to see you Tricks?"

"You don't waste no time, do you?"

"No. Too scared you may slip away again."

"You're not going to let me live that park situation down are you?"

"Honestly? No. Maybe once you say yes to my dinner offer...."

Tricks boldly interrupted. "Okay. When?"

"Tomorrow night. I'm in D.C. I'll be back tonight. I'll call you when I get in tonight and we can make arrangements."

"Okay. I'll be here. I have a little more unpacking to do, so I'm not leaving out."

"Unpacking what?"

"Oh, I just moved."

"Oh, I have to get you a house warming gift. Oh shit!!! I'll call you later my plane is about to leave."

"Okay."

She hung up and blew out a sigh of relief. "Yes"!! She shouted and jumped up and down. "I did it"!!

The next day came almost too quick. This being Tricks' first date (her only date) she was kind of in the dark about what to do and how to prepare. She wished she could call her friend Charlene at a time like this, but for some reason she didn't want her or any of her friends to know of her date with Ray. Once she sat down and thought it out she realized she was scared of failure with Ray, so if that was the case she rather her friends not know about it. In a lot of abusive relationships, women seem to lose a big chunk of self esteem. Is it because deep down inside they know the situation they're in is incorrect and it's embarrassing to let people see them stay in that relationship? It tears away at certain parts of their confidence, their belief in themselves. Sometimes it seems to me that abused women seem to take on the abusers negativity, in some form or fashion. Whether it be negative thinking or negative actions. I think in Tricks' case it was negative thinking.

For hours she sat on her couch and brainstormed on everything from what to wear to what to say. The scent of the incense burning in Tricks' apartment soothed her somewhat, but it also always reminded her of Ticky. She only had an hour and a half left to get ready and still she hadn't decided on what to wear. It would have helped if she knew where they were going. She didn't want to over dress or under dress. She just wanted everything to be perfect, but from her experience with Ticky she felt nothing could ever be perfect. After sitting longer on the couch taking up thirty minutes of the hour and a half she had left she got up and went to her bedroom and opened her closet reaching way in the back. Where she kept, what she called her 'forbidden' clothes. The clothing she would never have worn if she was with Ticky. Most was bought while she was with Ticky on what she used to call "Dream Shopping Sprees". She threw six or seven different outfits on the bed and finally came up with a Prada dress. Tags still on and in its same condition when she bought it. She laughed a soft smooth laugh to herself. She thought back to the day she bought the dress.

She was up in the city walking around when she passed the Prada store. The window... the window had the prettiest dresses. She stopped and stared for almost ten minutes before going in. She walked straight to one of the dresses that was in the window, the one that now lay on her bed. She touched the dress on the rack as if it were a new born kitten. She could just imagine herself in this dress. She didn't know where, but she could just imagine. She finally looked at the price tag, knowing it would be an arm and a leg she still looked. Nineteen Hundred Dollars!!! She screamed to herself. God Damn! She knew deep down it was going to be a pretty penny, but she just didn't want it to be! She took a deep breath and walked out the store, looked at her watch saw she still had an hour to make it to the bank. She later returned to the Prada store and bought that sucker!!!! She didn't care if she had to wear it around the house and imagine all day long she was getting that motherfucker!!! So, now she has a reason to wear her favorite dress and it's not to imagine.

It was eight-o clock when the door bell rang. Damn she thought to herself he's right on time. Something she didn't expect. She really didn't expect him to show up. She took one last look in the mirror and hoped she looked good to him. She answered the intercom and buzzed when she heard Ray's voice. She lit scented candles while she waited for him to arrive at her front door. The front door bell rang. She opened it with a warm smile.

"Hello, Ray."

He stood with flowers. "Hey, Tricks." He answered and bent over and kissed her on the cheek.

She took the flowers and thanked him. As he walked in the apartment he looked around and smiled. "It smells good." He said as he seated himself on the couch (without an invite from Tricks.) "You're still into pretty smelling things, I see."

"How do you remember?"

"What, I'm not supposed to?"

"I'm not saying that, I just thought you.... I don't know. I"

"It's been along time, I guess."

She started getting a feeling of discomfort. Here is this person she's known for so long, so many years, but still he feels like a stranger. They both sat in their own silence, thinking to themselves. Ray thinking and wondering to himself what has Tricks become. He felt that she was not the person he once knew. As a matter of fact he knew she wasn't. Something happened in between the time he last saw her and now. That secret innocence she once held had been gone. How? In which way he didn't know. All he knew was it was gone. And he felt he could bring it back. He could bring her and what they had back.

It was nine or so when they arrived to where Ray decided to take them to dinner. She looked as the valet drove off to park the car. The lights from the sleek restaurant awning reflected in the middle of her eyes. People dressed in the best clothing, entered and exited the restaurant. She smiled to herself. Happy with her decision to wear the Prada dress, she fits in perfectly she thought to herself. They looked so good together. Ray was looking pretty good himself. She felt a sense of security when he softly and sleekly slipped his hand into hers as they walked up the stairs and into the doors of the restaurant. This dating thing started becoming more comfortable. Now either Ray frequented this place on a regular basis or he has grown to have a lot of friends over the years, Tricks thought to herself.

"Hello Mr. Ray. How are you." A bald white man said to Ray as they were walking to their table. At least two others stopped him and shook his hand on the way to their table. It had totally slipped her head the NBA thing Ray had going on for him. But could these people know him like that? Was he really good and popular like that? Tricks didn't know much about basketball, she actually didn't know nothing. She didn't care either. The night continued nice and smooth. With talk of the past and the present. More of the past. Tricks got scattered when she was asked by Ray about the relationship she had just departed. "I'd rather not talk about that, Ray. At least not right now." She answered when Ray pushed the issue.

"Okay, we don't have to talk about it. I just wanted...."
"Don't get me wrong Ray. I just don't want to go there right now."

"It's okay. I understand."

They fell back into that silence they fell into earlier. Breaking the silence Tricks asked with a funny type of smile, what about you? What's going on with your love life?"

"Me? I don't have a love life. I got ball."

"Oh."

"See, I had a girlfriend in college. We broke up in my last year. Just didn't work out. We're not even friends. Since then I just been dating, and I don't do much of that."

"I don't at all."

"Don't what?"

"Date. I haven't been on a date since I broke up with Ticky. As a matter of fact I haven't been with another man, sexually, since Ticky or besides Ticky. Except for you. You broke my virginity. You remember?"

"No. We broke each others. Ticky? You're just breaking up with Ticky? You've been with him all that time? God damn! You're good, at least you stayed with the man you dumped me and broke my heart for. Ticky.... really?"

"Yup." She answered feeling more comfortable about the situation now. She hadn't realized until now how good she was. Most women these days went through a lot of men before they got to her age. And she was with her childhood sweetheart for an exceptional long time, rather her second childhood love. Ray was truly her first. But how much of that time could she really consider "being with Ticky". The relationship had so much static and pain. But at the same time love, mostly from her end she felt. Should she have stood Ray up? Maybe she wouldn't be in the predicament she's in now. All types of thoughts went through her head. The thoughts and the long moment of silence was broke when she heard Ray's voice calling at her.

Snapping his fingers in Tricks' face, Tricks.... Tricks. You okay? Earth to Tricks." After finally catching her attention, "what were you thinking about so long and hard?"

"Nothing." She replied with a fake smile, which came from an inch of embarrassment.

He picked up his drink and took a long sip before replying. "Nothing? Come on you have to do better than that, Tricks."

"It's nothing worth talking about, trust me."

"When will you start to trust me? Like you used to? Now I know you were thinking about something worth listening to."

"Maybe one day I'll share that thought I was thinking. When it's the right time."

"Well, I have no other choice but to respect that, baby."

They drove in silence, similar to the kind they had fallen into a couple of times earlier. This time they would catch each others eyes every now and then. This proved to Tricks that she wasn't the only one with funny feelings about the reunion. She just didn't know where his feelings were coming from more or less what they were about. She decided to break the silence this time.

"Now who's party you said this was again?"

"A friend I play ball with." He answered with a warm smile.

"Oh." She paused for a minute. "Is it in a club or what?"

"No. It's in his house. He just bought it, it's really like a house warmin'."

"That's nice."

"Tricks why are you acting like I'm a stranger? When are you going to trust me? Like you used to?" He pulled the car over and parked it. "Tricks do I make you uncomfortable? Are you feeling guilty?"

She looked at him straight in his face trying not to show him she knew that he knew what he was talking about. "Guilty!? Guilty about what!?"

"Come on Tricks you don't have to put up a front for me. I won't think no different of you."

"What would I be guilty of?"

"Maybe Ticky..."

"Ticky!!? Me and Ticky are over with."

"Look Tricks, I want you to know that I'm your friend before anything." He sat his hand on her lap at that moment she felt a warm secure feeling run through her, like earlier at the restaurant when he had slid his hand into hers. "I know this must be awkward for you, and trust I understand that."

He was so sensitive, and caring. This was something Tricks wasn't used to. All she knew was Ticky and Ticky's ways. She still loved Ray in her own little way, how couldn't she? She wanted to believe in him. She figured she would just have to pray on it, pray on him............ .

" I'm not ready, Ticky."

"So, when will you be? You keep tellin' me your not ready."

"I don't know. I need more time."

"Time for what? Don't you think we got enough time in with each other? We can't even meet and talk?"

" I'm just not ready......."

"Well, when are you going to be?"

She wasn't too sure if Ticky was ready. She didn't want to get caught up in his bullshit. "Tell me something, Ticky do you feel that the things you did to me and the way you treated me was wrong? Do you feel that you are an abuser?" She was using an exercise she had learned in "Group". Group was a program for battered and abused women that she'd been going to. Ray had helped her pick out the proper program for her. "I mean are you ready to tell me how you feel about our situation."

"What!! What the fuck are you talking about, Tricks? What you tryin' to say? You don't love me no more?"

"What!? That has nothing to do.... you know that has nothing to do with anything, Ticky!!!! How could you even fix... fix your mouth to say anything like that?!!!! I knew you wasn't ready!! You know I don't even wanna talk to you right now!!!" She fiercely slammed down the phone and stood in place for a few minutes. She felt hurt. Hurt by Ticky's reaction. How could he say something like that? She was more angry with herself, for allowing herself to allow him to get her so angry. She had learned in Group that anger could be your worst enemy in some cases. Never allow somebody else's frustrations get to you. After breaking out of her thinking she sat down on her couch and thought how she sometimes wished Ticky could be like Ray. Have his ways and disposition. Not that she didn't like Ray as Ray, but she wished and wanted so badly for Ticky to change. But she had to think about getting herself together.

After an hour of meditation she was back to herself. She took a shower, turned on some relaxing music, and got into herself. After trying to reach Charlene and the rest of the girls, and getting no luck, she plopped down on an over sized pillow on the living room floor and sipped on a glass of Red Passion Alize. She hadn't heard from Ray all day, but she didn't want to call him. For some reason she felt like she would only be calling cause she had nobody else to call. She had built this wall in front of her. Whether she believed it or not that wall was built with nothing but fear. Fear that Ticky helped build over a long period of time.

Where was her friends when she needed them? She thought to herself as she gulped down her third glass of Red Passion. Where was Ray? Her head was getting heavier with every gulp. That didn't stop her. She started thinking more and more. After paging Ray and getting no answer she thought (drunk thought) maybe she should give Ticky a chance. Maybe she was being too hard on him? All he wanted was to go out to eat or something. How could that hurt so bad? Just as she got up to page Ticky the phone rang.

She felt at that second like she had relapsed. She felt like she was in recovery and relapsed. So caught up in her own guilt and her own embarrassment she didn't even realize that her phone rang out and the answering machine had answered.

"Hi, Tricks.... you there? It's me....Ray. Well, call me when you get......"

She ran to the phone and answered it as calm as she could. "Hello.. Ray?"

"Tricks, what's up?" He replied on the other end of the line. This was a voice she wanted to hear so badly. This was the voice that saved her from continuing to relapse. She got one of those warm secure feelings she usually get from time to time when she either heard Ray's voice or whenever she was around him. "I'm sorry I didn't get back to you. My pager was in my work out bag in the locker."

"Baby" she thought to herself, a pleasant thought. It made her feel special. Like she was the only one.

"Oh, that's okay. I figured you was busy. It's no problem." She knew she was fronting. She knew she was a minute away from breaking. She also knew she wanted and needed to hear his voice, but that wall, always got the best of her. "So, what's up, Mister Ray?"

"Nothin' Ms. Tricks. What's going on with you?'

Trying not to let her vocabulary slur from her six glasses of Passion. "Nothing. Chilling out."

"You got company? I hear "company" music playing."

"What does company music sound like?"

"Like what's playing in the background."

Feeling flattered by his interest of who she's keeping company with. "Oh. I didn't know there was such a thing as "company" music." She replied with flirtation in her voice.

"Well, I'd like to accompany you and your company music. If that's all right with you?" He caught her off guard. She answered before she even realized what her answer was.

"Sure."

"Okay, I'll be there in an half of hour. Okay? You need anything?"

"No. Maybe another bottle."

"All right I'll see you in a minute."

"What the hell are you doing, girl?" She whispered to herself. She looked at her watch seeing that it was eleven-o-clock, she felt she had made a bad decision telling Ray he could come over. At this time of night what else could happen? Why? Why did she act in such a way when it came to him? Was it that in all reality she wasn't over Ticky? Of course not. Who was she fooling? How could you be over someone you've been around basically your whole life? Even in her situation, going through what she's been through with Ticky love is love. And why was she always comparing Ticky to every situation she goes through, it's like she was still subconsciously being considerate when it came to Ticky.

She learned that she should not even have Ticky in her everyday thoughts. It would only lead her to grief, she would just end up putting him in her daily living. Everytime she thinks about Ray she some how ends up either thinking about or comparing him to Ticky. She had to stop that. She knew it, she just seemed to be having a hard time. She took a deep breath, as if it was a new beginning for her. You know one of those "Waiting to Exhale" breaths. Well, it was done already. She already told the man he could come over no need to cry over spilled milk and trust Ray was everything, but spilled milk!!!

The sun shined so bright and heavy through Tricks' bedroom window. So bright it stopped her from opening her eyes immediately. Her head turned in circles at its own rhythm. One that she was not too familiar with. Her eyeballs throbbed like someone had punched her in them. (That feeling she was familiar with! But she had promised

herself she would not think about anything that had to do with Ticky).
Once her struggle of getting her eyes open was over, she laid on her
right side scared to turn to her left not knowing what kind of feeling to
expect. After a few minutes she tried to remember who, what, where,
and how she got in this state. She remembered drinking on her living
room floor and feeling a bit stressed. Then she remembered talking to
Ray...... Oh, my God!!!!! She thought to herself. Ray. I must have
fallen asleep and didn't hear when he came, shit!!!! She turned quickly
to the other side and reached for the phone...... What the fuck!!!!!!! Oh,
shit!!!!!! Oh, my God!!!!! She quickly turned back into the position she
had turned from. She was paralyzed. Stuck in place.

She looked over her shoulder to see if what she had seen was
correct. It was. It was correct. It was Ray!!!! It was then she realized
she was butt ass naked. It started coming to her slowly but surely. She
remembered sex. Good sex. She started to remember the way he
touched her. In such a way it would be in every way unfair to call it
"sex". She remembered making love. Real love. Like the first time. It
was a little stronger than the first time and he was definitely bigger than
the first time!! How could she she thought? Why would she? Then
again why shouldn't she? In her optic view she spotted three empty
condom wrappers. At least she wasn't that drunk and at least he was
responsible she thought. There was a lot of thinking going on in her
head. Damn!!!!! Three times, I still got it!!!

She turned on her left side and stared at Ray while he slept like
a new born baby after feeding. And I knocked him out! She had forgot
about the hang over that she had woken up to just a few minutes ago
and replaced it with her memory of last night. She closed her eyes and
slid closer to Ray until she had gotten right up under his arm. There she
was secure and comfortable. She began to gather her thoughts on last
night's event.

She remembered slowly. She remembered how he had been so
gentle. How he had entered her with grace and ease. How he had kissed
her breast just right (that was something you know who didn't do
properly). And once it got in....she remembered feeling wonderful. He
held one hand on the bottom part of her back and the other hand
supported her neck. And he moved so slow at the right times and so fast

at the right time that she thought he was love making. But what would she do now? What's next? See, she thought too hard about certain things instead of letting things happen. Instead of going with the flow. She had made love to another man. She has never made love to nobody else, besides Ticky. Well it wasn't like she made love to someone else, cause she had slept with Ray before she ever slept with Ticky. Stop it, Tricks! She said to herself. Stop trying to justify sleeping with Ray. You're grown and Ticky is out of your life you're not cheating on him you're starting a new beginning.

Ray woke up to the same sun light that had woken Tricks up. It shinned in his face just as fiercely as it did in Tricks' face. He, unlike Tricks remembered instantly what happened last night. It was a good feeling. A feeling he had been waiting for. He'd been waiting for years, actually. It was the best he thought to himself. When he entered her, he thought, it was so tight and even through the condom he knew it was warm. Warm with love. He was in love with her. He had never stopped loving her. To him it was the same as the first time too. It was just a little more mature now. He opened one eye lid with a smile. He knew the night could only be topped off with the morning beauty of her face. But, she was gone!

He opened both his eyes and sat up. He looked around the room and into the bathroom, but no Tricks. He got up and wrapped the sheet around the lower part of his body and walked through the apartment, still no Tricks. He went back into the bedroom and sat on the edge of the bed, he picked up his watch on the night table and looked at the time. It was then he noticed the note. He picked it up and read it.

"*Ray,*

> *I had to go run some errands. You were sleeping so good I didn't want to wake you. Hope you don't mind. The door slams locked. Thank you for a beautiful night, I enjoyed it. Hope you did also. Maybe we can hook up later and catch a movie or something (if you're not too busy) Page me, Okay.*"
> *Love Tricks*

"Well, maybe you should just let it go, man."
"You must be crazy. I could see if she would just talk to me.

All I want is to be friends. And she won't even give me that."

"Well, I hear... I mean the word out on the street is her and that N.B.A. dude, Ray, is an item."

"Stan, can't no man have nothin' on me when it comes to Tricks."

"Okay. Well, I know she be drivin' his Benz and Rover. 4.6 that is." Stan said with a teasing laugh.

"Yeah, right. You can't believe everything you hear motha' fucka'!"

"Okay. And not to mention that watch and friendship ring he went and copped her."

"You know, you're as bad as a bitch!!! If you believe that shit you're crazy!!"

"Okay." Ticky pulled out his cell phone and dialed Tricks' number. The phone rang four times before she answered it. "Hello." Tricks answered out of breath.

"What's up? Caught you at a bad time?"

"Ticky?"

"Yeah, what's up girl?"

"Oh, what's up? Naw, I was just coming in from the supermarket. What's going on with you?"

"Nothing much. Was just checking if you were ready yet?" "Are you?"

"Come on Tricks. How much longer do I have to suffer?"

She started putting her groceries away as she listened to Ticky blabber on and on about how much he had missed and loved her. But not once did he display a change. Not once did he show that he was ready. And not once did he sincerely apologize to her. She knew him so well. She knew what this phone call was about. She just didn't know how long he was going to beat around the bush. She knew he called about Ray. And just that second after he had came up for breath he hit her with it.

"So, I hear you and that Ray nigga' is some type of item."

"Oh."

"Oh. That's all you can say, is Oh?"

"Well, what else am I supposed to say?"

"What you mean what are you supposed to say?"

"You heard me..."

"What do you have to say?"

"Shit. I didn't know I had to answer to you, anymore. You don't hear me calling you and asking you 'bout all those hoochie bitches you be running around with, Ticky."

"What hoochie bitches you talking 'bout!!!!" They went through a screaming match for about three to five minutes before she realized that she was relapsing again.

"You know what Ticky, I'm not going through a screaming match with you. Now if you want to call and say hello and see how I'm doing I don't have no problem with that. But don't call here starting no shit!!!"

"Well, I hope you're happy with that clown ass nigga'."

"And I hope you're happy with those hoochie ass bitches you be fuckin' baby." She replied slickly. "Now I got to go. I have to cook dinner before I go out tonight. Talk to you later." She hung up the phone without waiting for a reply from him. Just as quick as she hung up was as quick as the phone rang back. She answered it with an attitude. "Look Ticky, I don't feel like hearing your bullshit. Just leave me...."

"Tricks... Tricks.... It's me."

The sound of Ray's voice instantly calmed her down. "Oh, Ray. I'm sorry. I thought you were..."

"Ticky? I figured that. Are you okay?"

"Yeah. I guess."

"What happened?"

"Nothing. He just called here asking me what's going on with us."

"How does he know?"

"Shit I guess everybody knows. You know how Ghetto Press goes. And there's a picture of us at that party you took me to last month at the Trump Towers. I saw it in one of those sports magazines."

"What! Get the fuck out of here. When.. where?"

"On the newsstand. I was shopping for dinner tonight and I passed the newsstand, I saw your name on the cover, they were doing a special on rookies. So, I picked it up and opened it up and dead smack on the second page of your story there I. I mean there we was. Hugged up and smiling. You mad?"

"No. Hell no I'm not mad! How I look?"

"Good. I bought it. I'll show you it when you get here later. You're still coming aren't you?"

"Yeah."

"Okay. See you later. I'm a start making dinner."

"Okay."

They hung up and Tricks started smiling. She felt like a girl out of a story book. That god damn big mouth Tammy. She knew Tammy had to been talking her business to Stan and Stan told Ticky. That big mouth bitch! She picked up the phone and started to dial Tammy's number to curse her out, but then she hung up the phone. Why should she? She thought. Why should she even bring that negativity into her space. (Something else she learned in Group.)

Brenda had started messing with this drug dealer from uptown. Which wasn't like her. Of course Tricks didn't know nothing about it. She really hadn't been around the girls a lot lately, although she spoke to them on the phone almost everyday. That was something Charlene forgot to mention. Tricks was so wrapped up in Group, home and Ray. Even though she didn't realize it, but she was moreso wrapped up in Ray than anything. She was also looking for a good art school to attend. Last week she brought her a whole bunch of art supplies. She had promised herself to get serious about her painting. That's how she had found out about Brenda.

She was up in the City shopping for art supplies, when she had bumped into Brenda. She didn't even recognize her, when she rolled down the window of the passenger side of a '98 two door Benz. When she heard somebody call out her name she didn't bother to even look in the car's direction. Until the car pulled up on the side of Tricks at the light. "Tricks... Tricks!!!" Brenda yelled with a Kool-Aid smile out of the car window.

Tricks turned around and looked. After a few seconds she had realized that it was her friend Brenda. "Brenda?" Tricks said as she walked closer to the car. "What's up, girl?"

"Nothing. On my shopping. Where you coming from?"

"Oh, buying art supplies." Tricks and Brenda looked at each other in silence for a few seconds. They both knew what was going on, Tricks never saw Brenda with this guy before (she rarely even dated). And Brenda knew how shady her friend was. Brenda knew Tricks was wondering who this man was.

"Oh! Tricks this is Barry. Barry this is my good friend Tricks."

Barry reached over and Tricks stepped off the curb closer into the car and they shook hands. "Hello, nice to meet you." he said to Tricks.

"Nice to meet you too." She replied with a smile. She had knew him, but didn't know him. It was more like she heard about him and saw him a few times at different events. She knew he was a big time drug dealer from Harlem. She always heard stories out in the street, occasionally, about his baby's mother. She was known to be a crazy bitch! She was known to go from Harlem down to Brooklyn and out to New Jersey to fight another female over him. And he was known for always cheating. Knowing how crazy she was, he didn't care. Shit she had done three years for him. I would have went tick-tick boom-boom too, if that motherfucker would've tried to play me!

Tricks wasn't too happy about Brenda's new choice of company, but she didn't want to display her feelings in front of Brenda or Barry. So, she just smiled and kept it to herself, it wasn't the right time she figured. After Brenda and Tricks had departed with promises of seeing each other for drinks later on in the week, Tricks headed home. Home straight to the phone to call Charlene. She could not believe Brenda! "Girl, it just slipped my mind. I thought you knew. She been fucking around with Barry for a minute now. And if you ask me she's kind of open."

"But... but.... where did she meet him? And when? Where was I?"

"Probably with Ray. You kind of open too. But anything is almost nice next to Ticky. Who's been running around like a nigga' tryin' to fulfill a dick wish."

"Who you tellin'. And then got the nerve to call me questioning me about me and Ray. Girl, when are you coming to see me. We should go out tonight for some drinks."

"All right. Lil' Keith went to his cousin's for the weekend."

"So, call me later. I'll be here."

After they hung up Tricks went into the living room and stared at the host of different colors and styles of paints. She hadn't started any painting yet. What would be her first painting? She thought to herself. She always had a thing for black art. So, there it was she was to start on her first portrait. She named it before she even started it. It was to be called "Black Beauty".

In The Middle of The Beginning

Brenda had not been seen or heard from in over two and a half weeks. It was obvious to the rest of the girls that Brenda had gotten a little out of hand with this Barry situation. Now don't get it wrong, they were not hatin' on Brenda. If it was with anybody else they would have been happy for her. But it wasn't, it was Barry. And Brenda wasn't exactly Barry's cup of tea. You know? Brenda was a girl from the hood, but wasn't exactly from the hood (you know?) How can I put it? See, she wasn't a product of her environment as some people would say. She lived in what some people called the ghetto, but she graduated and went on to community college. So, she always dated guys from her school or her job. So it was natural for the girls to worry about their friend. They had been calling her job, but no luck. She had missed a whole week of work. That's what got their eyebrows raising. That wasn't like her. She never missed work. Her patterns started changing. But the girls didn't want to be too persistent about the issue. Brenda got very touchy when it came to Barry. So, as time went on they just let it be.

Of course she went through her arguments with his baby mother. And it was well known around town that she (Brenda) was his new girl. He stopped fucking around with his baby mother all together. But you know how that go. I feel if you gon' stop messing around with someone then stop!! Don't do certain things to lead that person on. Like I always say "you never know what a man is telling or have a next girl thinking". They moved in with each other in Queens. Nice house and everything, but who wants to live how she was forced to live? She couldn't let nobody know where she lived, which meant her friends couldn't visit. She barely was allowed to give their number out.

For some reason Tricks had privileges others didn't. Barry said he picked up good vibes from Tricks. So she was the only one who was allowed to have their direct number and after a while the only one that knew where they lived. Barry started going out of town more often at one point. Then that stopped. He started being more in N.Y. than anything. Brenda never knew too much about his business life. It was better that way. But after a while something wasn't right. Something about Brenda wasn't right.

Her change became the topic of discussion often between the girls, but never brought up to Brenda, being she had become very touchy when it came to her personal life. The girls just noticed the changes as time went on and talked about them when they were not around Brenda. They tried to figure out what it could have been. Kim came up with stress. But that was ruled out by Tammy, who came up with Brenda being pregnant. But that's nothing that she would keep from the rest of the girls. They came up with everything from AIDS to abuse, ruling all of that out just brought them back to the drawing board. With no answers.

Brenda's mother came up to New York to visit, but never got to even see Brenda. The weekend she came to visit she called Tricks' house looking for Brenda. The day she was to leave to go back to D.C. Brenda had her waiting Downtown Brooklyn for over an hour. Brenda never showed up. Brenda had issues.

"Look, somebody need ta' talk ta' da' bitch! 'Cause she's gettin' out of motha' fuckin' hand. I'm tired of us talkin' 'bout it and not doin' shit. Now, if y'all 'ain't gonna say nothin' I will." Tammy said in her sarcastic voice she usually talked in.

Tricks took a sip of her drink and mumbled under her breath, "I bet you will, wit' ya' big ass mouth."

"What?" Tammy asked her.

Talking much louder than the first time and more cocky, Tricks repeated herself. "I said, I bet you will with ya' b-i-g- a-s-s- mouth."

"What da' fuck is dat' supposed to mean?"

Tricks had a couple of drinks and never got to confront Tammy about her thinking she had talked her business to Stan. "It means what da' fuck I said it meant. You got a big ass mouth. And you stay talkin' somebody's business!"

"What business you talkin' 'bout? Huh? Stop talkin' in sub...."

Charlene interrupted them, "look, stop that shit. This 'ain't about you two. It's about Brenda. Besides y'all are both drunk."

"Drunk my motha' fuckin' ass, Charlene!!" She stood up and faced Tricks, who was still sitting on the floor. "Now, you got something you want to say to me bitch? Tricks jumped up quick like a bunny rabbit. Which was to everyone's surprise. See, Tammy thought she was gonna bad mouth Tricks and Tricks wasn't going to say nothing and mind you they both were a little tipsy. "First of motha' fuckin' all, BITCH! That callin' motha' fucka's bitches is played the fuck out!!! Second of all I said what I wanted to say. I said you got a big ass mouth! Now if you would like to make a reply to that be my mother fuckin' guest! And third of all, don't be jumpin' up in my face like I'm some crab ass, as you would say, bitch you don't know." By the time she got to her last word she was all up in Tammy's face with her finger pointed between her two eyes. "I'm a grown ass woman and you won't be talkin' to me like I'm some fuckin child!" Charlene and Kim jumped up in between the two girls to separate them before any blows were thrown.

"Y'all gonna stop this bullshit. In my house at that. Calm the fuck down!" Charlene shouted as she stood between the two girls.

Tricks shouted over Charlene's shoulder, "No fuck that shit, Charlene! I'm tired of that bitch talking to motha' fucka's how she wants to!!"

Of course Tammy had to answer her back. Well, too motha' fuckin' bad B-I-T-C-H-! You should've jumped up in Ticky's face, like this, when he was wippin' ya' motha' fuckin' ass!!!!"

"Well, ya' big mouth ass should'a been runnin' around tellin' ya' business, too, while you be tellin' everybody else's. Like how you fucked Stan raw and he burned ya' dumb ass. Twice!!!!! At that big mouth bitch!!!!!"

Kim yelled at the top of her lungs. "Shut the fuck up, already!!!!!!!!! Y'all dumb asses just need to shut the fuck up!!!!" The both of them stopped in their argument and just stared at Kim for a minute. Sometimes friends need to get stuff off their backs. Those are usually the things they hold in to save their friends' feelings or to save an argument. Well, Tricks and Tammy let the dogs loose tonight!! Even though things had cooled down, a bit, after a while there still was tension in the air. But the main concern went back to Brenda. They went back and forth about how they was going to approach Brenda. Finally they all agreed to just call her and tell her to come over to Charlene's house. But what they were to find out, I don't think none of them were prepared for.

Being Tricks was the only one who had Brenda's home number, everybody else had only her pager number, she had to make the call. The phone was busy for an hour, straight. They contemplated going over to the house. Nobody's supposed to know where Brenda lived. How would they explain? Kim kept pushing the issue. Tricks tried to make the girls understand that she gave Brenda her word that she wouldn't tell no one where she lived. Of course the others couldn't relate to what she was saying. What if nothing is wrong and they go racing over there like Charlie's Angels or something. Tricks insisted that maybe they were just getting carried away, maybe they needed to sit down and think things over first. But Tricks lost her battle, so there they went. Next thing you knew they were driving, on their way to Brenda's house. Everyone agreed that Tricks would go to the house, while the others would stay in the car on the corner. If everything is okay, they came up with a story Tricks would tell Brenda and Barry (if he was home.) She would act like she was stressed out over Ray and she needed someone to talk to. Once they got to the corner of the block, in an eye's view of Brenda and Barry's house the girls stopped the car.

"Which one is it?" Tammy asked

"God damn! Their neighbor's sure is throwing some fuckin' bash." Kim said.

"Tricks, how we supposed to see what's going on? All you can see is a whole bunch of cars and people partying on that lawn." Charlene asked Tricks.

Tricks just sat silent as the girls went on and on, from how nice the neighborhood was to wanting to crash these people party. Then Tricks finally spoke. "Why couldn't she say nothing. I'm sure she don't know all these people, but they can know where she live. They can come to the party? And we, her friends forever can't?" The girls sat in their own silence, with their own thoughts, and their own hurt.

"What? That's.... that's the house, where all them people are?" Kim asked without moving her eyes off of the house.

Tammy pointed out the car window with a look of astonishment. "That big ass house! That house is bigger than yours, Tricks. What the fuck is she having a house warming or something?

And whatever she's having, why couldn't she invite us. Ol' selfish witch."

Tricks turned to the girls and paused for a minute. "What y'all think I should do? Think I should still go?"

"Yeah!!!" They all said at the same time.

"And make sure you bring her to the car. I got a couple of words for her." Tammy said. The girls looked on as Tricks made her way to the crowded house. Tricks didn't know why she had butterflies in her stomach. She looked at the crowd of people and didn't notice not one face. Maybe she got the wrong block? She thought to herself. She had only been to the house a few times. But one of the cars was parked in the driveway. This was definitely the house. She made her way through the unfamiliar faces. Once she got to the front door the music got louder and louder. She couldn't believe how crowded the house was. Especially for somebody who didn't want nobody to know where they lived. She didn't see Brenda or Barry nowhere. All she saw was a bunch of drunk people. This is really a party. She went out to the back and all she saw was more drunk people by the pool. She spotted the most sober person she had seen all night. It was a young lady maybe twenty-five or six. She was standing on the side of the pool smoking a beanie. Tricks walked over to the girl and tapped her. "Excuse me, do you know where Brenda or Barry is?" The girl turned around and looked Tricks up and down, not in so much of a disrespectful way though.

"Who?" She asked

"Brenda and Barry. They live here."

"I don't know them. I don't know who lives here. I don't know nobody in this place. Except the person I came with and I can't even find his crab ass!"

"Oh, I'm sorry. My bad."

"No, it's okay. But if you happen to see a tall dark skinned guy, with a bald head, name Chucky would you let him know I'm looking for him Please?"

"Okay." Tricks said and walked away.

"Hey!" The young lady called out to Tricks as she was walking away.

Tricks turned around to the girl. "Yeah?"

The girl walked up to Tricks and pointed up to the top of the house. "You might want to check upstairs. You know how it goes with these people." She looked at her watch. "It's about that time. You know?" Then she walked pass Tricks and went into the house.

Tricks didn't quite understand what just was said and what just happened, but she figured it wouldn't hurt to go look upstairs. So once again she trooped her way through a whole bunch of people, she didn't know. But who happened to be piled up in one of her best friend's house. It was like a lot of these people didn't know each other. They were just here. Nobody paid her any mind as she walked through the crowd. She started up stairs, not knowing what to expect. She went to each bedroom, knocked before entering, but nothing. Nothing in their bedroom and nothing in the other two bedrooms. She walked to what Brenda and Barry used as a study or office. Once again she went to knock before entering, but just before her hand hit the door she could hear voices. She recognized two of them. It was Brenda and Barry. She held her knock and thought for a minute. The other voices she didn't recognize. She didn't want to walk in on some type of business shit. So she figured she'd just tap on the door, stick her head in, and play it off. She did it. But, like what was said earlier she was not ready for what she was about to find out.

The girls rode in the car in silence. Nobody knew what to say. Nobody knew what to think. It was like they were talking in silence. Like everybody knew what each other was saying in their minds. Anger, hurt, and confusion. Tricks held a paper towel on her right arm, to stop the bleeding from the cut she got fighting Brenda. She tried to bring Brenda outside but she had refused and started fighting with Tricks. It seemed it took them longer to get home than it took getting to Brenda's. Charlene broke the silence. "What did she say when you went in the room?"

"What else could she say in the state she was in?" Tricks replied without looking at her.

"Well, what the fuck did dat' nigga' Barry say?"

"Shit." Tricks answered.

After twenty minutes of silence, Kim turned from the window and spoke. "I heard that mother fucker got down like that, you know.

But I just couldn't believe it.... he just didn't seem like it." She paused for a minute. "Well, what kind..... what was she doing?"

"Hell if I know. It was all types of shit there. By the way she looked, it seems like she was doing a little bit of everything and for a while. It looked like she hadn't just started today. She lost about ten to fifteen pounds!"

"What!!!" Tammy shouted. "Do you think she was shooting up, too?"

"Tammy, it look like she's been doin' a lot of shit. The girl is strung out. That nigga' got her strung the fuck out!! Her face don't even look like her face anymore. Everybody in that room was getting high. But, Brenda, she looked like shit. That nigga' looked like nothing was wrong with him. But he was high as a kite."

See, Brenda was getting high. Since none of her friends got high she took on new ones that did. Barry introduced her to drugs the second week they had started going out with each other. It started off with weed. Then came the cocaine. Barry got high for years, but somehow knew how to control it. He sniffed coke and dope. He did a little dust every now and then, but not as much as he did coke and dope. But, Brenda she wasn't used to it. She didn't know how to control it. And by the time they moved in with each other (Brenda and Barry) she was doing dope and coke. In many different ways, sniffed it, cooked it up and put it in her weed, and worst of all shooting it up. At this point they knew they had lost their friend, but was not ready to accept it.

They called Brenda over and over, but no luck. After finally getting an answer Brenda didn't want to speak to none of them. Then she just changed their number. After a while Tricks would just ride pass Brenda's house and sit. Sit thinking what could make her want to live like this. She hoped to at least get a glance of her, but no luck. Maybe they moved. She thought. Or was she just coming at the wrong times? Brenda had gotten worst since the girls popped up at her house. But, she didn't want help. She couldn't even admit she was an addict. Well, Tricks figured she better let it just lay for a little while then she'd try again.

After two months of letting it lay Tricks had to know what and how her friend was doing. Charlene, Tammy, Kim felt the same. This was their friend from childhood. They could recall when Brenda didn't even want cigarette smoke around her. Brenda was a crack head, dope shooting, and dust sniffin' skeleton. Only difference between Brenda and any other junkie on the Ave. is she had a roof over her head, so she didn't have to walk the street. She had all the money she needed to supply herself, so she didn't have to rob, steal, or sell her ass. But, it didn't matter, what it all boils down to is a junkie is a junkie and she had a disease. After hearing about Brenda's condition, from the street, they decided they should call Brenda's mother out in D.C. They heard that Brenda was looking like she weighed a hundred and ten pounds, a big difference from the one forty she used to weigh. She was still dressing decent, but she looked a funky mess. Her mother came down with her husband and went over to Brenda's house. Brenda opened and closed the door right in her face in one breath. After pleading with her daughter, after tears still came rejection. Her mother cried every night from that day on. She said she was cursed. She said she had to be, she lost her first child (her son) five years ago and now she was losing her little girl. She cried from that day on. One of a mother's worst nightmares, Brenda's mother was living it. She decided to go back to D.C. put her stuff in storage and come back to New York for a while. She wasn't giving her daughter to the devil that easy, she kept telling the girls. The night before she was to go back to D.C. to pack she got a call in the middle of the night, it was Brenda.

"Ma." She said sobbing. "Ma, I need ya' help... Ma.... Please I don't want to live like this no more."

"Baby?" She answered crying. "Oh, baby I'm here. You stay strong, mamma is going to go to D.C. put my things in storage and move back here. Okay? You stay strong 'til I get back."

"Okay, but don't forget about me. And tell the girls I'm sorry and I love them. Tell them don't be mad at me."

"Oh, they love you too. And they're not mad, baby."

"I love you ma. See you when you get back." They hung up with the love a mother and daughter could only give each other. That was the first night Brenda's mother didn't cry in a while.

She went to D.C. and Brenda tried to stay strong until she returned, but the night before her mother was to return Brenda was killed. Her and Barry. Barry had some type of bad dealings with some people and they rushed into Brenda and Barry's house tied them up, tortured them, and shot them both in the head. Brenda was two and a half months pregnant. She was waiting to see her mother the next day to tell her. She felt she had to come clean, for the sake of her child. The police back tracked to Tricks being the last one to see them alive. She had stopped by to check on Brenda and bring her some shrimp she had cooked earlier. Everything was fine when she left. In fact Brenda gained back some of her weight and was looking good. She was so happy about her mother coming the next day. Tricks dropped to the floor when she got the phone call, she didn't even bother to ask how they got her number or how they knew she was there. She just called the rest of the girls and told them to meet her at the hospital.

She didn't know if she could go through with identifying the body. Death, death was something they were not ready for. Charlene was still not over her baby's father. As Tricks walked down the hall to identify the body her knees numbed up. She could hear the girls crying down the hall behind her. She took a deep breath as the doctor took her into the cold room. He pulled back the sheet off of a body that laid on a table in the middle of the room. Next to that table was another body up under a sheet. She didn't even pay any attention to the other bodies in the room. As the sheet pulled back she grabbed her mouth with both of her hands and lost her breath for a couple of seconds. Brenda was not recognizable. She stared for a minute.

The doctor asked in a soft voice. "Ma'm? Is this Brenda Call?" Shocked Tricks couldn't answer right away. She stood still in place before answering. I... I... I can't really tell. Where is the rest of her face?" She asked crying.

"She.. she was shot three times in the back of her head...."

"Tricks interrupted him. "Look on her right thigh. There should be a little butterfly tattoo on it. She snuck and got it when she was sixteen years old."

The doctor pulled back the sheet more and checked the thigh on the body. He looked up and nodded his head up and down to Tricks. Confirming that the body was Brenda's. Tricks held herself and walked out of the room. By the look on her face there was no need for the girls to ask if it was Brenda or not. A piece of them was gone. And it would never return. How do you tell a mother that her child is gone? Another one of her children. Her last child. When you lose a friend it's like you lose half of yourself. Sometimes you share things with your friend that you wouldn't share with your sibling.

After the services for Brenda, her mother called the girls and told them to come over. She was going through Brenda's things and wanted them to have whatever they wanted. It was understood by Brenda's mother that the girls were like sisters to Brenda. And like daughters to her. Brenda's mother returned to D.C. two days after they had sorted through Brenda's things. Tricks had shut herself down. Even to Ray. She just couldn't function. Ray tried to be there for her, but she didn't want to be bothered. All she did was painted and cried, cried and painted. Ticky called her often to check on her. To her surprise not once did he pressure her into seeing him or getting back together. All he wanted was to make sure she was all right. Realizing, after meditating, that she would never get over her friend's death. But she also realized that she still had a life and she had to live it. So, that day she came out of her depression and started getting back to her regular routine. She went back to Group and learned it was time to face her "situation" which meant it was time to face Ticky. She decided not to call him and wait for him to call her. She figured when he propositioned her for a date or something she would accept. Just to let him know she wasn't intimidated by him. But he never called. Could he have been over her, finally? Fuck it. She thought. She still had Ray. But, after beeping him ten times and not getting an answer she felt chumped. She hadn't even realized what she had done to Ray. She was in a state of shock when Ray was trying to reach out to her. He loved her, but he loved himself too. He couldn't stand taking a chance of putting himself through what he went through years ago when she left him in the park. So, he decided to make his distance from her. He was her support system, but she couldn't take a fall. She kept on with her life. She kept painting, she got accepted to an art school she had been trying to get in. She kept going to Group sharing her stories, working through her "situation". What she didn't share with her fellow abuse survivors was that she started seeing her ex again. Which later down the line she realized was because she knew it wasn't quite right. She knew she was seeing him for all the wrong reasons and at the wrong time. It had been a month and some weeks since she had spoken to Ray. She now allowed Ticky to visit her at her house. Things were running smoothly. Ray became a memory in the back of her mind, but she truly missed him. She loved him, but just didn't know how to deal with it. We sometimes overlook what is good for us and choose just the opposite. She didn't see it as that. Sometimes in life we just don't learn from the first lessons God set on us. But he always finds it in his heart to give us another chance to learn. I guess this is her other chance.

Tricks ran raggedy around the house. She went from room to room looking for her red shoe. Charlene sat on the couch reading a magazine, not paying her a bit of mind. She rather not even speak about Tricks going out with Ticky. What she didn't know was this wasn't the first time. Finally, she spoke her piece. Whether she liked it are not. She felt she had to say something. "You know Tricks, I don't think that this is a good idea."

Tricks sat on the couch and struggled to get her shoe on. "Look Charlene, I got this under control. Trust me."

"I... I don't know girl. What happened to Ray?"

"What happened to him?"

"I thought you two was a couple. I thought you two was doing all right."

"Yeah, me to. I don't know what happened." Realizing she was talking to her friend, her best friend. She knew Charlene had known her better than anybody else. Charlene could see right through what Tricks thought she was hiding. "Look, I can't concentrate on no man. I got to move on."

"Tricks you call this moving on? I've..... I've watched you die slowly and slowly bring yourself back to life. I've cleaned your cuts and bruises. I've cried when you cried. All due to the man you're going out with tonight. And you call that moving on? Charlene tried so hard not to let the tears that was building up release from her eyes. Tricks why go backwards. Why don't you just try calling and speaking to Ray?"

"For what? I tried that already. He's a sensitive ass! Ol' pussy!"

"Oh, come on girl. You know you don't mean that. Number one, look how you treated him during the time of Brenda's death. Number two, just 'cause he was caring about your needs and showed you a side of a man you never saw before don't make him no pussy!! And you know that. And going out with Ticky ain't gonna make things no better."

"It's just a date, for god's sake, Charlene. We're not getting married or moving back in with each other."

"So why go out with him? What's your whole point...." Charlene's speech was stopped by the phone ringing. Tricks picked up the phone knowing that it was Ticky. Charlene could tell. That's how well she knew Tricks.

"All right, I'm out. That was Ticky. He's downstairs. I'll be back later. If somebody calls from Group just tell them I won't be making the meeting tonight."

"Should I tell them where you're at?"

"Don't be a smart ass Charlene. I'll see you later."

"I still don't feel good about this, kid." Charlene told Tricks as Tricks slammed the door in Charlene's face. Charlene worried herself for hours. After Brenda's death nobody knew what to expect. You have men who kill their girlfriends everyday. She had just read in the paper the other day how this guy sliced his girlfriend's throat and stabbed her to death. Charlene fell asleep on the couch, worrying.

Tricks felt different around Ticky. She felt uncomfortable riding in his car again. Although it was a new car, it was the same ol' trip. With the same ol' person. Ticky felt a little funny too. He was more surprised that she was in his car. He had almost given up on her. Most of the ride she looked out of the window, thinking. Mostly about some of the things Charlene had said. Still justifying her decision to go out with Ticky. She felt like she was on her first date. She didn't know what to say or rather how to start a conversation. They had hardly spoke since they left from in front of her building. She looked at her watch and noticed that they had been driving for fifteen minutes. That fifteen minutes felt like an hour. Ticky noticed her looking at her watch. That gave him the chance to break silence.

"What, you got to be somewhere?"

He had caught her off guard. "Huh"? She asked him. Finally turning from the window.

"I saw you looking at your watch. I thought maybe you had to be somewhere at a specific time."

"Oh, no. I was just looking at how long we was driving. I haven't been to Mr. Chow in so long I forgot how far it was."

"What....you want to go somewhere else? We can go somewhere if you want." He just wanted to satisfy her. She hadn't seen him like this in a long time. A very long time.

She nodded her head at him. "No. I want to go there. It's nothing." Pausing for a couple of seconds and deciding to change the topic, since he had made the first step for conversation. "So, what made you buy this car?"

"Nothing really. I like how it ride."

"Oh."

"So, aren't you wonderin' what happened to your car?"

"No. Not really."

"Why?"

"Cause. I mean... you have to understand when I left I didn't want to take anything that was connected to you. Or that would remind me of you. So, I left the jewelry and the car."

"I can accept that. I just wondered why. I had that feeling though. But it's still in the garage, if you need it. Trust it won't mean that you have a connection to me. It belongs to you and I'm not gonna drive it."

"Why didn't you sell it?"

"Sell it? For what?"

"Cause you're not going to drive it."

"Well, honestly at first in the beginning I was hoping you was coming back. Then when I realized that you weren't coming back I just figured that you would need it to get around."

Tricks couldn't believe what she was hearing. Was he truthful with the words he spoke. Could he really have cared how she got around or was this part of some act? "Well, I learned the public transportation system very well. Sometimes I rent cars or take cabs."

"Well, like I said you can come for it whenever you want. It was a gift."

"I'll keep that in mind, thank you."

Tricks thought to herself how badly she wanted to tell him she would be there in the morning! But being the stubborn person she had grown to be, she kept that comment to herself. Once they pulled up to the parking garage the tension had lifted a bit. It kind of reminded her of her first date with Ray (the tension). By the end of their dinner tension had lifted totally. And by the time they had reached in front of Tricks' building things, to Ticky, were like they used to be. When he asked her for a little kiss goodnight, she took a deep breath and refused him. She had a couple of drinks and she still indeed loved him a little. But, she caught herself and gave him a cute hand shake and said goodnight. All night she sat up weighing her options, which she didn't have many. She had a really good time tonight, but a part of her felt a little guilty. She didn't have nobody to talk to about tonight. Charlene had gone home. She left a note on the table telling Tricks she couldn't sleep, so she went home. She didn't have any messages on her machine, which she never did. Then she began to think about Ray. The good part of her conscious kept saying, "Girl, you letting a good thing go. You better go and get that man, if you know what is good for you." And the other part of her conscious kept saying, "Look, live your life. If he wanted you he wouldn't have let you go!" But, deep inside she knew what was right. She figured that the ol' saying was right, if you love something let it go. If it comes back to you it was meant to be. If it doesn't it wasn't meant. Something like that. She thought herself to sleep.

A month later

    Tricks was on her way home from Ticky's house (their old house). She was stuck in traffic and knew she had to go to her place first to pick up her art stuff. She was already late. Stopping at her house first was only going to make her even later. Her art thing was about the only thing she hadn't taken to Ticky's house. That's right, she went and took her ass back in that house. She thought it made it all right cause she still kept her apartment and stayed at her place once or twice maybe a week. She shouldn't had never fucked him! She started driving her old car again. She didn't pay no mind to what the girls had to say about the matter. She insisted that Ticky had changed. She continued with her regular scheduled life, without no hassle from Ticky. Things was running so smooth. Until that night. That night that marked her REAL new beginning.

    Tricks had told Ticky she was going to stay at school late and that she would meet him at his house later that night. She had to go to her place for a few minutes, then she would head over to his place. Well, that's what she had truly intended to do. But by the time she got to her house she was drained out and tired from school. Plus Ray was playing his first game at ten-o-clock and she didn't want to make Ticky feel no way. So, she figured that she would just catch the beginning just to see how Ray was looking. As soon as they did that thing where they introduce each player from each team and Ray's turn came she smiled and closed her eyes. She feel asleep. Ticky called and called, but she was sleeping too hard to hear the phone. He had called twenty-five times and left twenty messages. The other five times he just hung up in frustration. Poor child, so tired she laid on her stomach with her mouth open slobbering all over her arm. Of course Ticky being the man that he is didn't think maybe she was home sleep. Instead he thought of everything else.

    After a couple of drinks he left his house in a rage. He drove ninety miles an hour and ran every stop sign and every red light on the way. He found a way to get up to Tricks' apartment and banged on her door like a maniac. After about two minutes of banging, she moved for the first time since she had fell asleep. Waking up in a daze she looked at her watch. It was one thirty! She jumped up and fully noticed the banging on her front door. Once seeing Ticky through the peep hole she woke up all the way and opened the door. He burst in like a ball of fire. Yelling and screaming. At first she thought he was joking. But when he started looking through her apartment and hollering about having some nigga' there and ignoring his calls. He kept asking her something, but she was so in shock she didn't even hear what he was asking her. She just saw his lips moving. Then he raised his hands and slapped the shit out of her!

"You don't hear me talking to you?! I asked you a fuckin' question. Who da' fuck you had here, Tricks?!"

She looked at him like he had raised his hands for the last time. She took her foot with all her might and kicked the holy shit out of him. Right between his legs. She snatched one of her good smelling candles from off her coffee table and busted him in the middle of his head, while he was still knelled over in pain from her first blow.

She yelled at the top of her lungs. "MOTHERFUCKER! I told you not to ever put your motherfuckin' hands on me again." And as she spoke she swung with every symbol, like when a mother beats her child in the street for embarrassing her. She kicked him in his head, she didn't give him a chance to get up. "I will kill you NIGGA'!" She had lost it. She didn't even realize it. All she knew was she was sitting in the back of a police car and Ticky rode off in the back of an ambulance. She couldn't even remember if she locked her front door when the police took her a way. More or less when the police came all she knew was he had knocked the shit out of her and she clicked. She couldn't even remember how bad she had hurt him. Why did they take him away in an ambulance she thought to herself? She also wondered if he too had thought so deeply about her after he had beat her so many times. Of course not.

It seems battered people are so passive, very passive people a lot of times. She looked at her reflection in the cop car window. She could see dried blood on her lip and what was to be a bruise after a while on her cheek. He must have hit her twice. She could only remember the first hit. Then she looked at her forehead where she had stitches. Then she thought about that time he had beat her. But she got the best of him now. After hours sitting in the police station they finally allowed her a phone call. Who would she call? She was too embarrassed to call any of her friends, but the truth of the matter was she didn't have anybody else to call. She decided to call Charlene, she had to call somebody sooner or later. Anyway Charlene was the only one without a block on the phone. The operator let the phone ring three times then on the fourth ring Charlene picked up with a sleepy voice.

"Hello." She said clearing her throat.

"Hello. This is the operator, I have a collect call from Tricks. Will you accept the call?"

"Yes... Yes I'll accept."

"Thank you for using Bell Atlantic. You may talk now." The operator replied and cleared herself off the line.

"Tricks?" Charlene said in a whisper, scared. Tricks didn't answer. "Tricks, are you all right?" Tricks tried to talk, but couldn't get nothing out. She felt like she had a bag of apples stuck in her throat. Then she busted out crying in a discreet way. "Charlene.... I'm in jail,"

"What!!!!!! Jail... What.. What happened?" She woke up now. "Tricks sobbed. She tried speaking, but her throat felt like she had a bag of apples stuck in it. "Please, come and get me. I should be going to court soon. I'm downtown in the bullpen. Please come... now." She hung up the phone leaving Charlene holding the phone on the other line, baffled. Charlene sat up in her bed for a few seconds. Trying to digest the phone call. She jumped up and threw on a pair of sweats she had worn earlier. She ran through the house frantic, trying to get herself together. She tried to figure out what could have possibly happened. She dialed Tammy, and Kim. By the time she had gotten downtown the sun was on its way up. The girls hadn't gotten there.

By the time she finished her thought the girls pulled up. They jumped out of the cab with blank looks on their face. They ran frantic through the court house trying to find Tricks. They went from counter to counter trying to find out where Tricks could be. After finally finding out her court room, they raced to the third floor. All the girls could see was Tricks' back turned and the judge banging down that damn stick. Tricks must of felt her friends' presence. She hadn't flinched or turned around the whole time until her friends entered the courtroom. The girls sat on the bench, stuck. Tricks knew that her friends had just walked in. She knew that the girls didn't hear what had happened or what the judge had said. Tricks turned around as the officer walked her out through the doors in the court and said silently (barely moving her mouth). "Please get me out of here." Then she disappeared through the doors. The girls sat in shock.

They caught Tricks' lawyer. After having a long conversation with him they had found out what had happened with Ticky and Tricks. He said it would have helped if she would had reported the beatings. All she had was doctors reports from the beatings, but no police reports to match the hospital reports. Everything that the lawyer had said wasn't a surprise, accept her bail and how bad she had hurt Ticky. Her bail was Fifteen Thousand dollars!! And Ticky was hurt bad. Fifteen Thousand Dollars!! Even the lawyer felt that was outrageous! All they could do was wait for her call.

It had been a few days and Tricks was to go back into court today. She had told the girls not to worry about her. Tricks had the money to get out, but she said she didn't want to use it for bail. She was feeling guilty about Ticky. Which she shouldn't had. She was hoping that her bail would be reduced this court trip around. Charlene sat up every night worrying about Tricks. How could such drama hit them back to back? First Brenda's death and now Tricks. Charlene and the girls had been communicating with the lawyer on a regular basis. He really believed in Tricks. He acted more like a paid lawyer than a court appointed one. Ticky was still in the hospital. Tricks worked a good one on him.

Tricks hadn't mentioned to none of the girls what had happened that night with Ticky. They, over and over, came up with their own version of what happened that night. Tammy and Stan was going through one of their break up things, so she couldn't get any info from him. Anytime that Tricks would call she never would mention it. The last few days she sat on the Island (Rikers) to herself and in a silent shock. The girls all met up in front of the court house, like the first night Tricks had gotten arrested. This time they knew where they were going ahead of time, and they got there in time this time. Nobody knew what to expect. They only knew what they had prayed for.

After listening to four to five cases, they called Tricks. Just as they called her name, he came in. He slid in next to the girls, sitting in the next to last bench. He sat at the end. The girls looked at the same time, looked in shock. It was Ray. How did he know? Tricks hadn't mentioned about talking to Ray to none of the girls. He spoke to them and then they brought Tricks in. She looked different. Even though it had only been a few days she looked like she had lost weight. She didn't even look to the back of the court. The judge looked through her paper work for a few moments. They all sat still and prayed their own prayers to themselves. It only took about ten to fifteen minutes before her case was finished.

Her bail was lowered and she was ordered to attend a program for abused woman. Something like Group, but all the woman that attended was ordered by the courts to attend the program. Upon release, she would have to go five days a week and could not miss a day or she would be ordered back to jail. She would have to take urine tests once a week and would be evaluated by a psychologist. She stood hand cuffed the whole time. This time she sat on the bench on the side of the door that lead the prisoners back to the holding cell. She looked over to her friends and Ray and cracked a smile. The first in a long time.

The female officer came over after two other cases was called and carried Tricks and two other young women back to the back. At this point their facial expressions showed they were all thinking the same thing. And that was to bail her out, no matter what Tricks felt. She wasn't in her right state of mind to think properly, so they had to think for her. Ticky was still in the hospital. He was doing a tiny bit better, but still not too well. So, Ray put bail up and went out of town for a game. It was like it was mandatory that he paid for the bail. It never was no questions asked. He just paid and told the girls he had to leave for a road trip and he would be back in a few days. He instructed them to have Tricks page him as soon as she got home. And that was done, but Tricks seemed like a different person when she came home. She seemed so distant.

She had asked about Ticky once or twice the most. And she didn't page Ray right away. She felt a little uncomfortable. She was thankful, but she felt some what embarrassed. She thought it would be more easy if she called his pager and left a voice message. That way she would not have to talk directly to him, at least that's what she thought. She called the pager and thanked him for bailing her out. And made up a quick lie about how she was sleepy when she got out she slept the whole day and night away, and didn't get a chance to call until the next day. She felt bad for ducking him knowing how much he cared for her. She looked around her apartment. Everything was just how it was the night she got locked up. She had come in the day before and walked over the mess and when she wasn't walking over the mess she just sat in it. She stood in the middle of her living room with her hands on her hips for a few minutes. After taking a deep breath she started cleaning up the mess. Trying to remember what had happened that night. She could only remember so much. She blanked out at some point.

She wanted to find a way to check on Ticky, but didn't know where to start. She wasn't really worried about him as much as she was wondering about him. She wanted more so to know how bad he was hurt. She knew she had fucked him up pretty bad, but didn't know how bad. Motherfucker shouldn't have touched her! If you asked me. See, he better be lucky her ass ain't get old fashion and throw some hot grits on his ass!! She was finished cleaning before she knew it. She had daydreamed her way through the majority of the cleaning. She wondered why the phone ain't ring. Then she remembered that she had turned the ringer off to avoid Ray's call. She had lied at the end of her message and told him she was going out for a walk.

She went over to look to see if the answering machine had any messages (the machine still picks up with the ringer off.) It flashed rapidly displaying she had six messages. Five out of the six was Ray. The other one was Charlene checking on her. Ray basically said the same thing on all messages. He was trying to catch up with her and he guess he would try again later. She figured she needed to meditate before speaking to him. She lit a few scented candles and incense around her apartment and took a nice long bath.

After her bath she sat in her living room and meditated for an hour or so. She wanted to be mentally prepared before she spoke to Ray. Before she spoke to anyone. She knew it wouldn't be long before she had to communicate with someone. After her meditation she fell into a deep sleep. She was awakened by the phone still half sleep, she didn't think twice before answering. She had been screening her calls since she got out of jail, but this time she just answered the phone.

With a scratchy sleepy voice she answered. "Hello."

"Hey, there sleepy head. Did I wake you?" The familiar voice responded on the other end of the phone. It instantly woke her. She wasn't prepared for this. She hadn't expected to speak to him before preparing herself. There was a silence between the two phone lines. A silence that seemed to be hours long, but only a few seconds. She responded in a way that let him know he had caught her off guard.

"Oh, no. I just was dozing off. What's up? How are you?"

"Nothing much. I'm fine. And you?"

"I'm okay."

"Are you sure?"

"Yeah, I'm sure." By now she's sitting fully up in the bed and well ready for the conversation. "I'm just a little out of it, but I guess it will pass.... Thank you, Ray. Thanks for being there for me. And I'm sorry for pushing you away. I've been doing a lot of thinking and....."

He interrupted her. "Listen Tricks, I've been doing a lot of thinking too. And you don't have to explain nothing to me as long as you understand how I feel about you. As long as you know that I love you. I don't want to look on the past. I'm gonna be straight forward with you.... All I wanna know about is the present and the future. Basically, what's up with us. Now I know that it may be too soon, but I need to know something Tricks. 'Cause I'm not gonna make a fool of myself. If you think, honestly, that we can't have a future let me know. Because I'm gonna have to walk away. Don't get me wrong, I'm gonna always be there for you if you need me, but I can't keep holding on to something that's not going to be nothing. You know?"

"Yeah." she responded after minutes of sitting in her own silence, with her own thoughts. Her response puzzled him. She knew it did. She repeated herself. "Yeah."

"Yeah, you understand?" He asked in a soft voice. "When you say yeah, you say it meaning what?" She took a deep breath, so deep it scared him. He didn't know what to expect to come out of her mouth next. Then she spoke. She spoke the words she had thought about from the time she was locked up 'til earlier that evening while taking her bath. She knew she had to let that brick wall down now. She knew this was her last chance. "Yeah, meaning I'm with you. I'm there for you, all the way. I wanna be with......"

Once again he had stopped her in her words. "I'm on my way. I'll be there in a half." He hung up the phone before he could get a response and before she could respond. She jumped up, finally really realizing what was going on. She finally did it! She finally made peace with herself. She dug in her drawers for some sexy sleep wear. She felt refreshed. She thanked God for her blessings and asked for forgiveness for what she done to Ticky. She spoke to Mamma Pots, something she hadn't done (in this way) in a long time.

The time was going by faster and faster. She lit her scented candles and incense and dimmed the lights. Before she knew it Ray was at the door and they were in the bed. He had made love to her like he had never done before. Each stroke was deep, but passionate. Each kiss was wet, but loving. Each lick was unbearable, but delightful. And after they had reached their climax, together, he asked. He asked what she never thought she would hear in her life, but always wanted to hear. "Will you marry me?" It rang in her ears well after it was asked and answered. She couldn't believe that he had come prepared! With a ring and everything. What if she would have said no? Ray had had the ring for a while. He just was waiting for the right time to ask. But once she started pushing him away he thought he would never need to pull it out. But still, he saved it and didn't give up.

From that night on she didn't look back. Ticky went through therapy and never regained feeling in his right hand. He walks with a plate in his head. Tricks never knew his exact injuries. She never knew when she blacked out that she beat fire out his ass!!! She had almost killed him. She knew somebody was looking over her. And nothing since that night, with Ray, could stop her.

She finished art school and opened an Art Gallery. And her paintings are hanging in some of the most established black businesses. As for me... Well, I'm doing okay. I still keep in contact with Tricks and use life and her life story to help me go on day by day. I remember her story like the back of my hand. Never forgot it since she shared it in Group. See, I was her silent friend and we were friends ever since we met in Group. Tricks, Tricks is the best!!! And she made the best out of her situation. See, I can relate to her. So, I can tell the story like I was there!

Choices

At the time of coming across him, again, I was coming out of a relationship. And before that relationship, I was involved in an unhealthy relationship. So I was kind of messed up anyway.

I remembered going to my cousin's job and her mentioning his name. At first when she had asked if I had known a teacher by the name of "Mr. Abdul" I didn't....it didn't register. I knew a few Abduls. A teacher I thought to myself. What Abdul do I know that's a teacher? After busting my brains a few minutes, it came to me. Oh shit! It couldn't have been. After all this time. She said that when he found out that I was kin to her, he had mentioned that we were old friends. I wondered for years where he had been. The first cultural man I had ever dealt with on a personal level. Most of the young men back then I dealt with, were street guys. But he... he was different. Although back then he was young also, but still a little older than me. He had a little touch of that untamed animal in him. He had a little ghetto mentality in him, but at the same time he had knowledge of self. In other words he did a little wrong and at the same time he knew it was wrong. You know what I mean? Some motherfuckers don't even know when shit ain't right, but he recognized his wrong. He was a brother who knew he wanted something out of life. Back in a time when so many young brothers didn't want nothing but fast money and fast life to go with it.

I broke off into a daydream. I thought about the last time we had seen each other it was foggy. My cousin was at her desk taking a call when I came out of my daydream. I wondered if she was talking to me all that time before taking the call. I was in another world.

"Tiyer. You okay?"

"Oh, yeah. I was just thinking about something. Now what were you saying?"

"Oh, nothing. I was looking to see where Mr. Abdul was at this period. Come on let's see if he's in the lunchroom. He would want to see you."

As we were walking looking for him I found myself getting a little nervous. Why? I didn't know. After looking in two different places and still not finding him I started to get stressed because I wanted to see him.

"Ms. Jay. Have you seen Mr. Abdul?" My cousin asked some lady outside of the lunchroom.

"He was just in the lunchroom. You didn't see him in there?"

"No."

I was distracted by some kids pointing and whispering about me. One of the students had recognized me and had spread the word through the lunchroom that I was in the school. I was right in the middle of saying hello to some students when I heard my cousin a few feet behind.

"Hey, Mr. Abdul. Come here for a second."

I didn't want to turn around. I had gotten nervous all over again. I had already prepared myself not to see him after we were unsuccessful finding him. I took a deep breath and turned around with a smile. There he was. It was him and he had not changed in years. He looked the same. Just a little older.

"Hey you. How ya' been stranger." I said. And as soon as the words rolled off my tongue, I felt like a corn ball.

He wrapped his broad arms around me. "Hey, baby. What's going on? You looking good." He whispered in my ear. I wanted to melt. All eyes were on us. I felt it. They were trying to act like they weren't looking, but they were.

"So, Tiyer how you been? What you been up to?"

"Nothing much, working on my second album. And you?"

"You know me, maintaining."

"That's good. I had a baby you know? Last year."

"So I heard. Congrats. Married yet?"

"Oh, no. I'm gonna give you my number, give me a call keep in touch."

He went and got a pen and I gave him my numbers. We talked a little longer and then I said my good-byes. When I got to my car I was still shocked and at the same time I knew we probably would not speak to each other. It had been a long time and he, knowing the kind of brother he was, probably been happily married with kids. He always came off to be a brother that had true family values. You know come home to his wife every night type. He was the perfect husband. I could also tell he had grown a lot too. My cousin mentioned that he had gotten his masters. I was proud of him. Whether we spoke again or not I was proud of him. And he brought back a good memory. And I thanked him for that, to myself I thanked him and pulled from the school.

I ended up back at the school. A few weeks later. I wasn't thinking about Abdul until I walked through the doors. It took only ten minutes of me being in the school before I saw him again. He looked as good as he did last time I saw him. I hadn't given any thought to him not calling me since then. Until that moment. I wanted him and I was rather bothered that he didn't call. I have a problem with rejection. I got that from my mother. I felt the tension between us. Later down the line I asked him why didn't he call when I gave him the number? He said he wasn't sure if I really wanted him to call. Poor excuse.

Everything after that happened so fast. Next thing I knew he was outside with me at my car writing his cell number and asking what I was doing later. All day I thought about him and our past. I couldn't remember a lot. All I knew was that I was digging the brother back then... and not much had changed. What really bothered me was I couldn't remember details about our past. I knew we had fucked, but I wasn't to sure...about a lot. It didn't matter, cause I had a funny feeling that my mind would be refreshed.

And I wasn't wrong. We went out for something to eat later, rather I ate. I had to show my face at this industry party first. Then we stopped and I had a bite and a drink. That's all I needed. My juices started flowing. I don't know what it is about liquor that makes a person feel the way I was feeling. It's a feeling that can't be explained. I made up my mind though. I wasn't going to give in, not tonight.

We talked a lot that night. His mind was so strong. It's very rare that a man's mind would make you wanna give it up. Usually it's something physical. The more he explained his situation the more I just didn't get it. That's probably because I wasn't used to a real man. He had been with someone for a number of years, but was not happy. They had a child together and the whole nine yards, but he wasn't happy. He had a mistress also. He had feelings all over the place. I didn't want to add on to his problems. And I've become more passionate and considerate with age. I've learned how to respect other women. Me coming into the picture would just make his situation much more difficult. I knew it was wrong, but I couldn't stay away from him. We had a funny kind of connection. I always told him we must have been lovers in our past lives.

We made love all night. It was much different than back in the days. It was more authentic. More deep. Our minds had seriously connected prior to us laying in my bed. It was out of this world!! I was able to let it loose! My seeds wasn't home either. Shit he touched me like a man is supposed to touch a woman. I hadn't been touched like that in so long. You know when you meet someone and it feels like you could be with that person for the rest of your life? No matter what faults, if there's any, you can just stay there with them forever. When you don't care what your closest friends have to say about that person, you just don't want to be without them? I had to see if it was more than the sex that made me feel like that. But the sex sure helped! He entered me with respect. When he stroked me I could tell he had my satisfaction and nut in mind, before his own. I wouldn't mind going to bed and waking up with him!

When I woke up he was already dressed and ready to go to work. He kissed me gently on my lips and said goodbye. I wished he could have stayed. I fell back asleep and just as I got in a deep sleep the phone had to wake me up. I was in one of those "worn out from sex" sleeps.

"Hello...Hello. Nothing I was sleep. What? Look I'm not in the mood. I'll call you when I wake up. Bye."

He always got to call me with some bullshit. It seems when I don't pay him no mind he pays me some. And when I'm all on his shit, he don't want to be bothered. Nevertheless, I'm tired of the back and forth relationship we have. It's time for me to keep it moving. And I know I said that before, over and over again, but it's real this time. I don't even feel the same way about him like I used to. So why even bother trying to hold on.

When the phone rang, again, it caught me right in the middle of a good sleep. I didn't know who it was, but who ever it was wouldn't give up. I snatched the phone from off my night stand. "Hello?!"

"Peace. I'm sorry, did I wake you?"

It was him. My whole disposition changed. You know how a man can do that. Depending on who he is. I felt a warm feeling run through my body, as I sat up. "No...no it's okay. What's up with you? Did you make it to work on time?"

"Oh, yeah. I've been working like a dog grading these papers. I've been thinking about you, though. What about you baby, how you been?"

I looked at the clock and saw that it had only been a few hours since I saw him. I was souped! "Well... I've been okay. Thinking about you too."

"Yeah... that's what I needed to hear right now. So I'm gonna get back to work. I'll call you later."

It was something about the way he talked. It just made me feel secure. It was just so convincing.

We made plans to see each other the next day. I always looked forward to seeing him. He just took me out of the world I was living in when I was with him. Those old feelings started to come to surface.

Two Months Later

I was preparing myself for a show I had to do in the Bahamas. It was in casual conversation that we had realized we both were going to be in the Bahamas at the same time. His girlfriend had set up the trip for them. All he knew was the date. He didn't know where he was staying. All he knew was they were going to be there when I was. How scary is that? We joked about seeing each other while we were down there. And how he would sneak away to come to my show. I knew he wasn't serious. Even though he had me kind of convinced for a minute. I thought a lot about how we were having a lot of static between each other the past few weeks. He just was changing. You know the way a lot of men do after a while? He became less reliable. I didn't know what was going on. Maybe he and his girlfriend were finally working things out? Maybe she's come to her senses and finally appreciates him? Who knows what the problem is. All I know is I can't waste my time trying to figure out why we're not how we used to be. Sometimes when people start to catch feelings they push away, subconsciously. We had a special bond. We both knew it. It was just not the right time. It was just all wrong...and still it was all right. Fuck it! I'm not going to stress myself out no more about the shit! I'm going to do me. I'm going to concentrate on doing me. Why is it that us women always take time to focus on a man instead of ourselves. For example, you know how we could have planned to go out with our friends for weeks. Or even at the spur of the moment. If our man calls and says he don't want us to go or he wants to do something with us (all of a sudden) we would drop our plans to be with him or to stay in the house. And if we don't drop our plans we would take time out to consider it. Men! Shit! They wouldn't even consider leaving their boys! You would see him when he's finished, maybe. But he's not just dropping what he has to do. We go out our way to satisfy men. Not saying you don't have some men that appreciate it. It's just the way we do things, as women, and our patterns. But, anyway I don't want to fall into that pattern. So, it's best I just let it go. Whatever happens... happens.

In the middle of packing I fell into a deep sleep. When I woke up it was four-o-clock. Shit! I got to be at the airport in an hour! I looked through my caller ID to see if maybe he called and I slept through it. There I go again. As late as I was I still took time out to worry about if he called or not. Deep inside I knew he didn't, but still I insisted on checking. If things were right with us....he would have called and wished me a safe trip. I wished he would have called.

The whole trip I looked over my shoulders. I looked for him. Why? Why was I even thinking about him. If he wanted to see me or was thinking about me he knew where I was. He knew where he could find me. I enjoyed myself though. At least I tried. Until I woke up throwing up. Shit! What the fuck did I eat? More so what did I drink? Them Rum Punches are nothing to play with. I felt like shit. I had to be downstairs in an hour to go to this function. I jumped in the shower and threw my clothes on. When I got down stairs I bumped right into Kevin. I had met him last night at the dinner party. He was supposed to be some big time football player, I don't know. I don't know much about those sports guys. I only know about Mr. Jordan and Shaq.

"What's up Tiyer? How was ya' night, did you sleep okay?"

"Yeah. I think I had one too many of those Rum Punches, but otherwise I'm straight. What 'bout you?"

"Oh, I slept good. I went to bed right after the party."

"You did disappear... have you seen Sharon?

"Yeah, she's in the lounge."

"Thanks. I'll see you later."

He grabbed my hand as I was walking away, not in a disrespectful way. "Hey, what you doing later? Want to have a drink or a bite to eat or something?"

He caught me off guard. "Umm...Okay. What time?"

"Nine-thirty. At the bar on the Royal Towers side."

"Fine, I'll be there."

When I walked away I asked myself what the fuck was I doing? How I'm just gonna tell that man I would meet him? What he thought I was, some groupie bitch? I didn't know who he was, but it wasn't hard to tell a lot of these other women in the hotel did. I didn't feel up to it. I just wanted to crawl under my sheets and sleep.

I must have had twenty-hot flash episodes by the time the sun went down. It was nine-o-clock and I told that boy I would meet him for a drink. I could hardly stay focused at the awards ceremony. I don't know how I'm going to sit at a bar, drink, and hold my head.

Well, I made it. I did my best, plus the fact that his conversation was good and he was an interesting person, that helped. But for some reason I couldn't stop thinking about Abdul.

We ended our night with a walk on the private beach of the hotel. I was definitely attracted to him. I didn't know if it was lust, me being lonely, or just me reacting to the first thing that came my way. And only God knows I didn't need to react to the first thing that came my way, even if it looked like a good package. So......I let him walk me to my room, gave him a soft kiss on the lips, and said goodnight. My panties were a little wet, but I couldn't play myself.

By the time I got out the shower and lotioned my body, Kevin was ringing the phone.

"Hello."

" Tiyer?"

"Yeah." He caught me off guard. "What's up?"

"I didn't wake you up, did I?"

"No. I just got out of the shower. What's going on with you?"

"Nothing. I just wanted to tell you I had a good time tonight and I hope that we can see each other again sometime down the line. What you say 'bout that?"

"Well...I guess so. You seem to be a busy man. I guess whenever you get time we could hook up."

"I'm sure you're busy too, working on ya' album and everything. But I can make time."

"We'll see. What you doing tomorrow? We don't have to do no publicity work or nothing until the dinner."

"Seeing you I hope."

"We'll see how you feel tomorrow."

"What's that supposed to mean?"

"Who knows you may wake up and feel totally different about me."

He laughed. "Girl, you crazy. That's why I like you. I'll call you in the morning and see if you are up to having breakfast, all right."

"Well, I don't eat breakfast...."

He cut me off. "Well, there's a first time for everything. As a matter of fact I'll meet you down stairs in the morning around ten-o-clock." He hung up.

I can't believe it. He just hung up.

On the way home I just thought about life. My life. I know the lady sitting next to me on the plane, thought I was crazy. Isn't it crazy how we seem to believe what WE want to believe? We can know something is one way, but we will insist on believing it's another way. I knew it wasn't no rum punches. But I insisted on believing it was. Well, not exactly believing. But, I kept telling myself it was. I know my body, very well. I knew I was pregnant. I just didn't want to face the facts. Damn! What a fucked up predicament for me to be in. How could I let this happen? I just cried. I didn't care who was sitting next to me and what they thought. I was so empty inside. I knew what my options were, but neither one of them was benefiting. My career, my life, my family. His career, his life, his family. What a mess we made! I had to catch myself. This is my child I'm talking about. My own flesh and blood. I began to feel guilty about my thoughts. Should I tell him? Or should I just handle it myself?

I waited until the middle of the week to call him. I knew he was still in the Bahamas. Over and over I picked up the phone and hung it up as soon as it rang. I was hoping the answering machine picked up. It did. I felt a little relieved.

I paused before speaking. "Hey, umm... I can't really talk cause my mother's sitting here, but I know my body and something isn't right. Something is wrong. I guess I'll call you back."

I hung up the phone feeling like an ass. I didn't know what to say and if I should have said anything. Maybe I shouldn't have called. Maybe I should have just not let him know. Maybe I should have waited until I got home to call him. I could just die, I mean literally die.

It was not until about two days later when he returned my call. He left a message at my house. I had mixed feelings by now. I was hesitant at first, but I knew I couldn't put it off but for so long. I knew this would be the end of us for sure. It just would be too much for him to swallow. As well for me.

"Yeah, what's up?"

"What's going on, Tiyer? Now so you said something's wrong with your body? What's the matter?"

He said it like maybe I was getting ready to tell him I had VD or something.

"Yeah. I'm pregnant. I've been sick like a dog and lying around all day long. I know my body."

He paused. "Ohhh.....man. My God. Are you sure? I mean....shit!"

He kind of turned me off when he said that. What he thinks I'm a child or something? What did he mean, if I was sure. He thinks I have time to play?

"Yes, I'm sure. Look, I know my body. Very well."

"Well, we gonna have to do something about this. Umm....When are you leaving to finish your album?"

"In a few days."

"When will you be back?"

"Not for a while. Like a month in a half."

"Damn! I really did it this time. Look, we need to meet before you leave. We got to talk. What you doing tomorrow?"

"Not much. I just have to run around a little."

"Well, I'll be finished around one. Call me at twelve-thirty and we can meet, cause we have to talk about taking care of this. A month and a half is too long we need to take care of it sooner."

Oh, now I was pissed! He didn't even say sorry or are you all right. Motherfucker! He was a totally different person. He reminded me of the old him, from back in the days. He was incompassionate. I know he could tell the change in my voice and disposition. "What? I have to go and do my album. You talking about sooner and shit!"

"Look, we'll just talk about it tomorrow. Call me."

I just hung up. I could hear the fright in his voice. He was scared what would happen if his woman found out. For the first time in a very long time, at least since we had hooked back up, I saw him as a no good motherfucker! Probably because he hadn't even thought about my feelings and thoughts about the situation. Or it could have been just the fact that he had gotten me knocked up. I know I did my part and it wasn't just his fault, but I was considerate of him. I don't know what I expected. Once a nigga', I guess, always a nigga'.

Of course a few days had passed and I hadn't met with Abdul or spoke to him. I was packing my stuff to leave to go to work on my album. It figured he would avoid his responsibilities. I had already come to the conclusion that I was going to keep it.

Part Two

"Yeah."

"Yeah, what? What's this you talking about on my machine? You keeping the baby?! What....what are you talking about? You said something about I don't have to have nothing to do with the baby and something about health care."

"Yeah."

"Yeah, what?! I'm not having no more babies. And health care? I'm not ready to pay no health care. You done went down there and flipped the script on me. Yo, I cant have no baby."

Oh, he done caught me at the right time. "You don't have to have shit. I'm having it! And as a matter of fact you don't have to pay shit! You're so inconsiderate. All you know is what you want. Fuck me. Fuck what I have to deal with as far as killing it and having to feel guilty."

"What you think? I don't have to feel a way? Come on now Tiyer, I told you I don't want no more seeds! I already got a family, you already got a family! What are you thinking about?"

"You don't. You don't have to feel a way I'm the one who's going to have to deal with it. Once I go take care of it you'll be out in the clear. Everything will be all good for you."

"That's what you think? You think it won't bother me? Either which way. You're telling me you're going to have this baby and you think I can just walk this earth knowing I have a seed and not see it? Look, I'm not having no babies Tiyer. I'm ready to just walk off the set period. Cause you just don't seem to understand. Now I'm going to have to rearrange my whole shit. I'm going to have to tell my people what's going on."

"No you don't. You can keep your family. I don't give a fuck 'bout that. What you think I'm going to pop up down the line and tell your girl about the baby? That's some ol' late night movie shit. I'm not. Trust me."

"I don't know what you'll do. I don't trust.....

I cut his tired ass off. "What! You don't trust me you say? Come on you know me a little bit..."

He cut me back off. "Yeah, I know you a little bit. And I don't know what you're capable of."

"Oh, you don't know me now? You know what? I'm gonna do it. It's for you just know it."

"You gonna do what?"

"Take care of it. I'll find a place down here."

"Let me know, I'll drive down."

"Oh, no thanks. I don't want you there."

"Oh, come on. How does that sound, me not being there?"

"It's all right. I'll be all right. You know, before this situation everything was nice. You had me going I must admit. You really had me. You're good I'll give you that."

"Oh, so I guess you're going to hang up on me now?"

"No. But I am hanging up. Goodbye. Take care of yourself."

I had to sit there for a minute after hanging up. He made me, for some reason, feel like a piece of second hand meat. Like I didn't even matter. Especially when he started talking about his family. If he cared about the bitch that much why was he running around fucking people. Raw at that. I felt like everything he ever told me, before this point, was a lie. I guess he hadn't changed much since when I first met him. He just got more clever with his shit. He knows how to disguise it good. He called back in five minutes. I knew the shit must've been fucking with him.

"You know what?"

"What, Abdul?"

"I don't know who you think I am. You must think I'm some punk motherfucker, or something."

I hadn't heard him talk like this in years.

"What?"

"Who you think you telling what you gonna do. Like I'm not a part of this shit."

"Well, if that's how you feel, then you must be a punk ass motherfucker. You're the one who came to that conclusion. And you don't have shit to do with it! I dismissed you of your duties. I don't need you, you've done enough!! So you don't have to worry about your woman finding out shit cause you don't fucking exist motherfucker!!

And if I did keep this baby it wouldn't know you existed either. So you can stop worrying. You PUNK ASS NIGGA'!!!!"

I slammed the phone down. I never thought I would have ever called him a nigga' but he was acting like one.

Seven and a half months later

"My god damn feet hurt. I been on my feet all day. This is the hardest part of a new album, the promo part. Don't get me wrong, I'm really blessed to have the first single doing as well as it is. I...I'm just tired as hell. It's been a long time since I've had to go through this."

"Yeah, I know. But you also know you have to do what you have to do." My sister always had short answers. Straight to the point and that's that.

"If you wasn't my sister and I didn't know better, I'd thought you was crazy."

"Yeah, same here."

"How many more stations I got to do?"

"Umm...Two more. Then you have to do a lunch with the mix show dj's"

"Well, I guess that will be when I'll get to eat huh?"

"Yup. You need to lay off the extra meals anyway."

"Yeah, and what about you?"

"I need to, but I don't have to be on television either."

When we pulled up to the station I just took a deep breath. This was one of my favorite stations and I didn't want my stress to effect my visit. Me and the program director is cool. He made my day when I walked in the station. He had a big flower arrangement waiting for me.

"Tiyer!! My favorite girl. How are you?"

"Fine, now that I've seen you."

"Don't stroke my ego. How are you big sister?"

My sister always was good with people. "Hey, Damion. How are you?"

I had to do the regular, take pictures with the staff, radio drops, and a quick interview. Then it was off to the pop station. I fell out in the car. It seemed like as soon as my eyes closed it was time for me to get up. If it wasn't for my phone vibrating on my hip I wouldn't have woke up. I looked around and only saw the driver.

"Where's my sister?"

"She went in and checked out if they was ready for you. Your security is standing outside the car."

"Oh." My phone kept going off. "Hello. Hello. Hello! Asshole, you don't got nothing better to do than call people and breathe?!"

I've been getting crank calls for the past two weeks. It was time to change my number, not that I could afford to do that. Everybody had this number. It went off again. Caller unavailable it said. I just let the motherfucker ring. After the fourth time I couldn't ignore it.

"Hello. Hello."

I could hear a person talking low on the other end, like a whisper. "Yes."

"Hello, I can't hear you speak up."

The person just sucked they teeth and hung up. I was so into the phone call I didn't see my sister calling me outside the car. The whole time in the station I was agitated by the phone calls. I tried not letting it show. Obviously it worked, cause I walked out of the biggest pop station in LA with my song added. When we got in the car my sister didn't waste no time.

"Tiyer, what's ya' problem?"

"What you talking about?"

She looked at me with one of those give me a break looks. "You can fake them radio people out, but I know you too good and something is wrong with you."

"Oh, it's just those damn crank calls. The shit is aggravating."

"You're gonna have to change your number. And you know you can't let shit stress you out. Your pressure is high as it is." She started looking through her run down planner and whispering to herself. I knew she was about to come out with some shit I wasn't trying to hear.

"I know, I just was hoping it wouldn't have to get to that."

"I called and found an ob/gyn out here you can go see. I made an appointment for you in the morning before your fitting meeting."

I looked at her like she was crazy. "Well, when was you going to tell me?"

She nonchalantly said, "I just did."

"You know I don't like seeing no doctor except Dr. Kass."

"Yeah, I know but you're a week late for your prenatal check up, your blood pressure is up, and plus I already called Dr. Kass and he said you should see a doctor. So, that's that. And your feet are swelling up, I don't like that."

Just as she said that I felt a kick in my stomach. I guess that was the baby's way of telling me she was right. After the lunch with the mix show dj's I went to Mr. Chow and got something to eat. I didn't like the food they had at the lunch. Of course I had to run into everybody in the industry. Everybody looking and wondering who the baby father was. But they knew not to ask me shit. All they said was "Girl, that single is hot." And "You're looking good girl! You're carrying well." A bunch of bull shit! Phony motherfuckers. I was just happy to get out of there.

Why? Why do people have to call me early in the morning? Shit! They know I be sleep. And it can't be nobody, but someone from home calling my cell.

"Hello." I answered with the rough morning breath.

It was a long pause before the person answered. "Peace...How are you?"

I jumped up. My heart started beating over time. He caught me off guard. I couldn't even answer right away. I wasn't even sure what I should say.

"Hello?" I figured I couldn't go wrong with saying hello again.

"Yes. How are you feeling? I was hoping your number was still the same."

"Why? What made you wonder how I was doing?"

"I just....Look, you've been on my mind, I figured I would call and find out. You know instead of wondering. Plus I saw you on the awards the other night and it made me really realize our situation. I guess visibly seeing you pregnant made me realize....."

I cut him off. "Our? Our situation? We don't have shit. I have a situation. I mean who do you think you are, Mr. family man? What makes you think you can just call me months later?"

"I know. But I just felt I needed to make this call. I knew you would react this way, but I needed to do this for me. The last time we spoke I spoke out of anger...I just wanted to let you know that. But you look good. I'm proud of you, Tiyer."

"Whatever, Abdul. You kill me. And I hope you don't think anything's changed. I still don't want you to have anything to do with the baby. She doesn't need you in her life. And you don't have to worry about me saying anything to your woman."

He paused. "It's a girl? Man....that's nice. Look Tiyer I don't want to be enemies. You don't understand what I've been going through. This shit's really been bothering me. I hope you don't think that I just been living my life nice and easy."

"Look, I don't know how you've been living and I don't care. I know how I've been living. And it's hard. You couldn't even imagine. By the way I'm just curious, does she know yet?"

"I almost told her."

"But? Oh, that's right, you didn't want to fuck up your home....I mean it's fucked up already. Isn't it? Look, I got to go to the doctor."

"Is everything okay? Are you in town?"

"I'm going for a check up. I'm in LA."

"Well I would like to see you when you come back. You think that's possible?"

"No. I don't think so. Go do you. Stay with your woman and live your life. Keep chasing that family dream. I'm all right. The baby is all right and will be all right."

I didn't even give him a chance to respond I just hung the phone up. What else was there to say? It's crazy though, it made me feel bad to have to handle him like that. Even after the way he handled me I still had feelings for him. That doesn't make any sense.

As soon as I stepped my foot outside the car, in front of the hotel, Kassy was waiting for me. I thought I could escape her for at least ten minutes.

"Tiyer, we have to go to get you fitted for the video."

"Good morning to you too."

She kissed me on my cheek, like when I was a little girl. "I'm sorry. Good morning. How was the doctor?"

"Fine. Let me run up and change my shoes. I'll be right back."

"Hurry up. I'll wait in the car for you."

I couldn't get my feet in the room before that damn cell phone started ringing. I could feel it vibrating in my pocketbook. I scuffled through my bag to find it.

"Yeah, hello."

"Tiyer, listen....."

As soon as I heard his voice I cut him off. "Look Abdul, didn't I....."

"No, Tiyer listen, don't hang up it's important..."

"Hold on somebody is on the other line."

I could still hear him talking when I clicked over. "Hello."

"Tiyer?"

The voice wasn't familiar to me. "Yes. Who's this?"

"This is Karen." There was a pause before she finished. "Abdul's wife."

I liked to die! I almost shitted on myself. She was the last person I expected to ever hear from. Then it hit me, wife? Did she say wife? Was she being sarcastic or was she serious?

"Yes?"

"I've been calling you for a few weeks now....but I never would say anything 'til now."

"So, that's you who's been calling and hanging up?"

"Yes."

"So, what's up? What can I do for you?"

"Well, I need to know what is what."

"As far as?"

"With you and Abdul."

"I don't understand. Why didn't you ask him? Hold on my other line. Hello."

I could tell in his voice he knew what was happening. "Tiyer, listen...."

"Listen to what motherfucker! Why is YOUR woman on my phone? Excuse me, I mean ya' fucking WIFE!!!"

"Look, I can explain."

"Ain't shit to explain, bye!" I clicked back over thinking she would have hung up. "Hello."

"Yes, I'm still here....That was him wasn't it? I know him so well. I guess you do too, huh? I mean you've known him for a while, right?"

"Yes, I have. But still what does that have to do with

Situations

Situations

anything?"

"Look, are you pregnant from him? I mean .....what is going on?" I could hear the tension in her voice.

"What!" The ghetto was coming out of me now. "You need to talk to ya' husband not me! And where did you get my number from any way?"

"Like you told me, you need to ask ya' baby father!"

"No, you need to get a grip and learn how to hold on to ya' motha'fuckin' man. And just for the record, get all ya' answers from Abdul."

She toned her voice down and took a deep breath. "Look, I didn't call to argue with you. It's just that some things aren't clear. I mean how would you feel if someone you've been with for years comes and tell you that he's gotten another woman pregnant? And on top of that, when you ask him how he feels about that other woman he tells you that he loves her. I've known what's been going on for a while, but we were trying to make things work. Things have been fucked up for a while with us." I heard a loud knock at the door. I could hear my sister calling my name through the door.

"Look Karen. You should be talking about this with Abdul. I'm not... I don't know I got to go."

It was like she just ignored what I was saying. "He told me how considerate you were on my behalf. He also told me you didn't know we were married."

"No, I didn't know. But I have to go. You need to talk to him not me." I just hung up and turned the power off the phone.

"So, Tiyer what did she say? I mean how did she get the number?"

"I don't know how she got the number. And she wasn't saying much. Just that she knows about the baby and that they're married. He told her that I didn't know they were married. He told her that he loved me. Well, how far we got to go? I'm getting motion sickness in this car."

"I don't know. So what did he have to say?"

"I didn't give him a chance to say nothing. She clicked through our conversation. As a matter of fact let me call and see what he has to say."

"I don't think that is a good idea."

"Why?"

"Cause, you need to just get over him. You talking to him is just going to give you mixed feelings about the situation. Just let it be." I sat for a minute or two in silence and thought about what she said. But, I just couldn't help it. I dug in my pocketbook and took my phone out. I knew what I wanted to say. I practiced it in my head while the phone rang. I pressed *67, so my number wouldn't come up.

"Peace."

"Yeah, what's going on? Why is ya' wife calling me?"

My sister just looked at me and rolled her eyes.

"Listen Tiyer, shit happened so fast. I was trying to tell you, but you hung up so fast."

"Still that doesn't answer my question. Why is she calling my phone. And she said she's been calling a couple weeks and not saying anything. Where did she get my number from, Abdul? Why didn't you tell me you were married?"

It was dead silence on the phone before he answered. "Can I see you?"

"What?" I heard him clear, but I didn't know how I should react. "I'm in LA. What are you talking about?"

"I know. I can fly down tomorrow. I'd rather discuss this face to face. And I feel we have a lot of other issues to talk about."

"I don't think so." Damn! I wanted to say yes so bad. I couldn't give in.

"Tiyer, come on. How long you gonna be in LA?"

"A week."

"All right, Tiyer. I'll talk to you."

"Aright, goodbye."

What the fuck he means all right goodbye? I was pissed! I didn't like how that conversation ended. I shouldn't have called him. My sister looked at me with one of those, I told you so looks. "I told you you shouldn't have called him."

By the time I had finished getting fitted it was three-thirty and I was starving. I didn't have nothing else scheduled for the day, so I figured I'd go to the Beverly Center and window shop. I couldn't get Abdul off my mind. That's what I didn't want. I didn't want to wreck my brain over him. Of course I ended up buying something. I've been buying stuff for after I have the baby. For some reason I seem to think I know what size I'm going to be after the baby. Rather what size I hope to be. I picked a couple of things up for the baby. People were telling me I should wait until I was seven months or more. They said that it was bad luck to buy stuff for the baby too soon into the pregnancy, so I figured I was far enough now. I picked up some cartridges for my boys. I thought spending some money would help get Abdul off my mind. I was wrong, cause I went to bed thinking about him. I wonder if men go through what we do? If they do they sure know how to hide it.

My morning started as usual, with the phone waking me up. Usually it's my cell. This morning it was my hotel phone. I looked at the clock, it was ten-thirty. Only person it could be is Kassy.

"Yeah."

"Peace. Good morning. Did I wake you?"

"Abdul?"

"Yes."

"How did you get my room number?"

"Come on, I know your alias name. Is it a problem?"

I didn't want to give in, but I didn't want to end the conversation like the last one. "No. You straight. What's up?"

"Look, just listen. Don't hang up or go off. After we hung up yesterday I was stressed. I sat with my thoughts and the only thing I could come up with was to throw some things in a bag, go to the airport and jump on the first flight available. So....."

"So what?"

"So I'm here, at the airport in LA. Listen....just listen before you say anything. If you want me to leave I will turn around and go back."

Shit!! What should I do? Should I give him an E for effort and accept him? Or should I stick to my guns and send him on his way? I paused for a while.

"Tiyer, you there?"

"Umm...okay...just come on. But I'm not promising you

nothing. You hear?"

"I understand. I'm on my way."

What have I done! I couldn't believe what just took place. I'm going backwards, I'm doing just what I didn't want to do. I jumped up and got in the shower. When I got out I knew I had to call and tell Kassy. She could not find out on her own. I couldn't be walking out my room and bump into her. I called her room, but I didn't get no answer. I didn't bother to leave a message. Damn! I'm falling again. Just when I was doing so good. I could kick myself. I waited with butterflies in my stomach. I just had to promise myself I would hold my head. I had to stick to my plan no matter what.

When the knock came from the door I knew it was him. My heart raced. I opened the door and there he was. With his bag and a dozen of roses. It just wouldn't have been him if he didn't bring flowers. He was neat and good smelling. I held my head and let him in. I thanked him for the flowers and set them on the table in the dining area in my room. I felt the tension. It was like a first date or something. I offered him something to drink from the mini-bar. And of course he said water.

"You're looking good, Tiyer." I could tell he was looking at my belly. He wasn't used to seeing me pregnant.

"Thank you. I'm trying to keep it together, so I'll be half way decent after the baby."

He reached over and picked up the clothes I had bought for the baby. He held them up one by one and smiled. He had such a beautiful smile. The way he was looking you would have thought he wanted the baby. I just wish things were different. And I promised myself I wouldn't think like that. It didn't make sense to think like that, cause things aren't different and they won't ever be. So, it didn't make sense to even wish like that.

"This is for the baby?"

"Yeah. Isn't it cute?"

"Yeah. So, you've been doing a little shopping?"

"Yeah, just a little."

His disposition changed. He got serious. "Tiyer, I wanted to kiss you when you opened the door. What would you have done?"

"I don't know."

He reached over and set his lips on mines, softly. It was like he wasn't to sure what my response was going to be, so he didn't want to go all the way. You know with the tongue and stuff. So, I did. I probably shouldn't have, but I stuck my tongue in his mouth. And it felt good! Nothing had changed with that.

Only thing was I felt funny afterwards. Like it wasn't right. I didn't know what the next move should have been. It was like he was a stranger to me. He rubbed his hand softly across my right cheek. Chills ran down my body. Then he spoke softly. So soft it felt like a little breeze ran across my face. "I love you. I know at this point that might sound bogus and there's a lot I need to explain. But just know once the smoke clears, no matter what happens, I love you." Then he got up gathered his bag and went towards the door.

Before I could even realize what I was saying the words rolled of my tongue. "Where you going?"

"To my room. I figured you would have been more comfortable with me staying in my own room."

"Oh. I didn't know."

"I just came straight to your room. I know you probably have a long day ahead of you, so I'll get with you later to talk."

"Well, only thing I have to do is a few phone interviews."

"So call my room when you finish. Room 219. We can grab a bite to eat."

Before I knew it he had disappeared out of my room. I sat on the couch and stared at the wall for a minute, rubbing my stomach. What just happened here? How did he get here? What was he even doing in my life again? I asked myself these questions over and over. And time after time I came up with the same answer. I let him. I let him back into my life, or should I say my atmosphere. I can't blame nobody from this point on, but myself and my heart.

"What!!!! Tiyer, are you out of your mind girl?!!!! I mean he just came on his own? How....I mean... what... what made him just get on a plane? You're on your own sister! I wanna see how you handle this one. Why didn't you just tell him to go back when he asked you what to do?"

"I don't know."

"You don't know? Well, where is he now?"

"He said he thought I would be more comfortable if he got his own room. He's in his room I guess."

"So?"

"So what?"

"So what's next?"

"I don't know. I got to just go with the flow."

"You don't need no stress. And I hope he didn't come to bring none. I'm gone. I got a lunch date."

"With who!"

"AHHH?. Wouldn't you like to know."

"Whatever. I'm going to get something to eat with Abdul. Call my cell if you need me." As soon as she stepped her foot out the door I picked up the phone and called his room. I got a recording saying, "the hotel guest you're trying to reach is on the phone."

I didn't bother to leave a message. I got kind of turned off or more so jealous. Who could he be talking to? Probably his Karen. The phone rang and broke my day dreaming. "Hello."

"Hey. What's going on? You still working?"

"No. I just called your room, you was on the phone."

"We probably was calling each other at the same time. I dialed you a second ago and got a recording."

It didn't matter if he was lying or not. "Oh. So, you hungry yet?"

"Starving. You want to get something now?"

"I'll meet you in the lobby in five minutes. That's good?"

"Yes."

I hung up and brushed my teeth. Of course he was downstairs before me. We hailed a cab and went to Sharks Bar. I wasn't even thinking. Sharks Bar was a hot spot for industry heads. And as soon as the thought popped in my head I saw everybody I didn't want to see. Now they knew Abdul wasn't nobody from the industry, so I could imagine what was running through their minds. They were thinking he was the baby's daddy. Everytime we would get into a deep conversation somebody would come over to the table and interrupt. Basically, they came over to be nosy!

We talked about everything. I felt at ease a little. But it's hard to keep a straight head when there's feelings involved. But, I spoke my piece and he spoke his. It was a lot to swallow, but I've been known to have a big appetite.

When we got out the cab in front of the hotel it was already almost eight-o-clock. I can't believe we were out that long. I walked in the lobby to the front desk to get any messages and packages. When Abdul came in from paying the cab he had a blank look on his face. It was like he was looking right pass me or through me. He stared right over my shoulder. You would have thought he had been stabbed in his back and was on his last breath. When he opened his mouth to speak, it was like he talked in slow motion. His words struck me like a sharp pain. I didn't want to turn and look.

He said, "Karen..... What are you doing here?"

Karen!!! What the fuck was he talking about? I swung around and there she was, there we were. Face to face. She was a petite woman. Very light and not bad looking. She just stared with confusion in her eyes. He walked pass me like I wasn't there.

He spoke more firmly, now. "I said what are you doing here?"

She held her teeth together and spoke with hate in her voice. "Maybe I should be asking the same question, Abdul." He never once turned around to me. He never once said anything to me. He just grabbed her by her arm and harshly pulled her to the elevator. I looked around to see who had seen and heard the little episode. Thank God the lobby was empty. Still, I had seen what happened and I was hurt he would leave me standing there like that. I felt like he chose her over me. I rushed up to my room and tried to call Kassy. Her machine came on. I left a message and dialed his room. The phone rang out. I wanted to go to his room, but I knew that was a bad idea. What the hell was she doing here? How did she know where we were?

I felt my heart racing. I could feel an anxiety attack coming on. A sharp pain in my stomach brought me to my knees. The pain shot to my back. All of a sudden I couldn't breathe. My head was spinning. I had not felt this feeling before, but I knew something wasn't right. It felt wet between my legs. I knew it was sweat, my whole body felt wet.

Now I wished I had shared with Kassy what the doctor had told me. Now I felt like I should have listened to him when he said I should stay off my feet for a couple of weeks. He said my pressure was sky high. I sat on the couch and took deep breaths. But a sharp pain ran across my stomach again this time more sharp and painful. All I could do was scream for help, in my head. I couldn't seem to get it out of my mouth though. Why did I allow him to come here? He's nothing but bad news. I picked myself up and found a way to get to the bathroom. I threw some cold water on my face and neck hoping it would cool me off. But it didn't. I just got hotter. The sweat ran down my legs. I grabbed a towel and reached up under my dress to wipe the sweat from my inner thighs and legs. Oh my god!!! When I pulled the towel from under my dress it was covered with the color red. I was bleeding!! What's going on? My stomach turned into a rock hard ball. I shook my stomach, trying to make my baby move. I guess it was mother's instinct, cause at that point I knew my child was in danger. By this time the pain was unbearable. I fell to the floor and pulled myself to the front door. Somehow I managed to get myself out to the hallway. I had let my security off for the day to visit some family members, so I knew he wasn't in his room which was right next door. I pressed for the elevator and dragged myself onto it. I didn't have enough strength to press any buttons. I just prayed it would move. I didn't care what floor as long as somebody would find me. I cried for help. I knew nobody probably would hear, but I still tried.

"Help! Please, my baby." Hot tears ran down my face. Where was he now? Now that I needed him. How could I put him before me and my unborn?

When I woke up, I could barely get focused. I had no idea where I was. I knew I wasn't where I had passed out at. It was too soft. I looked around the room. I definitely wasn't on an elevator. I saw a long plastic cord running from my arm to two bags of liquid. One clear liquid and the other almond color. I was hooked up to an I.V. What is going on? My stomach felt numbed. I lifted my head a little and saw Kassy standing at the foot of the bed. I flopped my head back down and closed my eyes. My mouth felt dry and heavy. The tears burned my cheeks as they hit them.

"How's the baby?" That's all I could squeeze out my mouth. I didn't even bother to open my eyes. My head was hurting too much. I knew she heard me. When Kassy didn't answer I got scared. I popped my head back up and opened my eyes. She just stood there with water-filled eyes. I slowly reached my hand down to my belly. It was fairly flat to flat. All of a sudden nothing mattered, the I.V., the headache. Nothing. "Kassy.....Where's my baby? Huh? Where's my daughter!!! Go get my baby!!! What did you let them do?!"

The nurse came running in. She tried to hold me down, but I wasn't having it. She tried to comfort me, but I didn't want comfort at this point. I wanted my baby! Kassy held me in her arms and rocked me while I cried. I didn't need them to answer any questions. I knew. I knew where my baby was. Gone. It took a shot from the nurse before I could calm down. Actually I felt relaxed after that. I still was hurting, but I couldn't help but relax.

"Oh, Tiyer. I'm so sorry baby." That's all Kassy kept saying as she rocked me to sleep. "Tiyer, I'm so so sorry. I should have been there, baby." I fell back to sleep. All I could hear was Kassy whispering in my ear. I wanted to die. I felt like I should've died instead of my daughter. A part of me died with her.

For three days I didn't talk to anyone. I just stared out the window. People talked to me, but I couldn't talk back. I didn't want to talk back. I was dead inside. I thought a lot. Mostly about what happened a few days ago. I cried a lot. Mostly when no one was around. I had a room full of flowers, teddy bears, and cards. I didn't even know who they were from. I never bothered to look at any of the little cards to see who they were from. I barely got out the bed. It had gotten to the point where the nurse would just come in and sit the bed pan up under me until I pissed. I didn't even want to get up to go to the bathroom. My sister came every day and bathed me. I heard her bitchin' about how she would wash me. And nobody touch me. Ain't nothing like family. About seven days later, I remember, Kassy coming into my hospital room. I was sleep, but not too deep. She rubbed my head and kissed my cheek. She put her mouth to my right ear and she began to whisper. Very lightly. She said. "Tiyer, baby. You got to get it together. You have to go home. The doctors are starting to look at your case as some psychological thing or something. You haven't spoken since...since you lost the baby. They're afraid your depression may cause you to be a threat to yourself. I know you, they don't. But you still have to help me on this one. I'll take care of you, but I can't do that without your help. I love you so much. You have to pull through. You're killing mom. She can't even come back up here. I know you're sleep, but I also know you can hear me. I'll be here tomorrow, early. I'm taking you home.

When It's Said & Done (Part II)

"Look, you better snap out of it.... You have to start realizing your situation. Trust me I know how you feel, but you're digging your hole deeper and deeper."

Toni turned her pale face away from the window, she often stared out and looked Tiffiny in the face. With a cold stiff look she spoke.

"You have no fuckin' idea how I feel. You come in here every day talking ya' shit and acting like you know how a mothafucker is feelin'! You can't imagine how I feel! You might got the rest of these mothafuckers convinced, but you ain't got me, so you could just go about ya' happy fucking way and live ya' happy fuckin' life. Cause at ten o' clock at night when these lights go off and my fuckin' day comes to an end...you somewhere outside these walls livin' ya' life how you please. So fuck you!!"

Tiffiny stood up, not bothered at all by Toni's reaction. "Fine. Okay if you want to sit up in the psychiatric ward and play fuckin' crazy, fine with me. See YOU think YOU got all these mothafuckers convinced. Ain't a god damned thing wrong with you, you just feel sorry for yourself. I tell you one thing these mothafuckers gonna take that baby from you as soon as you push it out, if you keep acting like your ass is crazy! Oh, yeah honey AS SOON as you push it out. Cause as far as the system is concerned you're crazy and being crazy adds up to being unfit." She turned and walked away and suddenly she turned back and bent down close up on Toni's face. "Oh, yeah... I do know how you feel. I had my baby in jail, both of them. Twins. So fuck you! I guess I can say you don't know how I feel, huh?" Before Toni could react Tiffiny walked out the room. Toni just sat in front of the window like she had done for the past five months.

She fell into a deep depression soon after she was locked up. The loss of her brother, the baby, and worryin' about what Big Man was doing. She hadn't seen Big Man in a couple of months. She had turned away his visits. She turned away everyone's visits. Even Shelly and Stacy. She spoke to her lawyers about her business once every

week. She had already sold ten and a half million albums. The whole
jail situation brought a lot of attention to Toni. Letters from fans
poured in from everywhere.

Every now and then she would get a kite from Dex and J.R., not
often though. Dex was too scared that the Feds would read the letters
before it got to Toni. He wanted to break everything down to her, but
he couldn't get to her. He got word from another cat he was locked up
with, that she was in bad shape. He knew she wasn't weak. She never
had been, but she was alone.

The whole night Toni had cried to herself. She crawled into the
corner and cried. She thought about her life and how it had been turned
upside down. It wasn't until early morning when a guard found her.
"Are you okay, Toni? Do you need a doctor?" The young guard asked.

"No, I don't need a doctor. Can you call Tiffiny for me please..
I need to see her."

The guard agreed and rushed out the room. Toni picked herself
up and went over to her bed. She looked around the room at the other
women, only a few, that shared the large room with her. She realized
she didn't belong there. She realized she had so much more going for
her than the other women. She realized that these women were far more
gone than her. She didn't want her baby to be taken away from her.
Her unborn was the only thing she had left. She had to come up with a
plan. She needed to know what happened to her brother. She needed to
start communicating with the outside. She needed to get to Big Man
and she had a strong urge to find Shorty. But she had to find a way to
convince the system that she was ready to go into regular population.
And Tiffiny was the key. Tiffiny was about the only person that
believed in her.

Big Man held the phone to his ear with a blank look on his face.
The phone call from Toni caught him off guard. She was the last
person he had expected to hear from, especially since the last words she
had spoken to him were "I don't ever want to talk to you again a day in
my life!".

"Hey, are you there?" Toni whispered through the phone.

"Yeah....I'm here.. How are you? Is the baby all right?"

"Yeah, the baby is strong and kickin'...How you been?.... I like the new joint and video."

"Thanx. I've been okay, considerin' the circumstances. And you?"

"I guess I could say the same."

There was a long pause between the two before he answered. "So..."

She cut him off before he could continue. "I'm sorry for the things I said last time we spoke....I want to come home." She whispered. She tried to hold back her tears, but they snuck out.

"Toni...Toni...?"

She wiped her eyes and took a deep breath. "Yes."

"Baby I'll fly up tomorrow to visit you. Please stop crying."

"I can't help it, I miss Link so much. He was all I had Big Man. I'm so sick to my stomach thinking 'bout him everyday. I can't eat nothin', I try to eat for the baby but I just can't function. My nerves are so bad. And it's not cause I'm locked up, I can handle that. It's just all the other shit. I've been sick all day. My nerves are so bad my stomach is bugging out."

"What you mean? Did you tell the doctor?"

"No. It's probably nothin'. I've just been stressed a lot lately, that's all. Please come up here tomorrow, boo. I got to go into count.....I'll see you tomorrow, right?"

"Yeah. I promise I'll be there."

He held the phone long after Toni hung up, thinking about her. She was the first girl that had his heart like she did. It was her realness that drew him to her. He had given up on her after her last phone call. It wasn't until then he realized he didn't want to be with Lisa. He finally hung the phone up and walked over to the couch, where Lisa was lying asleep. He stared for a few minutes. He felt guilty. He knew he shouldn't have taken Toni serious when she flipped on him. How could he not understand that she was under a lot of pressure.

He bent over and shook Lisa. "Yo, Lisa. Yo.."

She sat up half sleep. "What happened?"

"I'm goin' out of town for a few days."

She sat all the way up and got fully alert. "What? Where you goin'? I thought you took the week off, what 'bout our Trip Big Man?"

"Somethin' came up that I got to take care of."

She stood up in a fury. "Somethin' like what! We've been planning this trip....How you gonna just wake me up out of no where and tell me you got to go somewhere and somethin' came up! Where you goin'?"

He talked and walked out the room at the same time. "I'm goin' to NY." And he disappeared out the room, leaving Lisa yelling behind him. He went up into the bedroom and started packing. He looked around the room at all the things Lisa had there. "How did this happen?" He asked himself. Lisa had basically moved in. She caught him at a weak point.

She came storming up the stairs into the bedroom. "I know you are not fuckin' serious!!"

He just kept packing like she wasn't even there. He picked up the phone and called his travel agent to make his flight and hotel reservation. She waited for him to hang the phone up before jumping in his face. "You are fuckin' funny you know that? This must be a personal trip if you're calling to make ya' own reservation. Why can't you tell me where you're goin', huh?" She started getting frustrated. She started to swing at him. He in return gave her one good slap across her face and she fell to the ground. She jumped up and ran down stairs to call the police. Big Man continued to pack his things until he heard a loud knock at the door. He went down stairs to find Lisa in the corner crying holding her face. The knocking continued. He heard a man's voice through the door. "Hello, this is officers Bark and Jackson... Please open the door."

Big Man walked over to the very tall window and peaked out. It was a cop car and another one pulling into his long driveway. He turned and looked at Lisa and asked. "What, you called the cops bitch?" She just started crying. He walked over to the door and opened it.

"Yes, may I help you officers?" He asked blocking the doorway preventing them from entering.

"Yes, sir. We got a domestic violence call. Is everything okay here.?" The officer asked peaking into the lavish home.

"Yes, everything is fine, officer."

Lisa stood up in a rage, thinking of the whole situation that had just took place with Big Man. She knew whatever he had planned had something to do with Toni and she wasn't letting that go down. She ran to the middle of the living room screaming. "No everything is not all right!! He hit me!!!"

He turned around in shock. By the time he could turn back to the officers they had pushed their way in. The first officer ran to her aid. "Are you okay?" He asked

"No! He just hit me for no reason at all!" She shouted. The officer walked over to Big Man, then turned to Lisa. "Do you want to press charges, ma'm?" He asked. It was a long pause before she answered. "Yes...Yes I want to press charges.........."

Toni sat in the rec. room dressed and ready for her visit with Big Man. Time passed and still no Big Man. She stood looking out the window drowning out the noise in the background. The yells from the girls standing in front of the TV broke her thoughts. "Oh shit! Dat's dat nigga' Big Man!! De' got his ass cuffed up!! Yo, Toni, look its ya' baby daddy on the news girl!!", one of the inmates yelled.

Toni ran over to the television in confusion. She didn't recognize the house that Big Man was being escorted from. She couldn't even see his face fully. She reached over and turned the T.V. up. "Yes, Sam we're standing here in front of the home of Rapper and Rolla's Records owner Darius Jones also known as Big Man. Sources say police were called to the home of the famous rapper on a domestic violence complaint. Apparently, Lisa Rock, the rappers live-in girlfriend called police after an argument broke out between the two. The twenty-five year old girlfriend claimed that she was beaten after a dispute between them. She was taken to St. Mary's hospital for treatment. Now back to you Sam."

Toni stood in front of the television stunned. Who the fuck is Lisa? She thought to herself. And when did he get that house? Her insides were numb. Why didn't he tell her about that bitch? She couldn't understand. And why would she call the cops on him? What kind of bitch is she? Her heart raced with anxiety.

****

The cameras and mics raced toward Big Man as he walked out the court room with his lawyers. He just walked straight to the tinted out black Suburban. He couldn't believe he had such a high bail of $60,000. Probably because the police found three guns in his home. The fact that his home was illegally searched seemed not to matter to the prosecutor. "Yo, did somebody check on Toni, like I asked?" he questioned one of the lawyers.

"Well we tried, but she rejected our visits. She said she didn't want to have nothing to do with you" he replied.

"What you mean?!"

"I'm sorry Darius, but it was nothing we could do.... And she wanted to inform you that she was removing your name from her visiting list." He answered.

"Take me to the airport."

TO BE CONTINUED – SITUATIONS 2!

ORDER FORM
QP PUBLISHING
P.O. BOX 1752
Wyndanch, NY 11798-1752

"Situations"	$15.00
Sales Tax	$ 1.24
Shipping/Handling	$ 3.20
TOTAL	$19.44

PURCHASER INFORMATION

Name: _____

Reg, #: _____
     (Applies if incarcerated)

Address: _____

_____

City: _____ State: _____

Zip Code: _____
Quantity?
For orders being shipped directly to prisons,
$5.00 will be deducted from the sale price of the
books.

"Situations"	$10.00
Tax	$ .83
Shipping/Handling	$ 3.20
TOTAL	**$14.03**

CREDIT CARD ORDERS
Visa, MasterCard, Discover, and American Express
(866) 622-1224

FELICIA JONES

"A successful attempt to display situations in everyday people's
story is short, but deep and sure to touch home for a lot of people.
Teri Woods - author of best selling novel "True to the G

"Situations" is a hot collection of urban stories that are just as rea
writing them. QueenPen has mastered the rap game. Now she
onto the literary scene with a vengeance. "Situations" is a must-rea
**Zane - National Bestselling Author of "Addicted", "Sha
All", and "The Sex Chronicles: Shattering the N**

Lynise "QueenPen" Walters

ISBN 0-97142

9 780971 424609

QP Publications
$15 in U.S.A.
$18 in Canada